THE CHURCHWARDEN
by
Margery Roberts
ISBN: 978-0-9954805-8-2

Published by

i2i Publishing. Manchester.
www.i2ipublishing.co.uk

Chapter one

Christopher handed a service booklet to a latecomer and looked around the church for an empty seat. It was not easy to find one but, thinking that an extra person could be squeezed into the fourth pew from the front, he conducted the elderly man up the aisle and persuaded the hymn-singing occupants of the pew to move closer together. He then returned to his post at the back of the church where, as churchwarden, he could keep an eye on things. His fellow-churchwarden, Mrs Knightly, was an acolyte on this occasion, watching over the servers in the chancel. The rector, the Reverend Julian Abbotsford, was on top form, conducting his farewell service triumphantly before taking up a canonry at Chichester Cathedral.

As there appeared to be no more latecomers at present, Christopher opened his *New English Hymnal* and began to join in the last verse of 'Love Divine',

'Changed from glory into glory,
Till in heaven we take our place,
Till we cast our crowns before thee,
Lost in wonder, love, and praise.'

The hymn ended with a crescendo and the rector stepped forward to welcome the congregation, his beautifully-modulated voice sounding just a little sad.

"My dear friends, it seems such a short time ago that I came to St Benet-by-the-Wall and now I must leave this exquisite church and go into deepest Sussex. Helen and I will take so many happy memories with us and think of you often. I thank you all from the bottom of my heart, and particularly the churchwardens, Christopher Jamieson and Caroline Knightly, for all the wonderful support you have

4

given me throughout my time here. In the name of the Father, and of the Son, and of the Holy Ghost. Amen."

And so, the Sunday Eucharist for this third Sunday after the Epiphany took its course, with a much larger congregation than usual.

Fr Julian had invited back all the couples whom he had married during his five years at St Benet's, and several were here, some with babies and toddlers in tow. There were also a number of young people and adults who had been confirmed during his time, along with some of the lawyers and accountants from nearby offices who had attended carol services and other special services in this church so close to the City. In the chancel were Caroline and her husband, Simon, both acting as acolytes, along with Justin, a student from the local Arts College, who was wielding the thurible. The choreography seemed a little ragged, although that may have been more because the cassocks and cottas of the servers were getting old and shabby than because of any lack of grace in the movements. Fr Julian, tall and distinguished, looked magnificent in the white and gold chasuble that he had persuaded the parish to buy.

By the time that Fr Julian mounted the eighteenth-century pulpit to deliver his last sermon, there was an impressive fog of incense in the church, causing one or two of the frostier-looking middle-aged women to cough pointedly and draw out their handkerchiefs. Christopher gave a wry smile as he sat down on the bench at the back of the church to listen to the sermon. It was funny how incense always had that effect, especially on people who did not normally go to church. Anti-papalism still seemed to lurk in the population of England, five hundred years after it had started. Well, Justin could be relied on to get up a good fug. Christopher gazed up at the coat of arms above the chancel arch, where a shaft of January sunshine was burnishing some of the tarnished gilding, and sighed. For twenty years, he had dreamed of having the interior of the church cleaned and refurbished, and yet the fulfilment of the dream seemed further off than ever. He forced himself to turn his attention to the pulpit where Julian was preaching an elegant sermon without notes.

"And so we turn to the poet George Herbert's sonnet *The Son*, in which he explores the relationship between the sun in the sky and the Son of Man – the very incarnation of God as our earthly saviour. He observes here that, although we have a humble setting for the entry of Christ on earth - the stable, of course – he is in glory and shines as the sun. Herbert was born in 1593 in the aftermath of the English Reformation and can be seen to represent the ideal of an Anglican parish priest, pious, intelligent and surprisingly humble for someone so well-connected..."

Christopher had no doubt that Julian had caught everybody's attention. Only the very youngest children were restless, although even they had been provided for. Julian's wife, Helen, had handed out toys from the church toy box at the beginning of the service and these were mostly keeping the children quiet. You really had to admire Julian. He was able to flatter people's intellects without seeming to be patronising. It was no wonder that he had his 'groupies'. He would thrive as a cathedral canon and probably go on to be a bishop. Julian's wife, Helen, was a doctor and so the couple did not have to survive on a clerical stipend. She was expecting their first child and was managing the pregnancy with the same cool efficiency she managed everything. The move to Chichester had been timed to fit in with her planned maternity leave.

The sermon ended and the service continued. When the time came for the congregation to receive communion, Christopher shepherded people up to the communion rail, row by row. Despite his efforts, there was a lot of jostling. Some people were going up out of turn and others were coming back to their seats using the central aisle instead of going around the sides. Eventually, he received communion himself and, as he stretched out his hands to receive the wafer, he unexpectedly felt a sharp pang of regret that Julian was going. They had not always gotten on well and both Christopher and Caroline had felt that Julian had caused them extra work and trouble. But Julian had brought new people to the church and had created a busy and sociable atmosphere that was new to St Benet's and was unlikely to persist in his absence. Christopher took the wafer. Then Caroline offered him the chalice and he sipped the wine. Was this, after all, Christ's blood?

When he returned to the back of the church, it struck him that the building was starting to feel cold. The boiler had been playing up for some time now and, although it had clearly been chugging away earlier in the day, it now seemed to have cut out. Christopher felt the radiator at the back of the church and was not surprised to find that it was only tepid. He made a mental note to telephone the heating engineer and ask for a visit. More expense! The parish's finances were beginning to be a source of worry to the churchwardens because, although Julian had been very good in many ways, he had been something of a spendthrift. Clergy always were. Various small trust funds had been plundered to pay for big events and outings and, despite the comparatively large congregation, regular giving – or 'stewardship' as the diocese liked to call it – was modest, to say the least. The parish treasurer was an elderly widow, Mrs Cook, who was quite efficient at adding up the money, but not very imaginative about finding ways of increasing it. Christopher shook his head slightly and returned to his seat. Julian was now giving out the notices and expressing his gratitude to the parish officers.

"And I should particularly like to thank Miss Deakin, our excellent parochial church council secretary, for all her hard work in taking the Minutes and keeping me in order. She has been a tower of strength throughout my ministry at St Benet's. And then, who could ever forget Mrs Cook, our wonderful treasurer? I shall miss you all. I know that my successor, whoever he or she will be, will be in good hands. And now, if you would like to stand for the Dismissal and Blessing..."

The service, Julian's last at St Benet's, ended and, for a time, Christopher had his hands full, handing out glasses of wine and answering questions - the main one being, "Do we know who will be replacing Fr Julian?" He did not know, of course, because nobody at the diocesan office had given any thought to it. The correct procedures would have to be followed and there would be meetings and consultations and correspondence before anything remotely resembling a name would emerge. He glanced across the back of the church to the table where Caroline was handing out cups of coffee. She caught his eye and gave him a bright smile. Christopher smiled back mechanically and went on supervising the wine glasses.

Caroline was a good colleague, nearly always helpful and optimistic and not usually sharing his underlying gloom about the parish. She worked part-time for a charity in the City and had two grown-up sons who occasionally came to the services. Her husband, Simon, was a harassed-looking government lawyer, not very senior, who seemed to spend his working life drafting regulations and codes of practice for little-known legislation. Christopher found him tedious at best.

When most of the congregation had said their goodbyes to Julian and Helen, and while Christopher was starting to gather up the dirty wine glasses, Julian approached him holding a neatly-wrapped bottle of wine.

"Well, Chris, you know that I could never have managed without you and Caroline. I have been very lucky with my churchwardens. Thank you."

He handed Christopher the bottle of wine and smiled in his peculiarly charming and boyish way. Christopher took the bottle and tucked it under his arm.

"That's very good of you, Julian. I didn't expect anything, you know. I was just doing my duty and trying to do the best for the parish. I – I'm sorry you're going. We've been getting some good congregations recently and that last confirmation was a record here – five people getting confirmed at the same time! I suppose that you couldn't turn down the offer of a canonry. Chichester too."

Julian nodded.

"Mm. Helen will enjoy working there as well. You know that she already has a place in a city centre practice for after the baby is born. London isn't such a good place for bringing up children. It would have been difficult finding good schools that we could afford, but St Benet's has been an interesting experience. I'm sorry that I will leave you with so much to do. The restoration and all that. Have you had any thoughts about getting the architect to draw up a scheme?"

Christopher shook his head.

"Not yet. The trouble is that Tony would charge us a small fortune for drawing up a fancy scheme and then charge us another one for scaling it down and doing what we asked him to do in the first place. I think Caroline and I will have to go through the last quinquiennial and make a list of the category A items. The parish can't afford to tackle anything else at present and, even so, we'll have to try doing some fundraising. That'll be very difficult without a rector."

"You won't have long to wait, I'm sure. St Benet's is such a fine church. It's bound to attract someone. The Bishop is the patron, of course, and he'll have someone in mind before too long. It's a pity about the house, though."

"The house?"

"Yes. Didn't I tell you that the diocese is thinking about taking it back and using it for the new Director of Ordinands? It's not a benefice house, after all. Wasn't your one sold thirty years ago?"

Christopher grimaced.

"Yes, and not replaced. But I thought that the parish was going to be allowed to carry on using it. What about the house that the last Director of Ordinands lived in? There's nothing wrong with it, is there?"

"Quite the contrary. It's probably worth about a million now and the diocese is selling it. It needs the cash pretty urgently. It was in deficit again last year, but something will be found for St Benet's, I'm sure."

Simon joined them, holding a glass of leftover red wine.

"I think I'd better drink this, although it's my third glass. Why do churches always serve red wine too cold? Well, Julian. How does it feel to be leaving? Your sermon was very good. Quite poetical."

"Thank you. I always like to give George Herbert an airing. I must go and say goodbye to Caroline. Will you excuse me?"

He nodded to them both, picked up another wrapped bottle of wine from the bench at the back of the church, and moved across to where Caroline was washing up coffee cups. Simon sipped his wine.

"That's that, I suppose. Julian and Helen can't wait to take themselves off to Chichester and we shall be left struggling. Do you think the Bishop will produce somebody quickly?"

Christopher shook his head as he placed his bottle of wine on a nearby pew. He then rearranged the dirty glasses on the folding table in front of him.

"Shouldn't think so. Did you hear what Julian was saying about the house?"

"The house? What about it?"

"It seems that the diocese wants it back. That's going to make it very difficult for us to attract someone. Do you think there are plans to join the parish up with St Andrew's? People have been talking about that for years."

Simon put his empty glass on the table, knocking over another one as he did so.

"Oh, sorry - it's not broken. I can't imagine so. The churchmanship is so different. They're bottom side of middle-of-the-road and we're Prayer Book Catholic. We don't even know anyone there. I've only been in the church once and that was for a confirmation about ten years ago. Isn't it by Street?"

Christopher nodded.

"Yes, G E Street, 1859. And it's got a Comper screen. Not his best, but quite fine. I don't think the congregation appreciate it. The tradition went downhill when the Reverend Mr Hardwick went there in 1951. He was there for thirty odd years and died of a heart attack at the altar on Easter Day, 1983."

Simon pulled a face.

"Hm, that must have been a thrill. Good Friday would have been better. At least everyone would have been miserable already. And what's happened since?"

"Oh, a succession of fairly dull middle-of-the-roaders. The present incumbent is the Reverend Jill Johnson – middle-aged, a bit tubby and hopeless over liturgy. Apparently, they had flowers throughout Advent. She doesn't wear vestments, of course. It's a surplice and stole sort of place. I've heard she's good pastorally, though, so there can't be any harm in her. I wish Julian had visited the sick a bit more."

Simon inclined his head towards the back of the church where Julian and Helen were now standing, ready to leave. Christopher and Simon both went towards them and they were all joined by Caroline, who was wiping her hands on a faded check tea towel. Julian shook hands with each of them in turn and gave Caroline a peck on the cheek. Helen gave perfunctory kisses to all of them and started to push open the main door.

"Well, we're off," said Julian, with a rueful smile. "You can still email me if anything turns up and I'll let you know how we get on in Chichester."

"And the baby," added Caroline, with a grin.

"Yes, of course, the baby. That won't be for a few weeks, but I'll be sure to let you know. Good luck all of you. Take care."

And Julian was gone.

"That's that, then," remarked Christopher, turning away from the big door. "We're on our own now. Ten people in church next Sunday."

"Don't be silly, Chris," smiled Caroline. 'We had eighty in church today, they can't all disappear. And the Archdeacon is asking Fr Bodkin from Holy Trinity to take our Sunday services. If the chaplain from the Arts College takes the Wednesday lunchtime ones, we'll be fine."

Simon pulled a face.

"Fr Bodkin! He's useless. He killed off about five parishes and then had to retire early because of rheumatism, or gout, or something. Holy Trinity will be glad to see the back of him. They don't need a retired priest anyway. They're the only parish in this deanery with a curate - apart from Christ Church, of course, which has dozens. But then, they're a law unto themselves, we don't want any of them coming near us."

Christopher started to carry wine-glasses to the table where Caroline had been washing up coffee cups in a large bowl of soapy water.

"We'd be better having Bob Bodkin than any of the Christ Church lot, at least he's sound. I think he went to St Stephen's House. He was a late ordinand and served his title in an Anglo-Catholic parish in Bradford. He's not bad as a celebrant. I imagine it was his terrible administration that killed off the parishes. Apparently, he never used to file anything – just left everything in heaps on the floor."

Caroline went back to her washing up and washed the glasses one by one, placing them on the table to drain. She nodded approvingly to Christopher who was ferrying the glasses across.

"How do you know things like that?" she asked. "I don't know anything about him except that he helps out at Holy Trinity. Is he married?"

"Yes," replied Christopher. "His wife is a bit batty but jolly. She keeps cats and they live in a ground floor flat in Stoke Newington. I don't actually know them personally, but I once sat next to his vicar, Fr Smith, at a dinner and he told me all about them." He turned to Simon, who was half-heartedly putting away hymn books in a cupboard. "Hey, Simon. Could you just take the rest of these glasses over to Caroline while I speak to Betty Cook? She's still stuck in the vestry counting the money."

Christopher walked up the central aisle, stopping frequently to hang up kneelers behind the pews on either side. The vestry was a smallish room leading off the chancel, and Christopher could hear the murmur of voices coming from it. When he entered, he found Mrs Cook sitting at the cluttered table with piles of coins in front of her and Mark Evans, the organist, leaning against the vestment chest. Mrs Cook looked flustered and Christopher guessed that Mark had been talking to her while she had been trying to add up the collection. Mark, thin, bespectacled and middle-aged, with sparse brown hair, was a passably good organist, but inclined to be less than good tempered.

"Hello, Betty," said Christopher, trying to sound kind. "You still here? I suppose we had a good collection today. If it's too much for you to count today, just put it in the safe and do it another time."

Betty, plump and with wispy grey hair, looked up at him gratefully.

"We do seem to have a lot of pound coins today," she replied, pushing some of her little piles closer together. "If you don't mind, I'll bank the notes and do the coins next time. I'm expecting my friend, Ann, to come for lunch and I'm already late. I'll just put all these coins in a bag."

She demolished all the piles and scooped the money into a cloth bag which she locked in the safe at the back of the vestry. Christopher then ushered her out of the vestry and turned back to address Mark.

"Thanks for the music today, Mark. Julian was able to go out on a high note. The choir sang well, I thought."

"They weren't bad," replied Mark noncommittally, still leaning against the vestment chest. "But I was just telling Mrs Cook that we need to pay them a bit more. It's difficult enough getting singers anyway and all the City churches pay more than we do. I can't guarantee finding four singers every Sunday."

Christopher frowned.

"But we don't really have more money to give them," he said. "In fact, I was wondering whether we ought to disband the choir during the vacancy. It's a decision for the PCC, of course."

Mark raised his eyebrows.

"Disband it?" he responded tetchily. "Surely that would be a drastic step? I thought that you weren't supposed to change anything very much in a vacancy. I realise that it may be up to the PCC to discuss the matter, but I should have thought that the Director of Music ought to be allowed to put his view. Julian always used to invite me to PCC meetings if anything to do with the music was on the agenda. I was naturally hoping that you and Caroline would do the same." He glared at Christopher, who glanced away and started to tidy up papers on the table. "Well?" urged Mark, when Christopher did not reply immediately.

"Yes, yes, of course," replied Christopher, still tidying papers. "But the finances might really be out of our hands. If we can't afford something, we just have to do without it. The choir's a bit of a luxury for a small parish like this. We managed without one before Julian came and I suppose that we could go back to not having one. I'm sorry, Mark, but running a parish is no joke. I thought you might have some sympathy."

Mark straightened himself and made a movement to leave.

"Well, Julian never seemed to find it difficult. But then, he did everything well. I'll be off now, Christopher. I take it that I can bring a choir next Sunday?"

"Of course you can," Christopher responded, trying to keep the irritation out of his voice. "Nothing will be decided for ages and we go on as normal for the time being. Goodbye."

Mark strode out of the vestry. Christopher sat down on the chair recently vacated by Betty Cook and ran his fingers through his wiry, greying dark hair. Why did everybody have to be so difficult, so unhelpful? He had never liked Mark very much, but he supposed that, in a parish, one had to nurture a sense of Christian fellowship somehow. Christopher thought that Mark made even less effort to do this than he did. The man was prickly, self-centred, vain and uncompromising. Just because he was an organist, everybody had to take care not to upset him. Was that typical of musicians? Christopher did not know. He glanced down at the papers which he was absently rearranging and noticed that one was an invoice for gas. That reminded him of the temperamental heating system and he made another mental note to call the heating engineer.

"Otherwise," he muttered, "the punters will claim they're freezing. I really don't care. Nobody else ever takes the trouble to find out what needs to be done. They just complain about it."

Caroline appeared in the doorway.

"Simon and I are just leaving," she called out, cheerfully. "I hope that's OK - we've done all the washing-up. Only, Adrian is home from college this weekend and I promised him we'd try and have some lunch with him. I don't think we've left too much for you to do. The white frontal can stay on for Wednesday. I'll check that the chaplain can come. I can't remember his name but it'll be on the diocesan website."

Christopher attempted to give a friendly smile.

"That's all right, Caroline. You get along. I'll just finish one or two things and then lock up. Have a good lunch."

Caroline gave a thoughtful look at Christopher's face and then left. Christopher knew that Caroline was thinking about his wellbeing in a maternal sort of way and found it irksome. His state of mind was no business of hers and he resented the fact that she was probably at this very moment saying to Simon something like, "I do hope that Chris is going to be all right. He seems very quiet today. I expect that the vacancy is bothering him. Poor Chris." Well, he couldn't stop her. Most women seemed to behave like that, wanting to know every detail of people's private lives and then indulging in amateur psychology. It was the worst thing about them. Even otherwise nice women did it and Christopher supposed that it had something to do with child-rearing or looking after aged parents. The funny thing about Caroline was that, despite all these instincts, she didn't seem to realise how dreary Simon was. Or, perhaps she did realise and made a martyr of herself. That was another problem with women. He couldn't imagine wanting to live with one.

Christopher picked up an old brass handle that served as a paperweight and placed it on the papers which he had shuffled. He then rose decisively, took his keys out of his jacket pocket and strode down the church to the main door. After a quick glance around the church to make sure that there were no stragglers, he closed the big door and locked it. He then flicked several switches on the wall near the door and the church lights went off, leaving the building illuminated only by the winter daylight which came through the clear, classical windows. He returned briskly to the vestry, where an electric light still supplemented the daylight, and pulled open the lowest drawer in the big wooden vestment chest. With fingers that were trembling slightly, he carefully drew out a folded chasuble and spread it out on the top of the chest with its back uppermost. It was old, but still magnificent. The white stamped velvet was edged in a border of blue silk, lavishly embroidered in gold. A central panel, also of blue silk, depicted the figure of St Benedict embroidered in brown, gold, green and red. Several of the threads had become unravelled, the white velvet was discoloured and the border had come adrift in a few places. Christopher gazed at it reverently and smoothed out some of the trailing gold threads as though he were stroking the tumbled hair of a loved child. His fingers traced the figure of the robed saint, lingering particularly on the halo, where the embroidery was exquisite.

For some moments, he stared lovingly at the garment, mentally drinking in its rich colours and beautiful workmanship. Because of its fragility, it was hardly ever worn at services these days. It had been made especially for the church in 1904 by the Sisters of Bethany, to a design by Comper. Julian had worn it once or twice and, of course, had looked wonderful. Most of the congregation did not know of its existence and probably would not have cared much about it anyway. Christopher cared a great deal about it. He knew also that there had once been a matching altar frontal but he had never been able to discover what had become of it. He suspected that a previous rector had chucked it out.

After a while, he began to murmur a restoration shopping list to himself.

"Carefully conserve and clean. Take in loose threads and rework. Restore worn areas of lining, replacing as necessary. Re-stitch areas of the border."

Even as he muttered these words, he reflected that it was all a vain hope. The parish had no money for work of this sort and the parochial church council would not think it worthwhile. Caroline might possibly vote for it but more because of her sympathy for Christopher than for any real interest in the project. She was not a philistine but she would have taken the view that things like the heating system or the electrics were more important at the present time. He gave a deep sigh and thought about the heating system. The winter had been quite cold up until now and, if the heating broke down altogether, the church would not feel very welcoming. It would also not be right to allow Justin to open up the church for visitors on weekdays. Justin had got into the habit of coming across from the college in his spare time to open the church and show tourists around. This even brought in some money because visitors tended to put a few coins in the church box.

Christopher allowed himself another five minutes' enjoyment of the chasuble before slowly folding it up and replacing it in the drawer. He then took his navy blue overcoat from a decrepit coat stand in the vestry, shrugged it on over his suit, picked up his shoulder bag from the floor, turned out the light, locked the door that led into the church and let himself out through the other vestry door into the narrow side street that ran alongside the church. He paused for a moment, thinking about his route home, and then strode down the street into the main road that went past the main entrance to the church. He always liked to go on foot to his flat in Islington, choosing each time one of a number of possible routes. He particularly enjoyed passing as many churches as possible, always lingering for a short time outside each one in order to appraise the architecture. He liked eighteenth century ones the best but, between St Benet's and his home, they were nearly all from the nineteenth century. Sometimes, he indulged in a detour which allowed him to see a few of the Wren churches in the City, but today he decided not to do so.

His route took him past St Andrew's Church, a rather shabby Victorian building in red brick and stone, with a narrow spire. Its west end was set back a little from the road, with a low railing in front. Next to it was the vicarage, a boring, boxy 1950's house on part of the site of the original one, which had been bombed. Next to that was a boring, boxy block of flats, built on the rest of the vicarage site and sold off to pay for the replacement house. Christopher, who had stopped outside the church, sighed deeply as he looked at it. He then glanced at the notice board in front of the church, where peeling paint announced that the Sunday services were. 'Holy Communion 8.00 am' and 'Parish Communion 11.00 am'. Weddings and baptisms were 'by arrangement'.

After a few seconds' quiet contemplation, Christopher continued his walk. He could have included Holy Trinity Church, which was down a side street, but he decided to give it a miss on this occasion. He pressed on until he reached Christ Church, that great nerve centre of Evangelicalism. As there were people gathered in the small churchyard and going in and out of the church, Christopher crossed the road and pretended to be waiting for someone outside a sports shop. He stared at the church disapprovingly, but was somehow fascinated by it. This was also a Victorian church, and by quite a distinguished architect, but there was a large modern extension on one side which spoilt the original symmetry. Nothing was shabby here. The church had been expensively, if insensitively, restored and there was a huge, electrically-illuminated cross over the main door. There was a much larger notice board here than at St Andrew's and numerous church activities were listed. The people who were chatting in the churchyard were mostly in their twenties and thirties, well-dressed, good-looking and voluble. One of them, a slightly older man, beautifully turned out in a dark suit, white shirt and blue tie with a motif on it, appeared to be the centre of attention. Christopher supposed that this was the vicar, Mr Newton.

On the low fence that divided the churchyard from the pavement was a long banner, printed in primary colours. Christopher read it almost unwillingly and frowned as he did so.

"Take part in the Christ Church Mission and help bring a million people to Christ. www.christchurchmission.org."

Christopher read it twice and then walked on.

Chapter two

Christopher stood in front of his bathroom mirror and shook his head as he tied his black bow tie for the third time. Once again, he seemed to end up with one side of the bow bigger than the other but, this time, he decided to leave it the way it was. He really should have set out by now for the February dinner of the Worshipful Company of Professional Institution Secretaries and Administrators, but he was feeling slightly sick and his preparations had been slower than usual. There was a bug going around his office and he hoped that he had not caught it. He was much too busy to be ill, what with the church work as well as his office work, and even the thought of it gave him a panicky feeling in his stomach.

He returned to his bedroom and put on his black jacket, only to feel that he needed to head back to the bathroom to relieve himself. He took off the jacket and then decided to extricate himself from his braces and cummerbund as well, but, when he eventually sat on the lavatory pan, he found that he could not produce anything. He then put everything back on, returned to the bedroom and took his overcoat from his wardrobe. As he pulled the coat on, he shook his head again, gulped down the sicky feeling at the back of his throat and then walked across the room and down the passage to his front door.

His flat was a ground floor one, not far from Upper Street, Islington, and Christopher walked the short distance to the main road and waited at the nearest bus stop. Much though he normally liked walking, he did not feel like walking to the City for the dinner. The weather was cold and damp with little occasional flurries of icy rain which stung his cheeks and made his eyes water. He shivered. All around him, people in coats and scarves were hurrying to their evening engagements, hurrying home from work, or just hurrying. Young couples, the girls mostly wearing short skirts, tight jeans or leggings, were looking at restaurant menus or going into noisy pubs. The rain, together with the bright lights from the street lamps and shop windows, made everything look slightly blurred. Christopher blinked and stared idly at a particular couple who were standing outside a pizza restaurant trying to decide whether to go in. The young man was of medium height, fair-haired and dressed in a dark fleece and blue jeans. His girlfriend was rather short and wore a red woollen coat over a long, ankle-length black skirt. She had short dark hair creeping out from under a striped knitted hat. Both wore trainers and there was not much to distinguish them from all the other young people milling around Upper Street. Normally, Christopher would not have noticed them or, if he had, he would have regarded them with slight contempt. Today, perhaps because he was feeling sick, he experienced a completely unexpected shock of envy.

He had never done what they were doing. He had never held hands with a girl in that close and companionable way, never taken a girl out for a pizza or been taken out by a girl for a pizza. He had known girls at university, of course, and there were women in his office, but his relationships with them had always been formal and remote or artificially playful and satirical. At university, he had joined the rambling club and gone out for walks in a group, but the girls had not shown much interest in him once they had discovered that he was fascinated by church architecture and furnishings. They had seemed aloof, in any case, and none of them had been very attractive. A friend of his, who had shared his interests, had managed to secure a girlfriend and Christopher had gone around with them in a threesome for a whole term. Amanda, that was it. A nice sort of girl with long hair tied back and sympathetic brown eyes. His friend had ended up by marrying her. Christopher had gone to the wedding but had not kept in touch much since. He seemed to remember that they now had two or three children and lived in Guildford.

Christopher glanced back to the street and could see a number 56 bus approaching. He looked at the young couple again and saw that they were entering the restaurant. Through the glass, he could see them being greeted by a waiter and shown to a table. Well, they were probably boring, after all, and would talk about silly things like clubbing or rock music. He boarded the bus and sat down towards the back. As the bus roared towards the next bus stop, he stared out of the window at the shops and busy pavements. Seeing a heating engineer's van parked outside a building, he started to think about the heating problems at the church, which were still unresolved. An engineer had come while Justin had been minding the church but, although he had spent quite a long time inspecting the thermostat and time switches, he had not made a positive diagnosis. On the following Sunday, the heating had cut out again, halfway through the service, and Christopher had had to telephone the heating firm to ask for another visit. Simon had been very irritating about it, saying several times that one couldn't expect people to attend divine worship in a cold church. Mark had also complained, claiming that his singers could not sing properly if they were cold, and Christopher had had to struggle to keep his temper. However, unexpected support had come from Justin, who had pointed out that the heating engineer had tried very hard to fix the problem, that the boiler was old and that it wasn't anybody's fault that the heating kept switching itself off. Justin was a good chap. He had remained loyal to St Benet's since Julian had left and often sided with Christopher in any dispute.

Christopher pictured to himself the church heating system, tracing the pipework from the boiler to the radiators, header tank and overflow pipe, and wondering which bit of it was going wrong. He felt sure that it was something to do with the thermostat in the vestry, although the heating engineer had not thought so. Could it be something in the boiler itself? It seemed unlikely, considering that the boiler was completely mechanical and very unsophisticated. Christopher bit his lip and swallowed down a sicky feeling again. How long was this dinner going to last? He hoped that he was going to be seated next to someone decent. At the last dinner of the Company, he had sat next to an elderly man who had gone to sleep during the speeches and actually snored, waking up only when the Master had sounded the gong to signify the end of the evening. Christopher had not been able to talk to the person on his other side because she had been deep in a conversation about the care of the elderly with the man on her other side. Christopher had felt frozen out, even though he had heard almost every word of the discussion about care homes, where "equal opportunities", "racial equality" and "human dignity" had been referred to a large number of times.

The bus stopped near to St Bartholomew's Hospital and Christopher got off. A cold draught attacked him and he turned up his coat collar in a futile attempt to feel warmer. The hall where the dinner was being held was not far away and he walked there briskly and without pausing. He knew all these streets and had mentally plotted a route when he had sent in his booking for the dinner. Light was streaming down some steps from an open doorway and he joined two or three other diners who were entering the building. They followed the usual routine of leaving their coats in the cloakroom, visiting the lavatory and then joining the groups of people who were waiting to go upstairs for the formal presentation. Christopher spotted a friend who was standing in a corner with his wife and another couple, and went across to join them. The friend smiled a welcome.

"Hello, Chris. May I introduce Jenny, my wife, to you? Strangely, I don't think you two have met. And these are the Clarks, Stephen and Heather. Stephen is deputy director at the Institute of Advancement. Heather is headteacher of Parnassus Specialist Science Academy."

Christopher shook their hands, saying, "How do you do?" to each of them in turn, ending with his colleague.

"Good to see you, Max. I didn't get a chance to talk to you at the conference the other day. What did you think of it? The presentations were a bit long-winded."

"Oh, not bad. I don't think you stayed on for the cocktail reception at the end, did you, Chris? The drinks were pretty good, and plentiful as well. But you're looking down in the mouth. Anything wrong?"

Christopher gave a wry smile.

"No, nothing," he replied. "At least, I hope not. There's a bug going around our office and I thought earlier in the evening that I might have caught it."

His companions backed away slightly and, before anyone could think of what to say next, a gong was sounded upstairs. There was a general movement towards the wide staircase and a portly man wearing a red sash over his jacket positioned himself at the foot of the stairs to direct the flow. Christopher joined the queue that was snaking slowly and somewhat erratically up the stairs. When he reached the top, another man sporting a red sash called out his name and Christopher stepped forward to shake hands with the Under Master, the Master and their wives. A few words were exchanged, but it was bad form to say anything more and Christopher moved on into a room where drinks were being offered. He accepted a glass of orange juice but, when he sipped it, the sicky taste came back into his mouth. He swallowed hard and threaded his way through the assembled guests to a large notice board on an easel where the seating plan was displayed.

"Hm, table F," he muttered, looking at the plan. "I have Tony Smith TD on my left and Henry Stamford on my right, with Mr and Mrs Matthew Patel sitting opposite. Don't know any of them, but the Patels look the best bet."

"Any good, Chris?"came a cheerful voice over his shoulder and he found Max standing just behind him, also studying the plan.

"Well, I don't know," he replied. "I'm on table F and I'm sitting next to Tony Smith TD and Henry Stamford. Do you know either of them?"

"I know old Tony," responded Max, moving forward to join him. "He's not a bad bloke. Likes to think he's a military man. He'll probably want to talk about wine. Henry Stamford, I don't know much, although I can remember admitting him to the Company a year or two ago. Jenny and I are on table B. The other names are vaguely familiar but I don't think I know them much. Jenny always manages to talk to people, whoever they are. It's funny how women can do that. She starts asking them about their children and that always gets them going. No good if they haven't got any, of course."

Christopher could not help smiling. There was a lot to be said for being an uncomplicated sort of person like Max. He was always cheerful, had a pleasant wife and two children and got through his work with minimum fuss and without any soul-searching. Christopher had known him for quite a while but usually only met up with him at conferences. He wished sometimes that he could be like him, straightforward and prepared to like everybody, but knew that he never could be. But, was he doing Max an injustice? Was Max really a very complex character who was good at putting on an act, a public face? Was Tony Smith TD really a complex individual? And what about Henry Stamford? Christopher gave his head a slight shake and then started as he realised that Max was staring at him with puzzlement and some amusement.

"Sorry, Max," he said apologetically. "I was deep in thought then. So you don't know Henry Stamford? Well, he can't be worse than the people I sat next to last time. I ended up eating my dinner in silence and reading the menu all evening. Oh, there's the gong. Here goes."

A gong had provided the signal for the assembled members and their guests to move into the large dining hall where the meal was to be served. Max went to look for his wife and Christopher joined the crowd that was spilling into the hall. He found table F and his place on it and stood behind his chair, waiting for the other occupants to turn up. A smartly-dressed couple took their places opposite and smiled across at Christopher, who dutifully returned their smile. Well, the Patels seemed very nice. Then, a tall, grey-haired man moved into the place on his left. Tony Smith TD. Tony extended a hand to Christopher and they shared a formal handshake. "Tony Smith." "Christopher Jamieson." "How do you do?" "How do you do?" After another minute, a plump, red-faced man materialised on Christopher's right. "Henry Stamford." "Christopher Jamieson." "How do you do?" "How do you do?" Grace was said by the Company chaplain, a sociable-looking priest with shiny cheeks, and everyone sat down.

Christopher's neighbours at the table turned to speak to their neighbours on the other side so, for a short time, Christopher was isolated. For something to do, he took up the menu card which was on the table in front of him and scanned it. Normally, he would have enjoyed anticipating the various courses but, today, the descriptions made him feel queasy. He read it over to himself, under his breath.

"Marinated herring with potato salad and beetroot. Roasted chicken with lemon, thyme, garlic, petit pois and pancetta. Rich soft dark chocolate torte with whipped cream. Coffee and petits fours."

It seemed strange that these descriptions, which normally would have made him lick his lips with pleasurable expectation, now only made him feel more ill. In fact, he began to notice a heavy feeling in his chest and the taste of the orange juice in the back of his mouth. It was actually more like the taste of vomit. Christopher realised with sinking spirits that his evening was going to become a battle with impending sickness. He reached across the table to the water jug and poured himself a glass. As he sipped the water, he noticed how noisy the hall was, with everybody talking and crockery and cutlery clinking. People always spoke at the tops of their voices on these occasions, trying to make their conversation intelligible over the hubbub but, of course, this only made the noise worse. There was subdued lighting in the hall, with candles burning in branched candelabra on the tables, and Christopher felt that he had blurred vision. He looked across at Mr and Mrs Patel, who were each talking animatedly to the guests on their other sides. They were probably in their thirties, very good-looking, with smooth, milk chocolate skin. Matthew was wearing a beautifully-cut dinner suit, impeccable white shirt and perfect bow tie. His wife, Amy, looked superb in a bright green dress, made of some glossy material, probably best quality silk, with a wide neckline and tiny sleeves. Her sparkling necklace and long earrings made her large eyes look lustrous and seductive. They were easily the best-looking people in the room. Most of the men were either a bit tubby or very tubby, with their black jackets stretched tightly across their backs or hanging loosely over baggy black trousers. The women were either smart and business-like, wearing expensive but plain dresses, or of the mutton-dressed-as-lamb variety, in low-cut frocks covered in sequins and with flowing scarves which failed to disguise their flabby upper arms and wrinkled necks.

Christopher looked thoughtfully around the hall and, in doing so, gained a friendly smile from Max who was seated at a table not far away. Max's wife, Jenny, was sitting opposite her husband, talking to an elderly member in an interested and kindly way. She was very sensibly turned out in a blue silk blouse and long black skirt. Christopher then directed his attention to the top table where this year's Master was beaming at his guests in a very self-satisfied way. Ranged on each side of him were the principal guests, who included a Member of Parliament and a senior investment banker. He hoped that the speeches would not go on too long.

"A bread roll, sir?" said a voice at his left shoulder, and Christopher automatically selected a brown roll from the assortment offered by the white-jacketed waiter. By this time, Tony Smith had finished his introductory conversation with the guest on his left and had turned to address Christopher.

"What are they giving us, then?" he said jovially. "The food's usually rather good here. Let me see." He grasped the menu card and peered at it. "Marinated herring, eh? With potato salad and beetroot. Then roast chicken and peas. Sounds good. Then chocolate cake and cream. Very nice, except if you're watching your waistline, eh? I must say, I do like this simple sort of food. You know where you are with it."

Christopher agreed politely and Tony continued.

"Y' know, I was at a restaurant the other day with a colleague – place just off Regent Street – and neither of us could make head or tail of the menu. We couldn't work out whether we were ordering meat, or fish, or whatever. And, when we got it, we still didn't know which it was. I must say, it looked very pretty though, with a little bunch of herbs on it and a trickle of sauce. Would have made a good still life. It tasted all right, but it was only two mouthfuls and the pudding wasn't much better. I can never understand what you're supposed to do with the squiggle of sauce. Eat it? Now, my idea of a really good pudding is a big slab of rhubarb crumble and custard. Don't you agree?"

Christopher had to swallow what felt like a lump in his throat before replying. The descriptions and smell of food were making his queasiness worse and worse.

"Yes, of course. Rhubarb crumble. It was my favourite pudding at school. But what do you think the speeches will be like tonight?"

"Oh, all right," responded Tony. "To be honest, I usually let them wash over me. You're always sleepy by that stage in the evening. But, what was I saying? Oh yes, rhubarb crumble. That's not the only pudding I like. My grandmother always made an excellent spotted dick, full of currants. And then there's steamed syrup pudding and bread and butter pudding. And you never see sago pudding these days. Goodness, I grew up on sago pudding. I've no idea where sago comes from, but perhaps they don't grow it any more. It's all this global warming."

Tony paused while a small plate of herring and potato salad was placed in front of him and then continued.

"Herrings are another example. We had them every week when I was a boy – kippers, bloaters sometimes, or just fried. You can't beat them for flavour but the bones are bit of a nuisance. Mind if I start?"

He ate a mouthful of herring and potato and Christopher tried to do the same, but he found it very difficult to force his throat to accept the food. Tony carried on talking and eating at the same time.

"Really good, this herring. Good flavour. I suppose it's all to do with the marinating. But, d'you know, I'm not sure that they've got the right wine to go with this. I would have said a good Syrah or even a quality Gewürztraminer would have been better. Alsace is the best place for that, of course. But, my word, other countries are catching up. We had an officers' dinner the other night – just ten of us – and the wine was a Pinot Noir. I've never tasted such a fresh and fruity Pinot Noir as that one. Tasted of ripe plums and raspberries. We all tried to guess where it came from. France was the most popular, but I didn't agree. I know my French wines. Somebody thought it was from Switzerland, but I didn't think much of that for an idea. But you'll never guess where it was from. New Zealand of all places! I'd never have guessed. But, actually, there are some jolly good wines coming from there these days. Oh, excuse me a moment."

He broke off his monologue to pour a glass of water for his neighbour, and then began talking to the neighbour. Christopher was glad to be spared for a few moments and he sipped his water before making another attempt to eat some of the first course. Conversation was buzzing all around him and he had an odd sensation of being invisible. He glanced up and found that Amy Patel's green dress and bright jewellery were merging into a shimmering and unstable shape. But, as he pushed his food around the plate, he became aware that Henry Stamford was discussing the Church of England with his neighbour.

"It's all finished," he was saying. "I can't see how it can possibly struggle on much longer. The congregations get smaller and smaller. Nobody wants to get married in church these days. Or married at all. They can't pay their clergy. And, anyway, no-one can see the point of having an established Church. Half the country isn't Christian, so why have an established Church? It doesn't make sense. Oh, I know that we'd have to look after the cathedrals and all that if the Church packed up, but that can be done by the heritage chaps."

"I don't think it's as bad as you suggest," replied the neighbour mildly. "I think the Church does at least give the country a moral basis. Wouldn't we be worse off without it? Who would do all the memorial services and the royal weddings?"

"You don't see my point," responded Henry slightly irritably. "I'm talking about being the Established Church. They can go on holding memorial services if they like, but I don't see why it has to be Established. But anyway, Established or not, it's all going to fold up sooner or later. I passed a church the other day and noticed that it had curtains in the windows. It wasn't a church; it was a house! It even still had gravestones all around it, but it was a house. That's what's happening. The churches are all closing and being turned into other things. The people of this country just aren't interested in religion any more. It's all celebrity stuff and sport."

"I do see your point about the Establishment thing," answered the neighbour in a patient voice. "That's what I'm saying. Because the Church of England is Established, it means that we have a moral and ethical basis in public life. I think everything would be a lot worse if we didn't have the Church, but I'm very sorry that churches are having to close."

"It's their own fault," said Henry. "If they can't make Christianity attractive to the rest of us, they deserve to close. It took the Church over a hundred years to accept Darwin and I'm not sure that half of it accepts his theories even now. Last summer I popped in a church when I was on holiday in the West Country and picked up a booklet about Creation. Ridiculous stuff. They'd ruined the church – loudspeakers everywhere and modern chairs. I'll tell you what I think…"

Christopher turned his face away and tried not to listen. A clammy sweat had broken out on his forehead and he kept having to swallow a sour liquid that came into the back of his mouth every few seconds. Suddenly, a different voice entered the discussion that was continuing on his right-hand side.

"Excuse me for interrupting you, gentlemen," said Amy Patel in a sweet and silky voice, "but I'm afraid that I couldn't help overhearing what you were saying. You have both made very good points. On one hand, it does seem to be an anachronism to have an Established Church in a multicultural and multi-faith country. On the other hand, it means that the government is obliged to listen to the moral and ethical views put forward by the representatives of the Church, even if it doesn't subsequently follow them. Don't you agree?"

"Well, yes," spluttered Henry. "It sounds so reasonable when you put it like that, but I don't think many people in this country could care less. You must admit the Church is on its last legs."

Amy drew herself up and looked almost defiant. Her eyes glowed.

"I don't think that's true at all. A few churches might be having difficulties, but some churches have been reborn. The Holy Spirit is drawing people in and giving them something to live for. At my church, people are absolutely flocking to the services. We have already extended the church once and we're having to think about extending it again, or taking over another church. We have a big children's group, a youth group, young adults' group, seniors' group – it's wonderful. If you were to come to Christ Church, you'd see what I mean. Last year, we had twenty people going forward for ordination. Now we're running a campaign, to bring a million to Christ. I can give you the link to our website."

Henry was almost silenced.

"Er, thank you. But my neighbour here, Christopher, is something to do with the Church. A churchwarden or something. Isn't that right, Christopher?"

Christopher hardly heard him. He knew that, unless he escaped as quickly as possible, he would be sick all over the table. Muttering "excuse me", he struggled to his feet, dropped his napkin on the floor and almost ran to the nearest exit. With his hand over his mouth, he fled down the stairs and into the gentlemen's lavatory. Just in time, he almost fell into a cubicle and was sick down the lavatory pan. He shivered as he gripped the sides of the lavatory and cold sweat beaded his forehead. The smell of his vomit was nauseous and he reached out a shaking hand to flush the lavatory. The water roared down the pan, taking most of the solid matter with it, but, just as the noise stopped, Christopher heaved again and poured more vomit into the clouded water.

For a few minutes, he could not think at all. The sickness seemed to have taken over his whole being and he shuddered wretchedly as he knelt in front of the lavatory, like an abject sinner confessing a lifetime's crimes. Gradually, however, he began to feel rational again and, when he could not spit out any more of the loathsome fluid, he lifted his head and unwound himself into a sitting position. His head ached, he had a dull pain just above his diaphragm, and chilly sweat was dripping off his face. He felt pathetic and he guessed that, if anyone had been looking, he would have looked pathetic as well. But nobody was looking. Apparently, nobody had bothered to follow him to find out if he needed help. Christopher would not have wanted anyone to do so, and yet he felt hurt and rejected. The people at his table had presumably gone on eating, drinking and chatting without wondering where he had gone. Well, he could not return to the dining hall in his present state and the only thing to do was to go home once he could gather enough strength. He groped in his pocket for his handkerchief and, with a trembling hand, used it to wipe the sweat from his face. He then rested his elbows on his knees and sat still for about five minutes, trying to muster sufficient energy to stand up.

At last, he dragged himself to his feet and stood for a moment, trying to get his balance. He then staggered out of the cubicle and went to one of the wash basins where he washed his hands, splashed water over his face and sluiced his mouth out, trying to get rid of the lingering taste of vomit. He could not avoid seeing himself in the mirror, but what he saw made him feel slightly faint. His face was white and drawn, with a slightly greenish tinge, his bow tie was coming undone and water was dripping from his flattened hair.

"Not a pretty sight," he muttered, taking his bow tie off and stuffing it in his pocket. "Now to try getting home."

The bored-looking woman in the cloakroom gave Christopher an odd look when she handed him his overcoat, but did not say anything, much to his relief. He did not feel like having a conversation with anyone at the moment, least of all a cloakroom attendant. But, as he struggled to do up his coat buttons, he heard his name called and looked up to find Max coming down the stairs towards him.

"Hi, Chris!" called out Max from halfway down the stairs. "Are you all right, old man? I saw you leave the dinner, but thought you'd just gone to the loo. Do you know, you look as white as a sheet."

Within a second or two, Max was standing beside him, looking with real concern at Christopher's pale face and damp hair. Christopher tried to smile but knew that the effect was probably rather ghastly.

"Oh, I've just been sick, that's all. It's this bug I told you about. I – I'm not in a fit state to go back to the dinner. I couldn't eat it anyway. I've just brought up the whole of the first course. I'm going home. Perhaps you could apologise for me."

"Now, look here," said Max, firmly. "Let me call you a cab. You can't possibly get home on your own in that state. It's no trouble, they won't miss me. We're still waiting for the main course. Take my arm."

Christopher shook his head.

"I'd really rather be left alone, Max. Honestly. I'll be all right. It's not far and there'll be plenty of buses. I think I just want fresh air at the moment. You get back. I'll be in touch."

He finished doing up his buttons and moved towards the main doors, leaving Max standing still with a perplexed look on his face. An attendant appeared from nowhere to open the door and Christopher went out into the cold night air. The evening had been a disaster.

Chapter three

It was a grey Sunday morning in March. Christopher had woken at 6 o'clock after having a nightmare about falling off Beachy Head. Just as he had fallen off the cliff, he had woken up and now he was standing at his bedroom window trying to capture the floating mist of his dream. Why had it been Beachy Head? And how had he known it was Beachy Head? Had anyone told him it was, or had he somehow recognised it? He had not been there since he was a boy and only dimly remembered what it looked like. He could remember his father telling him that it was the highest cliff in England and that people committed suicide there. In his dream, it had definitely been Beachy Head.

He ran his fingers through his uncombed hair and looked out at the paved yard outside his bedroom window, where some concrete tubs still held the straggly remains of last autumn's plants. The yard was included in his lease and he had meant to replace the plants with spring bulbs but had never gotten round to it.

"It's all this wretched work," he said out loud. "And now the bloody Archdeacon's coming. Why did I land myself with all this?"

Although his question was rhetorical, Christopher looked enquiringly at the chilly grey yard as though expecting it to answer him. A few shrivelled brown leaves were blowing around in circles, chasing each other in a futile game, as though they were spirits of long-dead occupants. A grim smile passed over Christopher's face as he remembered the estate agent's description of this yard. 'Private walled garden with shrubs and container plants.' How did a garden differ from a yard? His childhood home had had a garden where he had spent many solitary hours wandering around the lawn and up and down the path, but this was nothing like that. There were, however, shrubs. Two, to be exact – a forsythia and a buddleia, both growing against the wall opposite his bedroom window. In some ways, they had been well-chosen, because the forsythia bloomed in the early spring and the buddleia in the late summer. The forsythia had yellow buds on it and would have bloomed before now if the winter had not been so cold. It was a cheering-up plant which produced its bright yellow flowers when hardly anything else was blooming.

Christopher felt that he needed cheering up.

"I suppose humans are part of nature," he thought. "Perhaps in the past, we did follow the rhythm of the seasons, feeling perked up in the spring and planting things, and then getting mellow and fruitful in the autumn. It was a lover and his lass. Having it off in the flower meadows in May, full of optimism and the spirit of new life. We've lost something somewhere. I must have been conceived in the spring, but I can't imagine mum and dad feeling like that. I expect that dad was wearing his cardigan at the time. And I must have been such a shock to mum that she never wanted any more children. It's funny that you never really know what your parents were like at the time that you were born. Dad never seemed young to me and yet he must have been once. And mum always seemed so staid, as though she had always been middle-aged. But there was that photo of her in a mini-skirt."

He grinned, seeing in his mind the photograph of his mother in a mini-skirt and his father in a check shirt with a big collar. Then his face became serious again.

"Poor things. They never got much joy out of life. I could never work out which one was propping up the other. And I just felt embarrassed by them - I suppose that was horrible of me. There was that awful time when I invited Jerry Benson home to tea. How old was I then? About thirteen?

We all had to sit around the table and eat bread and butter and cake while dad tried to make polite conversation with Jerry. Dad must have thought that all families behaved like that. Jerry didn't know what had hit him. I never got invited back. I'm not sure that I was much fun either. My idea of conversation was to play at conjugating Latin verbs. And I read a translation of Homer's Odyssey so many times that the paperback fell apart in the end and I tried to stick it all back together with parcel tape. I wasn't interested in football or rock groups. They were boring. My heroes were Agamemnon and Odysseus. No wonder I didn't have many friends."

Christopher continued to stare out of the window, thinking about Latin verbs and Homer's Odyssey, until a raucous whirring noise behind him disturbed his train of thought. It was his alarm-clock, set for seven o'clock and not yet turned off. He made a dive for it and pressed down the button at the top. It was time that he got dressed and set off for St Benet's. The Archdeacon was taking the service today and then staying behind to talk to the parochial church council. Christopher had a sense of foreboding about this. The Archdeacon was an irritable little man who had little time for parishes which used coloured vestments or the Book of Common Prayer. He took the view that these put people off and deterred families from attending church. Although at least middle-aged himself, he liked to talk about 'modern forms of worship', 'new expressions', 'worship areas', 'the call of the Holy Spirit' and 'different ways of being church'; language which left Christopher cold. He could see no point in having slangy modern language when the stately and mellifluous prose of the 1662 Prayer Book was available. And he was not sure that he wanted families very much either – nasty, ill-disciplined children who paid no attention to the service and expected to be given biscuits and sweets by their parents. He had cynical misgivings about the motives of these parents, suspecting many of them to be attending church so that they could get their children into the local Church of England schools. He knew that Julian had written several letters in connection with that. But then people liked Julian anyway, because he was so charming and made them feel important.

Christopher had returned to the window while thinking these thoughts and continued to stare moodily out, reluctant to begin a day which he felt was going to be unpleasant. The leaves were still going round and round.

"Suppose," he thought, "I were to resign. What would happen? Well, Caroline would do her best, there's no doubt of that. But Simon would try to get his own way over things and Caroline would be torn between appeasing him and doing what she thought I would have wanted. Hm. Then, who would volunteer to be the other churchwarden? Simon might, although a husband and wife team would look a bit silly. What about Justin? He's young, but he does care about St Benet's and might volunteer if he thought that nobody else would. Betty Cook wouldn't and anyway isn't up to it. Neither is Hilda Deakin. But what if one of them did become churchwarden? They would give in to the Archdeacon and get rid of the Prayer Book. And the vestments! Oh, heaven."

Christopher rubbed the centre of his forehead with the fingers of his left hand as though trying to get rid of a nagging headache. His face took on a look of resolve. No, he would have to remain as churchwarden. Without question. There was no hope for St Benet's otherwise. In his mind, he saw the exquisite Comper chasuble with its rich colours and fine workmanship. Then, mentally, he opened the other drawers in the vestment chest and checked the contents. There was a drawer for each colour – white, red, green and purple. And, mixed up with the purple vestments, there was a rose-pink chasuble for use on Mothering Sunday and the third Sunday in Advent. Not many churches used rose-pink these days, but St Benet's did. The pink chasuble was a bit shabby and the braid was starting to become unstitched, but it was still very usable. Christopher thought that he would take his sewing kit one Sunday and stitch back that braid, ready for Mothering Sunday. Mothering Sunday. He sighed, thinking of the bunches of daffodils that he and Caroline would have to give out. These were given to all women, regardless of whether they were mothers or not, in order to prevent disappointment.

"And I suppose," he said out loud, "the men will soon want them too in these days of equal opportunities."

Christopher turned away from the window and started to get his clothes ready. He took a white shirt out of his wardrobe and put it on the bed. Then he selected one of his three suits and put that on the bed, too. The suits were all dark – one was dark blue, another was dark grey and the one he had chosen was also dark grey, but with a faint stripe. He then looked through the ties that were hanging on a rail inside his wardrobe door and fingered a couple of possibilities. After a few moments' thought, he pulled out a black tie which had red diagonal stripes and little motifs which looked like open books. This was the tie of his Worshipful Company. He then opened the top drawer of his dressing table, where underpants and handkerchiefs were neatly stored in little piles, and took out a pair of white underpants. From the other drawer, he took black socks and, when all this clothing was laid out on his bed, he went to his bathroom to wash and shave, first taking off his blue check pyjama jacket.

While he was shaving – and Christopher liked a wet shave – he reflected again on the Archdeacon's visit. He knew what it was for. The Archdeacon was going to tell the PCC that St Benet's was going to be placed under suspension of presentation. Christopher had learned this through Mark Evans, who had learned it through the grapevine. It was not official yet because the parish was supposed to be consulted, but Christopher knew that the consultation was likely to be nominal and perfunctory. The house which Julian and Helen had occupied was already being redecorated by the diocese, ready for the new Director of Ordinands. This meant that any priest who came to St Benet's would need to have accommodation provided by someone else, another parish, for example. Or, St Benet's could be held with another parish, or united with it. St Andrew's, probably. Christopher grimaced and nearly cut himself as he thought of the plump Jill Johnson in her large cassock and surplice conducting the liturgy in a mumsy way at St Benet's. Then again, would the Archdeacon want to put Bob Bodkin in as a priest in charge? Bob had taken the Sunday services since Julian's departure and was coping moderately well, if rather unexcitingly. The congregation had already dropped in size and some of the young families had mysteriously disappeared. Would Bob ultimately kill the place off, just as he had killed other parishes off? It would be a big risk, although Christopher quite liked Bob and his scatty wife. Bob was at least happy to wear the vestments and use 1662.

Christopher wiped his face on a white towel and returned to his bedroom to dress. While he was dressing, he continued to think about the Archdeacon and what he might be planning to say to the PCC. By the time he had finished dressing, he had almost convinced himself that Bob Bodkin was going to be licensed as priest in charge.

This would be a little dreary, but not absolutely dreadful and the parish would be able to struggle on for a while. Yes, that wouldn't be too bad, he thought. Not brilliant, but bearable. He could think of worse situations and he did not even attempt to think of solutions that would be worse still.

Three hours later, Christopher was sitting at the back of the church listening to the Archdeacon's sermon. His relative optimism of earlier in the morning was now rapidly evaporating in the prickly atmosphere of the Archdeacon's obvious grumpiness. Caroline, Simon and Justin were doing their best with the serving in the chancel, but nerves were causing the three of them to be clumsy and fidgety. Justin had accidentally knocked the thurible against the chancel step, causing hot charcoal to spill out on to the floor. Caroline had made the situation worse by fetching a dustpan and brush from the vestry when she imagined that nobody was looking, and then becoming the centre of attention for the small congregation. Mark was playing badly and the choir were singing raggedly and even, at times, discordantly. The Archdeacon, who was the main cause of all this, had become seriously bad-tempered and was now preaching a sermon designed to plunge everybody into black depression.

"My dear friends, let us remember that Jesus cast out the devils. Every kingdom divided against itself is brought to desolation. We - you and I - are Jesus's Church and we also have to cast out devils. And what are those devils? Murder, lying, dishonesty, I hear you say. Yes. But there are more subtle devils. There are the devils within our own walls that divide us and bring us to desolation, devils that put one church congregation against another, or are within a single congregation. Believe it or not, there are congregations in this diocese which never meet other congregations and certainly never meet anyone from another denomination. There are, I'm afraid, people who care more for fancy church music, for embroidery, for sickly-smelling incense, for metal ornaments, and for rules and regulations than for spreading the good news of Jesus Christ, our own personal Saviour. My friends, I urge you most earnestly to seek out the devils in your own lives and to confront them. Then, when you have taken the courage to get rid of them, look for Jesus. Let him come into your hearts, speak to him and, most of all, listen to him. He is there for you. He only can direct you towards a true Christian life, stripped of all the paraphernalia and trappings of any church which has become inward-looking and powerless. He is your own personal Saviour. Open the window and let the fresh air in."

"In my travels around my archdeaconry, I see all sorts of churches – rich ones, poor ones, ones with a lot going on and ones with nothing going on. Several are in between. I visited Christ Church the other day and felt elevated by what I saw. The church was packed with enthusiastic people, all lifting up their hearts to Jesus. There was a mother and baby group, a Sunday Club for the children and numerous other groups, all thriving. I'm not saying that every church needs to be like Christ Church. The Church of England is a broad Church. But this is just one example of a church which has grasped its mission with both hands and is moving forward. If you need some ideas about the future of St Benet's, I urge you, my friends, to speak to the team at Christ Church. I know that one of their ministers would be delighted to speak to your PCC or congregation. Please avail yourselves of the opportunity."

Christopher clenched his fists angrily. How dare the Archdeacon speak to them like that! The tradition at St Benet's was totally and utterly different from that at Christ

Church. The Archdeacon was being deliberately provocative and discourteous. This was clearly a foretaste of things to come, a warning and a threat. Christopher could feel his cheeks getting hot. He glanced at the servers in the chancel and saw Caroline looking pale and miserable and Simon looking cross. Justin was staring across at the Archdeacon, completely mesmerised by what he was saying. The four choir members were flicking over the pages of their music books, probably not listening to a word of the sermon. And Mark, seen in profile as he sat at the organ console, was rigid and upright. Christopher had a stifled urge to shout at the Archdeacon, to demand that he leave the church immediately, but quelling this instinct only made him angrier. His mouth felt dry and the palms of his hands felt sweaty. He knew now that the Archdeacon was an enemy.

The service struggled to its end and, when coffee had been served to the handful of people who stayed behind, the members of the PCC took their seats around the table in the vestry. Christopher had hastily tidied it up before the service had started and shoved all the clutter in a cupboard, so it was looking unusually clear. He had placed a chair at the head of the table for the Archdeacon but, when the latter entered the room, Christopher was told curtly to sit in it.

"Go on, you sit there. You're chairing the meeting, Christopher. That's only proper. I will sit here next to Justin and speak when it's my turn. Now, let's get on, please. Are we all here? I've got another appointment at 2 o'clock. Go ahead."

Christopher sat down and looked bleakly at the faces around the table – the Archdeacon on his left, then Justin and Betty Cook, then, on the other side, Hilda Deakin,

Simon and Caroline. Nobody looked very happy. Christopher inclined his head towards the Archdeacon.

"Would you like to begin the meeting with a prayer, Father?"

The Archdeacon raised his eyebrows slightly.

"Oh, do get on, Christopher. We've just had an hour of prayers. I don't think we need any more just now. Begin the meeting, please."

Christopher glanced down at the agenda in front of him.

"Apologies for absence. Do we have any apologies, Hilda?"

Hilda looked flustered.

"Er, does Mark count?" she pleaded, looking appealingly at Christopher, and then continued. "He's not a member of the PCC but he did say that he'd like to come when we're discussing the music. Only, I don't think we are discussing the music today. Oh dear, and then there's Gordon. He's never been to a meeting and someone said that he didn't know he was elected last year. Do I minute that?"

Christopher, with a sidelong glance at the Archdeacon, straightened his back.

"No, that's all right, Hilda. Don't mention Mark. And I think we'll just forget about Gordon for the time being. The Archdeacon wants to get on. The next item on the Agenda is the Minutes of the last meeting. I have my copy here. Has everybody got a copy?"

There was a general rustling of papers and Betty started fumbling in a large blue shopping bag which was on the floor. Caroline placed her set of Minutes in front of her and looked encouragingly at Christopher.

"I'm sure we've all got them, Christopher," she said kindly, ignoring Betty's bent head. "There are just a couple of paragraphs that need to be clarified. Would you like me to run through them?"

"More than a couple," Simon hissed threateningly, refusing to see the agonised expression which Caroline turned towards him. "I really don't know what we're expected to understand by things like *the plan was not taken kindly to by SK* or *it was agreed that this will have to be left to another meeting when there are more people here*. Some people don't know what reported speech is."

Hilda's cheeks went pink and she began to look upset.

"Well, if you don't like the way I write them, why don't you write them yourself? I'm only doing my best. We haven't all been to college like you have."

She put her pen down and groped in her handbag for a tissue. The Archdeacon started to pat the table with the fingers of his left hand and Simon shrugged his shoulders. Christopher groaned inwardly and, ignoring Simon's mutinous expression, addressed the sniffing PCC Secretary.

"Don't worry, Hilda. We'll sort it all out later. Now, please, go back to taking the Minutes. Is it everybody's wish that I should sign these Minutes as an accurate record of the meeting?"

Nobody answered him. He scrawled his name on the paper in front of him and passed it across the table to Hilda. The Archdeacon was making no attempt to disguise his irritation and Christopher started to feel very angry.

"The next item on the Agenda is *Matters arising* but, as the Archdeacon is clearly anxious to get on, we'll move to item four: the vacancy. Caroline, would you like to summarise the position?"

Caroline licked her dry lips and tried nervously to speak in a firm and pleasant voice.

"Yes, of course," she replied. "Well, the parish became vacant in January on the resignation of the Reverend Julian

Abbotsford – oh, gosh, I meant to tell you that Helen had the baby yesterday. A little boy, and guess what! They've called him Benedict!" A murmur went around the table but Christopher looked impassive and signalled to Caroline to continue.

"Oh yes, where was I?" she went on. "Yes, and since then, the Sunday services have been taken by the Reverend Robert Bodkin, and the weekday services..."

"All right, all right!" interrupted the Archdeacon. "We know all that. I think it would be better if I were to tell you how the diocese stands over St Benet's."

Christopher looked at him coldly.

"Our usual custom is to ask the Chairman's permission to address the meeting, Archdeacon," he said. "However, I have no objection to your proceeding."

The Archdeacon rounded on him.

"Your permission!" he barked. "You have wasted my time today with all this nonsense about reported speech and babies and I have to ask your permission to speak? I will continue. The diocese intends to suspend presentation to this parish pending discussions about its future. There is no parsonage house and it's unlikely that a full-time priest will be appointed."

Caroline opened her mouth to speak and then thought better of it. Simon looked sullen. Christopher folded his arms. The other members of the Council were silent, miserable and afraid. The Archdeacon continued speaking.

"You will be given an opportunity to discuss the proposals with a representative of the Bishop in due course. That will be me. In the meantime, I will give you some advice. You will stand a much better chance of being given a priest if you co-operate with the diocese and do not insist on using outdated liturgy and meaningless traditions which only alienate people. You must regard yourselves as a mission church and find ways of reaching out to families and young people. There was only one family that I could see in the congregation today, and I'm not surprised. Apart from anything else, the church was freezing cold. Is something the matter with your boiler?"

Christopher glared at him.

"There is a fault with the boiler which is being dealt with," he stated. "Do you want further details?"

The Archdeacon glared back.

"Just get it fixed, will you? I can't waste my time with that. But a church needs to be warm and welcoming if it is going to attract people. I couldn't find any mention of a crèche or Sunday Club on your pew sheet. What arrangements do you have?"

There was silence for a few seconds, Christopher pointedly declining to answer. Caroline attempted a smile.

"I am afraid, Archdeacon, that we've had to suspend anything like that" she replied. "Helen Abbotsford was very good with the children, but the rest of us have not found the time to organise anything. There really aren't many children who come. We used to get a lot of baptisms with Julian, but we haven't had any recently. It's funny, really. I suppose that St Andrew's or Holy Trinity have been getting ours."

The Archdeacon grunted.

"All right, all right. What about teenagers?"

Christopher looked at the ceiling and Caroline realised that it was again up to her to answer.

"Um, I don't think we really see many teenagers. You know what it is with young people. They don't seem to like going to church when they get to about thirteen. I know that my boys didn't want to come any more at about that age. They used to prefer to stay at home and play computer games. Is there anything..?"

But the Archdeacon had heard enough.

"I get the idea" he snapped. "It's completely hopeless. No babies, no families, no teenagers. Does anybody have any questions? I'm in a hurry, mind."

Nobody spoke.

"Well? Be quick now."

Christopher shifted his chair slightly so that he could look directly at the Archdeacon.

"Yes," he said, icily. "I have a question. Can the diocese explain why it has deprived this parish of its house, sent us a useless priest to take our Sunday services and then asked you to come here and insult the volunteers who have kept St Benet's going for years?"

The Archdeacon made eye contact with him for a split second and then looked away, flushing. Everybody else, including Simon, froze.

"Well?" persisted Christopher. "I think I am entitled to an answer. I am, after all, one of the churchwardens and a Bishop's officer. Could you answer me, please? I also am in a hurry."

The Archdeacon looked down and gathered his papers into a tidy pile, ready to put in his briefcase. Then he rose to his feet, scraping his chair legs on the bare floor.

"I will answer you," he said slowly. "But you won't like to hear what I have to say, Mr Jamieson. The fact is that you have done your utmost to keep this parish in the Dark Ages for years. You have blocked every reform. You have insisted on carrying on as churchwarden without giving anyone else a chance. You have resolutely forced the parish to use language and liturgy which, frankly, someone should have banned. You have just had a parish priest who was one of the most talented young clergy in the diocese and yet you failed to support him. In the end he could not stand it any longer and has taken himself off to Chichester diocese. You were not welcoming to his wife. You prevented the expenditure of funds on necessary improvements - even heating! – with the result that this church is one of the most miserable ones that I visit." He paused for breath and stared at Christopher's expressionless face with exasperation.

"And now you dare – you dare – ask me for an explanation! If you have a complaint, you can take it to the Bishop. I am wasting my time here. I came today with good intentions and with the purpose of consulting you and your colleagues in a civilised and helpful way. You are a disgrace and if I were the Bishop, I would remove you from office. Good day."

He shoved his papers in his briefcase and bustled to the vestry door that led to the street. It was, however, locked and, with everybody gazing at him in a state of shock, he turned and marched to the other door with as much dignity as his short stature would allow. For a very slow minute, there was absolute silence. Hilda and Betty both seemed close to tears. Justin chewed his fingernails. Simon stared at his agenda and Caroline tried to look at Christopher's white face without his noticing her. After a moment more, Christopher got up and pointedly closed the door that led into the church, left open by the Archdeacon. He then resumed his seat and tried to focus his eyes on the agenda.

"We will go back to *Matters arising*," he said, with a slight tremor in his voice. "Is there any item in the Minutes that anyone wishes to discuss?"

Nobody answered. Christopher was aware of the inability of everyone present to carry on with the meeting as though nothing had happened, and yet he could not think of anything else to do.

"If nobody wishes to raise anything under *Matters arising*, we will move on to the next item. I don't know if we finished with item four but, if you don't mind, I think we will defer any further discussion of it. We move on to item five."

"Christopher, don't you think -" Caroline looked across at him beseechingly, but he turned his head away.

"Christopher, I suggest that we adjourn this meeting to another time. The vestry is getting chilly and I know that people want to get home." She glanced around at the members, but Hilda, Betty and Justin all stared at the table. Simon was beginning to make impatient grumbling noises.

Christopher shrugged his shoulders and started to collect his papers together.

"All right. If that's what members want. But I don't know how I am supposed to run this parish if you all refuse to discuss the business."

"I wasn't aware that you were running the parish," responded Simon with a hostile edge to his voice. "For a start, there's another churchwarden. And, if you are running the parish, you're not doing it very well. You've completely mucked up this interview with the Archdeacon – Caroline, what is it?"

Caroline was pinching his sleeve in an attempt to shut him up, but it was Justin who intervened.

"I think you should leave Christopher alone," he said, gulping down his nerves. "He's doing his best and the Archdeacon wasn't exactly friendly. I agree with Caroline. We should adjourn."

Simon raised his eyes to heaven and got to his feet.

"Well, I for one have had enough. Come on, Caroline, let's get on. I can think of better things to do than sitting in this ice-box. You others, you might as well go."

Hilda and Betty looked at each other anxiously and started to pack up their papers. Hilda dropped her pen on the floor and disappeared under the table for half a minute while she retrieved it, emerging with a red face and the suspicion of a tear on her cheek. Within a few minutes, everybody except Christopher and Caroline had slunk out of the room. Christopher remained seated but Caroline stepped up to the head of the table and stood beside him.

"Christopher, don't take it too much to heart," she said sympathetically. "The Archdeacon wasn't being fair and he was in a bad mood the minute he arrived. But his intentions are good. I'm sure he didn't really mean what he said."

"He did," answered Christopher shortly. "He's always had it in for me. But don't bother to sympathise, Caroline. Isn't Simon waiting for you? I'll be in touch."

Caroline gave what Christopher always called 'her concerned look' and slowly walked out of the vestry.

Christopher leaned his forehead on his right hand and stared into the darkness of his closed eyes. He felt as though his brain was aching with a dull pain that would not ease and would not allow him to rest. Why had he been attacked in that way? Why did no-one thank him for all the effort he put in to keep St Benet's going? Why did the PCC members not support him? Well, Justin had spoken up in his defence and Caroline had been her usual self, but that amounted to very little. Simon was a bloody nuisance and the two old women were fairly stupid.

After a few moments of contemplation, he opened his eyes and looked around the vestry, allowing his gaze to rest finally on the vestment chest. The chest had always seemed like a box of delights to him. He remembered when he first became a server, back in Fr Kent's time, and had been shown the layers of chasubles, tunicles, burses, veils and maniples, all in their liturgical colours: green, red, white, purple and black. Some of those items had become too dilapidated to use and Julian had put them away in a cupboard, wrapped up in polythene. Christopher had plans to get them out again and have then repaired and cleaned when he could find the time. But his favourite chasuble, the white velvet one, was still in the lowest drawer and, for a minute or two, he pictured it lying there quietly, with all its beautiful embroidery undisturbed. He also thought about the white and gold chasuble that Julian had encouraged the parish to buy. That was handsome enough – and it had been expensive enough – but the decoration was nothing when compared with the venerable white chasuble.

He got up but, instead of going to the vestment chest, he turned and went into the church. The vestry door had been left open by Caroline, and Christopher also left it open behind him. The church was empty and peaceful, with the smell and vapour of incense still hanging in the air. Some hymnbooks had been left lying around on the cabinet at the back of the church and he went mechanically down the side aisle and started gathering them up. When he had a neat heap of them, he bent down, opened the cabinet door and started putting them away. As he fitted them into their place, he noticed that a prayer book had been crammed in on the wrong shelf and, taking it out, he weighed the small volume in his hand. It was dark red and had *Common Prayer* and *Cambridge* printed on its spine in gold letters. The congregation used cream booklets for the services, but there was still a large number of prayer books tucked away in the cupboard. He straightened himself, still holding the little book. It was an old friend and Christopher was familiar with almost everything in it. Today, he felt in need of an old friend and, sighing, he seated himself on the back pew and started to flick through the pages.

"Evening Prayer, Morning Prayer," he muttered, "the Litany, Prayers and Thanksgivings, the Collects, Epistles and Gospels, First Sunday in Advent, Second Sunday in

Advent." Smiling slightly, he recited the well-loved headings to himself, sometimes repeating them in a parsonical voice. After the Gospel reading for All Saints' Day, he turned the page and paused for a moment, looking down at the words.

"The Order for the Administration of the Lord's Supper or Holy Communion," he said slowly and then looked up as though he had heard a noise. But the church remained quiet in the slight mist of incense and he resumed his reading, this time almost silently and with close attention; the words acting as a balm for his bruised mind. After several minutes he reached the prayer which was called 'the prayer of humble access' and, standing up, he began to say it out loud.

"We do not presume to come to this thy Table, O merciful Lord, trusting in our own righteousness, but in thy manifold and great mercies. We are not worthy so much as to gather up the crumbs under – under - thy Table." His voice cracked and he swallowed hard before resuming his reading.

"under thy Table. But thou art the same Lord, whose property is always to have mercy. Grant us therefore, gracious Lord," he stopped again, this time really hearing a noise. Somebody was turning a key in the outer vestry door. Christopher stood still, keeping a finger in the prayer book but holding it behind his back. He heard the vestry door squeak open and, a second later, Caroline appeared in the doorway from the church to the vestry. She looked across the church at him, uncertainly.

"Do you want something?" he asked flatly. She tried to smile and took a step towards him.

"No, nothing," she replied. "Or, rather, I wondered if you were OK?"

"Why shouldn't I be OK?"

"Oh, well, you know, the Archdeacon and all that. Is there anything I can do?"

"No, I don't think so. Just leave me in peace."

Caroline hesitated, clearly not knowing what to say or do next. The she tried again.

"Don't be silly, Chris. Let me make you a cup of tea. Simon has gone home, so I'm not in a hurry. We could discuss things – what to do next." She took another step forward and rested her hand on the end of a pew. Christopher did not move.

"Chris, please. Don't get all worked up. You were right to keep your end up. I admired you for saying it. Only, perhaps we should be careful – just while the parish is vacant. We're not in a strong position. We could be forced to take someone we don't like or – or -"

"Or what?" he replied sharply. She looked down at the pew beside her.

"Or close the church. But that's very unlikely. We're grade 1 listed and the diocese wouldn't know what to do with it. We're much more likely to be sent someone. I shouldn't worry too much."

Christopher's hand tightened on the book he was holding. He wanted Caroline to leave but did not know how to make her go without being unpleasant. He hated it when she tried to be kind towards him, even though he could hardly blame her for doing so. While he tried to think of a reply, she started walking towards him, slightly warily but with sympathy in her eyes. Christopher put the prayer book on the pew and then sat on it in order to prevent her seeing it.

Caroline did not enter his pew but went behind it and placed a hand gently on his left shoulder in what was intended to be a sisterly way. He understood that and yet felt himself go rigid.

"Christopher," she pleaded. "Let's both have a cup of tea and recover from the Archdeacon. He's an ill-tempered little man."

Christopher twitched his shoulder in an effort to make her remove her hand. He tried to speak steadily.

"I've told you, Caroline, I don't want any sympathy. I know you mean well but I would rather you just went home and left me alone. For now, anyhow. Another time, we'll talk about tactics. I didn't sleep well last night and I want a bit of time to myself. Just go, please."

Caroline took her hand away.

"Well, if you're sure. But I don't want you moping. Promise you won't sit here all day. It's not good for you."

Christopher's patience ran out.

"Please, Caroline, just go!" he shouted and she backed away. "I tell you, I've had enough for now. Just go!"

Caroline hurried back to the vestry door and, with a last quick glance at Christopher's face, left the church and, a second later, the vestry. Christopher heard the door bang shut. Shifting his position, he recovered the prayer book and opened it again. But the words were blurred and, with a faint sigh, he closed it.

Chapter four

Christopher picked out a plastic badge with his name on it from those arranged on a table in the entrance hall of the conference centre. It was a mild day in April and he had come out without wearing an overcoat for the first time since the beginning of the year. While he was pinning his badge to the lapel of his jacket, he glanced over the other badges and, recognising several names, smiled faintly to himself, mentally producing an instant picture of each individual.

"Bossy Brenda is here, of course," he thought, "and that rather insipid woman, Sandra Jenks, who goes around with her. And there's Henry Stamford. I haven't seen him since that awful dinner. I expect he'll be pompous and blustering. And there's old Robert Leggs, he never misses these conferences. And good old Max, I hope he turns up."

A hand thumped on his shoulder and Christopher turned to find Max beaming at him. Max removed the hand and used it to pick up his own badge from the table.

"Good to see you, Christopher," he said, as he pinned the badge slightly crookedly to his jacket. "How are things?"

Christopher grimaced.

"Oh, all right on the whole. And how's everything with you, Max? How are Jenny and the, um, the kids?"

"They're all fine. Andrew is doing his GCSE's this year. He should be all right. They both always seem to be working on projects. Kate is doing a project about television advertising, which means that we all have to watch ghastly programmes every evening and try to decide why certain programmes have certain adverts in the breaks. It's quite interesting really. The other evening there were three adverts for men's fragrances mixed up with a motoring programme. It's psychology, you see."

Christopher pulled another face.

"Yes, but rather Kate than me. Shall we find the coffee?"

They walked across a corridor to the room where coffee was being served and pushed through the groups of dark-suited men and women to the table. A slim blonde girl wearing a black skirt and white blouse poured their coffee for them and they each collected a biscuit from one of the plates on the table. Christopher nibbled his meditatively.

"You know, Kate ought to do a project about the biscuits served at conferences. You can tell the type of conference from the biscuits. Charity affairs have horrible cheap ones because they don't want people saying that money was being wasted on the biscuits instead of being given to the poor and needy. Big corporate efforts have luxury cookies to impress clients, full of chocolate chunks and big raisins – the cookies, that is, as well as the clients. We're sort of in between. Ordinary cookies for us. I think I'll just have another."

Max smiled and then steadied his cup as someone pushed past him.

"Let's move across to that corner," he advised. "I nearly got this lot over me. How is the Institute of Professional Administrators getting along?"

"Oh, all right," replied Christopher without enthusiasm. "We're getting a new computer system. I don't know what's wrong with the old one, but the powers-that-be have decreed that we ditch it. I thought I'd come to this conference to get away from the business for a day. And, anyway, I suppose I'd better get up to date with the tax issues. Which sessions are you hoping to go to?"

Max took a sip of his coffee.

"I'm not sure. I want a decent lunch. They're doing a buffet effort from midday because the session on *e-admin* is timed to finish at 12.30, and one of the afternoon sessions begins at 1 o'clock. There's an interesting-looking session on management and ethics which I thought I might go to, but that starts at 1.15, which leaves the lunch break a bit tight if you go to the *e-admin* one as well. By the way, I saw Henry Stamford's name on the table. Funny he should turn up. Have you seen anything of him since that dinner you were sick at? I thought we might see Tony Smith here. He always likes a free lunch, but perhaps his employers have got wise to it."

Christopher managed a faint smile.

"I vaguely remember that he talked of nothing but food at that dinner. I was about to throw up at any minute and it didn't help. I haven't come across him or Henry Stamford recently. I've been a bit preoccupied."

Max looked at him enquiringly, but with sympathy.

"Is it that church of yours? How is everything going?"

Christopher finished his coffee and put the cup and saucer down on a side table before replying.

"Oh, not particularly well. The heating system is still playing up. I got the engineer in and he said it was working, but it turned itself off again a week later. I'm fed up with it, really."

"What, the church?"

"Well, the boiler, anyway. We also had a visit from the Archdeacon."

Max put his own cup and saucer down and looked sideways at Christopher's face.

"Is he a boiler, as well? I take it the visit wasn't a success?"

Christopher had an instant picture in his mind of the Archdeacon preaching the hated sermon and felt himself getting angry.

"He is a stupid, pompous, arrogant little man. He preached a sermon which was a barely veiled attack on me and the church council, and then I had a row with him afterwards. Apparently, I am personally to blame for everything that has gone wrong at St Benet's over the past fifteen years, I am standing in the way of any reforms and St Benet's will come to grief in the near future because of me."

"Surely not?"

"And more besides. In his eyes, I am the devil incarnate and I ought to be thrown into fire and brimstone, where there is wailing and gnashing of teeth."

Max raised his eyebrows.

"Well, I'm buggered. I didn't know you had it in you, Chris. You always seemed a decent enough chap to me. But I suppose the Archdeacon might be wrong. What is an Archdeacon, anyway? I suppose I should know."

Christopher paused before replying and watched other delegates take their cups and saucers back to the coffee table and prepare to leave the room to attend their first sessions.

"Oh, just a more high-up sort of priest than a parish priest. He has an archdeaconry, which is a lot of parishes, and looks after clergy discipline and church repairs and that sort of thing. I suppose you might regard him as senior management, or something like that. But it looks as though the first sessions are about to start. I think I'll have to go to the *Tax for Corporate Bodies* seminar rather than the *e-admin* one. But will you look out for me at lunch?"

Max nodded.

"Of course, see you then - if you're still awake."

Max strolled away but Christopher remained where he was for a little while longer, watching people get rid of their coffee cups and shamble off to the meeting rooms, some on their own, others in groups of two or three, and all – male and female – dressed in similar suits and light shirts. As usual on these occasions, he wondered what they were thinking, or whether they were thinking at all. Other people seemed able to make conversation about almost nothing and to find trivial things funny. He noticed that Bossy Brenda was laughing loudly as she left the room with Sandra Jenks. Brenda was stout and wore high-heeled shoes, so her large backside, tightly covered in black trouser, stuck out the back and wobbled when she walked. Christopher looked at it and shuddered. Involuntarily, he shifted his eyes to the fair-haired girl who had served the coffee and was now stacking up the cups and saucers. He sensed that she also had been looking at Brenda's backside. A faint suspicion of contempt was in her blue eyes as she looked at the retreating women and remained there when she glanced in Christopher's direction and met his gaze. He did not attempt to smile. He guessed that she felt no warmth for a middle-aged executive in a dark suit and boring tie, and he could hardly blame her. After a fraction of a second, the girl lowered her eyes and finished stacking a pile of saucers.

Christopher was the last to leave the room, apart from the fair-haired girl, but the seminar on tax had not started when he took his seat in the back row of the meeting room. In front of him, delegates were shuffling their papers or reading some of the literature which had been placed on the chairs and which appeared largely to be advertisements for the firm of accountants which was hosting the conference. Christopher shifted the documents to the empty seat beside him and looked around the room. He had been in dozens of rooms like this – plain walls, painted in the non-colour which paint firms called Magnolia; stacking chairs set out in rows; recessed spotlights in the ceiling; large, plain windows; a table at the front with a laptop on it and a couple of chairs behind it; and a screen on the wall. The word 'soulless' came into his mind. And then he wondered what 'soulful' would look like. Would there be comfortable old chairs, good paintings displayed on the walls, an antique table covered in one of those thick cloths that the Victorians liked and piles of leather-bound books? He smiled at the thought of attending a seminar room like that. His fellow-delegates would need to be shabby but intellectual-looking, with untidy hair but sharp, twinkling eyes; their sensitive hands clutching well-used copies of Kant or Burke, rather than this hard-faced lot, with their degrees in Business Administration or Finance. The cloth on the table would be dark-coloured, perhaps in a deep red and green pattern, and there would be one of those green-shaded brass lamps on it, giving just enough light for the speaker to read his notes. The speaker would be venerable, with white hair, wearing an old tweed suit and a slightly crooked bow-tie.

"Good morning, gentlemen and ladies. It gives me great pleasure to welcome you to this discourse on aesthetics in the late eighteenth century. It is my privilege to address you on a subject which has absorbed me for the past thirty years..."

Christopher suddenly noticed that the real speaker had arrived, a balding man in a grey suit, white shirt and red tie. This individual was talking to a colleague and pressing the keys of the computer until the words, 'Tax and Corporate Bodies' appeared in large letters on the screen behind him. But there seemed to be something wrong with his display because, although he kept on pressing the keys, the words on the screen did not change. The colleague then suggested various remedies which also did not work. After a few moments of this fruitless effort, the colleague, inspired by the speaker's irritation, left the room and returned with the fair-haired girl. She, completely ignoring the audience, strode up to the table and rapidly typed something on to the computer. Over her head, the presentation came to life and a series of charts passed rapidly across the screen, to the evident satisfaction of the speaker. The girl then strode out again, still without looking at the rows of executives, and the lecture began. Christopher tried to bully his brain into thinking about tax and, for a short time, was successful.

It was while he was in the lunch queue that Christopher again found his mind turning to his problems at St Benet's. It was something that Max had said. That was it: 'what is an Archdeacon anyway?' Max might just as well have asked, 'who is an Archdeacon anyway?' or even, 'who is the Archdeacon anyway?' Christopher saw again the scene in the vestry with the Archdeacon shouting at him, Caroline looking anxious and everybody else frozen into misery. He also saw himself, shouting back furiously at the Archdeacon, although it all appeared to be in mime and horribly enhanced. He felt his cheeks redden with anger as he surveyed the Archdeacon's fussy face and figure and the nails of his clenched fists pressing into his palms. What right had this irritating little man to lecture him about St Benet's or anything else?

"Chicken or vegetable lasagne?" somebody said, and Christopher discovered that he had reached the serving table and was being offered the inevitable choice between meat and 'veggie'. He looked distractedly at the legs of chicken wallowing in sauce and the dish of lasagne, seemingly full of carrots and peas.

"Oh, chicken please."

"Rice or veg?" enquired the plump woman behind the counter, brandishing a serving spoon over a huge pile of boiled rice.

"Er, rice will be fine. Thank you. Are the knives and forks somewhere?"

The plump woman inclined her head towards another table.

"Knives, forks and spoons are on the table. Chicken or vegetable lasagne?"

Christopher moved on and, holding his plate carefully in his right hand, he gathered up his cutlery and a paper napkin from the table with his left hand. As he did so, somebody lurched against his back and he nearly tipped his lunch onto the box of knives.

"Sorry, old chap," said a voice behind him. "Somebody pushed me. Hey, isn't it Chris Jamieson? You're not going to be sick again, are you? Sorry, only a joke."

Christopher swung himself round carefully and found Henry Stamford smiling at him jovially.

"Oh hello, Henry," he replied unenthusiastically. "How are you keeping? Have I seen you at these conferences before? Shall we just move away from this table?"

He guided Henry to a less busy part of the room and stood, awkwardly holding his plate and cutlery, wondering how to get rid of him so that he could find a seat and eat his lunch before it got cold. Henry seemed disposed to chat.

"Oh, I've been to a few," he replied to Christopher's question. "But I suppose that we haven't run in to each other before. I've seen your friend, Max. Nice chap. Got a very nice wife, too. Are you married?"

"No, I'm not. Look, hadn't you better go and join the queue before it all goes? They'll run out of the chicken at this rate and everyone will have to go veggie."

"No hurry, I'll get mine in a minute. You weren't at the *e-admin* seminar, were you? I didn't see you there. Where were you? Tax, I suppose."

"That's right," agreed Christopher. "Riveting stuff. My favourite subject. But the queue's getting quite long and I don't suppose you want to miss the afternoon sessions. I need to find a table so that I can put this lot down."

Henry turned away reluctantly.

"I suppose you're right. Perhaps I'll join you at a table," he replied, waddling away in the direction of the lunch queue. Christopher meanwhile had been looking around the room, hoping to see Max. He was unsuccessful, but he did spot a table in the corner which had nobody sitting at it. Once he had gotten rid of Henry, he made his way to it, sat down and started eating. Almost at once he found Max standing in front of him, holding a plate of chicken and rice and some cutlery.

"May I join you?" he enquired, giving an elaborate mock bow before sitting down on one of the two vacant seats. "I saw you talking to old Stamford and thought I'd better mount a rescue party. What's the chicken like?"

Christopher swallowed a piece of meat which he had been chewing and nodded.

"Oh, it's all right. A bit chewy, but I've tasted worse. I managed to persuade Henry to join the queue. Chaps like him always want their lunch. How was the electronic administration?"

Max grinned and then ate a mouthful of rice before replying.

"Wonderful. The presenter was the most boring man on earth, but your friend Bossy Brenda really let him have it. All she needed was a rolling pin. He was a pile of mincemeat by the time she'd finished with him. How was tax?"

"Tax was as thrilling as usual. I think I went to sleep halfway through. What are you going to next?"

Max ate another mouthful of rice.

"Well, I thought the talk on business ethics might be interesting. It sounds a bit out of the ordinary and I really think that ethics are important in the workplace. How about joining me?"

Before Christopher could reply, another delegate approached the table and picked up the only spare chair.

"Hey, guys. Do you mind if I take this?"

Max grinned.

"Take it with our compliments," he replied. "It will make sure that an unwelcome guest doesn't sit here." The young man looked puzzled, but took the chair to another table where he wanted to sit with his friends.

"Well, that's good," continued Max. "That should stop your friend Henry Stamford sitting with us once he's got his nosh. Oh, it's OK. I can see him nobbling someone else. Now, where was I? Oh yes, how about joining me at the ethics session?"

Christopher chased the last few grains of rice around the plate with his spoon.

"All right," he agreed. "It might be interesting, although, if it is, it will be the only session that is. I wonder what the presenter will say."

"Well, it must be important that people are decent to each other at work. There are all sorts of things that might be relevant."

"Name some," challenged Christopher. Max screwed up his face into a thoughtful expression.

"Let's see. Er, I'm not sure this is a good example. But, suppose you are in HR and management tells you that the firm has to get rid of x amount of staff. What would you do? Would you ask management to show you the evidence, because you did not feel that people should be deprived of their jobs unless it was really necessary? Or would you think of all the people you didn't like and make out a case for making them redundant? Or would you be really virtuous and suggest that you might leave yourself, provided it saved someone else's job? Or – let's think – would you point out that, if four senior personnel were to go, or retire early or something, that would save all the other jobs? This is all assuming there isn't a trade union to fight back. If there is, well, hm – difficult."

Christopher smiled at his friend, enjoying the spectacle of Max trying to look serious.

"You tell me what you would do yourself," he replied, screwing up his paper napkin and putting it on his empty plate.

"OK. Let me see. Well, it wouldn't be as easy as all that, because if you criticised management, you might lose your own job. And what if you had a wife and kids? Um. It wouldn't be very proper to dump all the people you didn't like, but some of them might deserve it. And what if they had wives and kids? I suppose what I would really do is to try to make the least number of people redundant on the best terms and offer them support and help in finding other jobs. But, wait. That sounds a bit weak and watery. I think that I should suggest to management that we ought first to have a meeting to discuss the ethical side of the situation. Yes, I think that's right."

Max cast a look of self-satisfaction at his friend and waited for Christopher to applaud. But, instead, Christopher got up from the table.

"People don't behave like that in offices. But I'll just get us a coffee," he replied, "and then I'll tell you what I think."

A few minutes later, they both had cups of strong, murky coffee in front of them. Max looked at Christopher expectantly.

"Well?" he said. Christopher sipped his coffee.

"OK, let's look at your proposition. You say that management tells HR that it has to make people redundant because, well, the firm can't afford them. That is not, in itself, an ethical situation. It is a business manoeuvre or a piece of expediency. Is management correct? And who constitutes management? Are the HR people part of management, are they the slaves of management, or are they quasi-independent? However, you suggest that the responsibility of HR is to look at the question in an ethical light, and that is not unreasonable. Looking at it in an ethical light presumably means applying a set of moral principles. But what are those moral principles? To your mind, it means vaguely being decent to people and mitigating their suffering. Well, there are some moral principles underlying such a response, because you are assuming that people should not make other people suffer. Is that right?"

Max looked slightly troubled and stirred his coffee with a plastic spoon.

"Yes, I do mean that. Our moral code is to treat other people fairly and not hurt them if we can help it. In fact, to do as you would be done by, or something like that. That seems obvious to me. I don't quite know what you're getting at, Chris."

Christopher drained his cup before continuing.

"But is it?" he questioned. "Do we really believe that? We might pretend to, but we act quite differently. In practice, we all try to take advantage of other people – to grab some of their share in order to increase our own – and we don't really care if we make them suffer, whatever we might say in public. In fact, suffering must be a by-product of our competitive instincts. If we are to get on, we can only do it by stabbing other people in the back. Everyone does that, but some are better at it than others. So, to get back to your HR proposition, the HR people will make sure that they make other people redundant in order to protect their own jobs. All the stuff about giving them help over job interviews and guff like that is only face-saving and window-dressing. It's whited sepulchres."

"Whited sepulchres?" repeated Max, looking completely puzzled. Christopher shrugged his shoulders.

"Oh, never mind. Superficiality, things not being made to look the way they really are. How is our time going?"

Max consulted his phone.

"Well, if we're going to the ethics meeting, we ought to be getting along. I didn't think much of the coffee."

"The fair goddess didn't make it," replied Christopher. "But I need to pop in the gents. I'll see you there. Can you keep a place at the talk for me – assuming anyone else will go."

As Christopher was leaving the men's washroom, he suddenly remembered that he hadn't checked his phone messages all day. As he didn't want to stand in the corridor listening to his messages, he made his way back to the entrance hall and got his phone out there. The only message was from the church heating engineer, who told him, at considerable length, that it was not worth tinkering with the system any more this season because it was about to be closed down until the autumn. He listened to the message twice and then deleted it. He was fed up to the back teeth with the church heating system. A passer-by brushed against him and he found himself looking at the fair-haired girl.

"Oh sorry," she muttered, adjusting her black shoulder bag. He tried to smile.

"That's all right. We missed your coffee at lunchtime."

She raised a finely-shaped eyebrow.

"At lunchtime? I only do the morning coffee. Haven't the afternoon sessions started?"

"Yes, I suppose I ought to be attending one of them. You're going home, I expect?"

She carefully buttoned up her closely-fitting black jacket before replying and then looked at Christopher coldly.

"Home? No, of course not. I'm returning to my office in Cheapside. I hope you have a pleasant afternoon."

Christopher watched her go out through the swing doors. He felt uncomfortably irritated by her manner towards him and yet knew that she was not obliged to behave in any other way. Did other men find her appealing? Some women had a strange quality of being attractive and repellent at the same time. Some were, of course, just repellent. He turned and made his way through faceless corridors to the room where the ethics seminar was taking place. The door was closed and, peering through the glazed panel, he saw that the room was full to capacity. There was Henry Stamford, sitting in the front row and staring at the speaker with unusual attention. Bossy Brenda was also in the front row. And there was Max, sitting in the back row, also gazing at the speaker, but with a hand placed protectively on a booklet on the empty seat beside him, probably the only vacant seat in the room. Christopher hesitated, wondering how he could slip in without drawing attention to himself. The atmosphere in the room was unusual for a conference of this sort: almost electric, if that was the right word. He craned his head to have a better view of the speaker and then drew in his breath with a sense of shock. The smooth-suited and well-groomed presenter, lecturing with an earnest and animated face, was Mr Newton, the vicar of Christ Church.

Chapter five

Christopher gave the brass tablet another rub with his rag and stood back to criticise his handiwork. There was still a streak of polish on the left-hand side, so he wiped the rag over it until the brass shone.

He had not been able to sleep. Or rather, to sleep properly, because he had glanced at his alarm clock at 3.24 am and then at 4.47 am without knowing what had happened to the time in between. At 6.00 am, he had got up, dressed and come to the church, where for the past hour he had been polishing brass, first the door handles and now the tablets on the walls. He had an uncomfortable feeling in his head, made up of tiredness, apprehension and discontentment, and he wondered whether some coffee might help. He had not bothered to have any breakfast. Perhaps he should have done. It then occurred to him that Caroline would fuss over him when she and Simon arrived, bringing him coffee and giving her concerned look. He decided to make his own coffee.

While he was filling the kettle in the tiny room under the tower, he considered the likely events of the morning. Bob Bodkin would probably arrive at the last minute, having left his sermon behind and gone back to fetch it. The congregation would then trickle in unenthusiastically, some of them arriving during the Gospel reading or even during the intercessions. A fortnight ago, they had celebrated Easter Sunday, and the number in church had been half that of the previous year. He switched on the kettle. Well, that was understandable. Julian's groupies had largely dispersed, leaving what might be called the rump. Bob tried hard, but he was not very inspiring, and some people had stopped coming. Christopher had heard that one or two had been spotted at St Andrew's, where the Reverend Jill

Johnson would be mothering them, encouraging them to stay. He frowned. He had also heard a rumour that former members of the St Benet's congregation had been seen at Christ Church. Surely the rumour was untrue. How could anybody go from being an Anglo-Catholic to being an extreme Evangelical? It was perverse. The kettle switched itself off and he grabbed it almost savagely and poured the boiling water into his mug, where a spoonful of cheap coffee granules covered the bottom. He added a splash of milk from a carton and carried the mug carefully back into the church.

After placing the mug on a pew with a Gift Aid envelope under it, he resumed his polishing, smearing a small amount of polish on a tablet commemorating a parishioner who had died in 1922. This was a fairly plain memorial, with no raised decoration on it where dried brass polish could build up in the crevices, and it polished up well. Christopher caressed it with his rag and then stood back to read the inscription. He knew it by heart, anyway.

'In fond and loving memory of Amelia Susan Stoddard, daughter of Colonel Richard Evans Stoddard and his wife Margaret, of Harefield in the County of Middlesex, who worshipped in this church for forty years. Born 23 March 1862. Taken to her eternal rest 19 December 1922. Blest are the pure in heart.'

The words had always irritated him. Did Amelia and both her parents worship in the church, travelling in from Harefield? Did only the parents worship in the church? Or did Amelia live somewhere else and come to church on her own? He had always half-meant to look her up in the public records, but had never got round to it. There was no mention of her in any of the church registers and he wondered who she was and whether she had really worshipped at St Benet's for forty years. Was it the wrong church? He shook his head slightly and had a gulp of coffee. The ache in his head was still there.

Christopher surveyed the brass tablets on the wall in front of him and then, gathering up his tin of polish and rag in one hand and his mug in the other, he moved to the chancel and placed his mug on the bench where the servers sat. There were just two brass tablets in the chancel, facing each other and both to former rectors. He decided to tackle the older of the two first, a handsome rectangular plate with closely-packed gothic lettering, commemorating the Reverend James William Seymour. This was a difficult tablet to clean because of the lettering and decoration and the task was made worse by the crusting of polish left by Betty Cook, who tended to cover all the brasswork in excess polish as part of her mission to the church. He gazed at it, frowning, for a few minutes and then had another gulp of coffee, draining the mug. He was not sure whether to add more polish or to get a screwdriver and try to remove the old dried polish. It was not his favourite memorial in the church, but he had great affection for it. The sun, shining slantwise through the dusty east window, lit it up.

'Sacred to the Memory
Of the Reverend James William Seymour
Rector of this parish 1852 to 1875
Beloved by all his parishioners, a man of great learning and wisdom, who served God as a labourer in the vineyard, never sparing himself but devoting his life to holy works, giving comfort and relief to the poor, who turned to him in their distress.
He fell asleep 2 December 1875 in full assurance of the promises of Jesus Christ.

For now we see through a glass darkly: but then face to face.'

He read it through twice and felt, to his slight annoyance, a lump come to his throat. Mr Seymour had been a strange character. The eldest son of wealthy parents, he had shocked his family by choosing to enter the priesthood. Despite having the education and ability to be a bishop – and it was rumoured in 1867 that he had been offered the See of Lichfield – he preferred to be an ordinary parish priest and to adopt a very simple lifestyle. Looked after by a devoted housekeeper, he had lived in the gloomy parsonage house, often providing shelter for poor families who had been evicted from their lodgings because of non-payment of rent. He had spent his personal fortune on trying to alleviate the poverty of his parishioners and had finally died of a heart attack on a cold December day, collapsing in the street while on his way to visit a sick old woman. Hundreds of people had lined the route of his funeral procession. The plaque in the church had been provided by public subscription.

As Christopher stared at the tablet, he saw in his mind a tall, stooping man, dressed shabbily in clerical black, hurrying along a filthy back street and then stumbling and falling. Within seconds, people in tattered clothing appeared from the houses and surrounding roads as the word spread that their saintly rector had collapsed in the street. Their thin, pinched faces showed fear and alarm as they gathered round the huddled figure. A young builder was sent to find a doctor. And then the picture changed. A horse-drawn hearse was slowly creaking its way along the street, with black-suited mourners, heads bowed, hands clasped, plodding after it. The pavement was packed with people, the men bare-headed, the women wearing ancient felt hats or with shawls pulled over their heads, the children silent and thumb-sucking. It was a Victorian genre painting.

Christopher closed his mind to any more and decided to fetch a small screwdriver and scrape off some of the clogged polish on the tablet. He went into the vestry and opened the top drawer of the vestment chest. He kept a few useful odds and ends in here, including a couple of screwdrivers. After selecting the smaller of the two, he closed the drawer and returned to the chancel. At once, he knew that he was not alone in the church, although, for a moment, he could not see the other occupant. There was a movement in the shadow at the west end of the church and the figure of a man emerged, dressed in an anorak and jeans and with a bulging holdall slung over his right shoulder. Christopher stood still while the man shuffled towards him. This was obviously a homeless chap. They all looked alike. The shambling walk, slightly wheedling expression, shifty eyes, unshaven chin, well-worn clothing and either a rucksack or holdall seemed to be obligatory, as was the usual request for a train fare. Christopher was not disappointed.

"Can I speak to the vicar?" the man enquired in a vaguely northern accent.

"We don't have a vicar," replied Christopher, looking him hard in the face. "I'm one of the churchwardens. Are you looking for money? If so, we don't have any."

The man put his holdall down on the floor and looked appealingly up at Christopher.

"No, it's not money I'm after. Don't worry about that. But, you know, my old father is ill in Newcastle and I just need to get a train ticket. You think I'm homeless, don't you? I'm not. I live near here. But I need to get back to see my old father and my wallet's been stolen. I only need the train fare."

"I don't believe you," Christopher responded briskly. "You are homeless and you are trying to get money out of me. Well, I told you. We don't have any money. Now will you leave, please?"

"Just the train fare," pleaded the man. "It's very important. The fare's not much for a guy like you. Churches have got money."

Christopher's face hardened further,

"I tell you, no. You would only spend the money on drink or drugs. I know your type. Now will you go? I've got to get the church ready for the service."

The man picked up his bag and put it over his shoulder.

"I'll stay for your service, then. It's not very Christian to chuck people out. I was only asking for a train fare. I'll sit at the back. Don't mind me."

To Christopher's annoyance, the man walked nonchalantly to the back of the church and sat down on the back pew, placing his bag on the floor beside him. Christopher turned his attention back to the brass tablet and, for a few minutes, scraped very carefully at the whitey dried polish. But the man's presence made him feel uneasy and he soon gave up the job and took the screwdriver back to the vestry. Coming back into the church, he glanced at the other tablet in the chancel, his favourite tablet. This one commemorated the rector who had introduced High Church ornaments and ritual to St Benet's, and who had bought vestments and furnishings of the highest quality, including the Comper chasuble and altar frontal. This was Charles Aitchison, who had been rector from 1888 to 1920. There had been riots outside the church in 1889 because Fr Aitchison had put six candles on the altar and worn a chasuble, regarded then as dangerously High Church.

Christopher looked at the tasteful plaque approvingly, but quickly turned away again, not wanting to connect Fr Aitchison in his mind with the slumped and probably malodorous figure on the back pew.

At the same moment, there was the sound of talking and Caroline and Simon came into the church, closely followed by Justin.

"Hello, Chris," called out Caroline, cheerfully. "I guessed you were here when I saw the door half open. We met Justin just outside. Can we help with anything?"

"I think I've done it all," responded Christopher, coming down the aisle to meet them. He inclined his head towards the visitor, whom Caroline had not previously noticed. "I've been here a while, cleaning the brass tablets."

Caroline looked around the church obediently but without much interest.

"Mm yes, they look very good. But I thought that Betty Cook usually did them. She'll be upset if she finds that you have cleaned them yourself."

Christopher shrugged his shoulders.

"She leaves them caked in polish. I wish people wouldn't do things they're not capable of doing. That's the trouble with this place. People do things badly and then expect to be congratulated."

Caroline looked slightly shocked and tried to draw him towards the east end of the church and away from the homeless man.

"There's something in the chancel I wanted to show you," she replied loudly, leading the way. Christopher joined her reluctantly.

"Look, Christopher," she said in a low voice, pretending to show him something on one of the seats. "Volunteers like Betty Cook do their best and really think they are giving service. If she hears that you have been running her down, she'll get really upset and then leave, and our congregation will get even smaller. You'll end up with the church all to yourself. Simon..." she paused.

"Yes?" prompted Christopher. "Simon what?"

Caroline cleared her throat.

"Simon thinks you may be throwing your weight around a bit too much. I don't necessarily agree with him. You know what Simon is."

Christopher flushed slightly.

"Yes, I know what Simon is," he replied. "But I have to keep my opinion to myself. In what way, pray, have I been throwing my weight around?"

Caroline began to look uncomfortable and, after a glance down the church to where Simon was holding a lengthy conversation with Justin, she continued.

"Oh, I don't really know. I think he may feel that you dominate the PCC too much. And, um, you make decisions without consulting the rest of us. And one or two of the ladies have told me that you have been sharp with them. Please, Chris, we're all in this together. I know you feel worried about the future but don't take it out on us."

Christopher turned slightly and faced the altar which had a plain white frontal on it.

"It's all very well for Simon to be critical," he said bitterly. "Only, he's not churchwarden. The responsibility for running a parish in a vacancy falls to the churchwardens and everyday decisions have to be made by us. What you call the 'ladies' are a load of moaners who want everything just the way they like it and expect praise when they bugger things up. And what happens when the heating goes wrong or a light bulb needs changing? Everyone assumes I am going to see to it. I'm getting fed up to death with it all."

"That's not fair, Chris," retorted Caroline, facing him. "I always do my share and so does Simon. You just ignore what we do. It's me who has to go round smoothing things over when you're in a bad mood. That's been quite a lot recently."

"Bad mood! And what sort of mood is Simon usually in? I don't know how you cope with him, always criticising everything. Sorry. I suppose he's different at home. I know you do your best, Caroline, and I'm not blaming you, but some people in this church make my job very hard. Simon...'" He paused and saw, with some irritation, tears starting to well up in Caroline's eyes. He was baffled as to the reason. Why didn't she just argue back?

"Oh, never mind. We'll have to get ready for the service. I can hear some of the so-called ladies arriving."

Caroline sniffed quietly and went into the vestry, leaving Christopher still facing the altar. He sensed that Betty and Hilda, with a couple of other women, had arrived and were generally fussing at the west end of the church, probably because they had spotted the homeless man. He knew from experience that he would have to throw him out after the service in order to lock up the church. He looked at his watch. Time was getting on. The congregation, or what was left of it, was starting to arrive and Bob Bodkin would no doubt soon turn up, flustered as usual but amiable. Christopher suddenly felt terribly tired. The woolly ache in his head was still there and he faced the morning service with apathy tinged with distaste. Well, he would let Justin, Caroline and Simon do the work and he would sit at the back and have a rest. Drat the homeless man.

For a few minutes, he lacked the energy to move and found himself looking at the woven pattern on the white altar frontal. It was a standard pattern of Tudor roses and was totally innocuous, if rather boring. There was a gold-coloured fringe along the bottom. He conjured up in his mind a substituted image of a sumptuous frontal, embroidered with interlaced branches encircling golden figures of St Benedict and the Virgin Mary. The branches had further branches sprouting from them, with leaves on curling stalks along the sides. Each branch ended in a Tudor rose, white and red, and a deep red and gold fringe ran along the bottom of the frontal. No such frontal existed at St Benet's or, to Christopher's knowledge, had ever existed, but it was the frontal that he would have liked the church to own. A light touch on his shoulder made him start.

"Sorry, Chris," mumbled Justin, apologetically. "I didn't mean to make you jump. Simon has been going on at me about the incense we use."

"What's wrong with the incense?" replied Christopher, turning to face Justin, whose face was troubled.

"Well, I don't think there's anything wrong with it. But Simon says I encourage Fr Bob to put too much incense in the thurible. I don't. But Fr Bob likes to use a lot. Simon says it wastes money when the parish is hard up. Can you have a word with Simon, Chris?"

Christopher summoned up the kindest expression he could muster. Justin was an ally and he did not want to antagonise him.

"Don't worry, Justin. You do a very good job with the incense. Just carry on as usual. If we try telling Bob not to use so much incense, he'll get nervous and not want to come any more. Leave it with me. I'll have a word with Simon. It's true that the parish is hard up, but I don't think the incense makes much difference. Have we got plenty?"

Justin nodded.

"Yes, heaps. Don't you remember that you bought a special offer – three boxes for the price of two? It'll last us ages. I'm still on the first box. And there's loads of charcoal, as well. In fact, when we thought we'd run out last time, we forgot about a great lot of it in the cupboard with the wafers. It'll last till Christmas at least. But I'd better get changed, hadn't I?"

Justin disappeared into the vestry. Christopher sighed and looked down to where Simon was arguing with the homeless man, trying unsuccessfully to get him to leave. Whatever he said to Simon about the incense, Simon would turn it into a row. And Christopher was too weary for a row. But how was he to keep Justin's goodwill? Justin was the least troublesome of everybody at St Benet's and was, in any case, a nice lad. He picked up his coffee mug and strode down the main aisle to the back of the church.

"I'm just going to wash up my mug, Simon," he said, trying to sound friendly. "Why don't you come so that we can have a quick chat? We haven't got all that long before the service starts."

Simon followed him into the little room under the tower but with no sociable expression on his face.

"Bloody homeless," he grumbled. "He won't leave. He says you're going to give him his train fare to Liverpool or somewhere. You didn't say that, did you?"

"No, I certainly did not," replied Christopher, closing the door behind Simon. "I told him that he would spend the money on drink or drugs. He's sitting there to spite me. I'll have to boot him out after the service. But I really wanted a quick word about the incense."

Simon bristled.

"Has Justin been talking to you behind my back? Wretched youth."

"He's a decent young man," responded Christopher, rinsing his mug in cold water. "You've made him very unhappy about the incense business. And, anyway, I don't really understand what your problem is. We've got plenty of incense and Bob does us a favour by taking the services. He happens to like plenty of incense."

"Well, I don't. It makes us look Romish, except that the Romans don't seem to use it any more. We have a church council to decide things, Christopher. You don't own St Benet's, even though you act as though you do. You should hear what people are saying."

Simon's truculent tone was making Christopher angry. Through the closed door, he could hear the organ playing and the choir practising a psalm.

"Mark's here," he said shortly. "I'll have to see to things. We can continue this discussion another time."

Simon stood with his back to the door and put his hands in his pockets.

"We've still got ten minutes," he replied. "You know you're making Caroline upset. She works very hard for this parish and you just snub her. She's always been very kind to you, although nobody would think so, judging by the way you behave. It's about time somebody had a word with you."

"Well, aren't you having a word with me? If Caroline is upset, she can tell me so herself. Isn't it a bit sexist for her husband to speak to me? This isn't the nineteenth century."

Simon flushed.

"How dare you talk about being sexist! You are the most sexist person I know, Christopher. You don't even know how to speak to women, let alone work with them. I have no idea how you manage to survive at your office, where you presumably have people of both sexes. We have a strict code of practice at mine, based on the Equality Act. In fact, I drew it up myself."

Christopher leaned across Simon and grasped the door handle.

"Yes, I would have guessed that. Anyway, I can hear the phone ringing and Bob will no doubt have arrived. Excuse me."

He pulled open the door and pushed past Simon who followed him out looking aggrieved.

Christopher moved quickly to the telephone at the back of the church and picked up the receiver. He was vaguely aware of a scattering of people in the pews and the homeless man still sitting beside his holdall at the back.

"Hello, St Benet's Church", he said hastily, pressing the receiver to his ear to blot out Mark's organ playing. "What's that? Oh, hello, Bob."

He could hardly hear the voice at the other end, especially as Mark seemed to be playing extra loudly in an attempt to drown it.

"Sorry, Bob, I can hardly hear you. The organ is a bit loud. Are you all right?"

The voice sounded apologetic.

"Yes, well, no, not entirely. I've gone down with a bad cold or flu or something and I just can't make it today."

Christopher had a panicky sensation in his chest.

"Not make it? Do you mean you can't take the service, Bob? Are you sure? We're nearly ready to start."

"I know," replied Bob feebly. "I'm really sorry. I got all ready to come and then had a coughing fit. Susan wants to ring the surgery. I'm feeling a bit dizzy. I'm so sorry. I'm sure you'll manage. See you next week, I hope."

Christopher slowly replaced the receiver. No priest! It meant that a churchwarden would have to take the service.

And the service was due to begin in five minutes. Bob might have rung earlier.

Within a minute, Christopher was putting his cassock on in the vestry, surrounded by the servers.

"But Chris," urged Caroline. "I can take the service. You don't have to do it. Or we could do a bit each. And Simon could help."

Christopher shook his head and did up the top button.

"Thank you. But I'm the senior churchwarden and I must take responsibility. I'll give out the consecrated wafers from the aumbry. Can you get Hilda to take the collection?"

Caroline looked thin-lipped and stubborn and did not reply. Justin chipped in.

"But what about a sermon? Do we still have a sermon when there isn't a priest? How will you preach a sermon, Chris? And what do we do about the Peace? Oh, and I don't think you can do the Absolution either. Can you?"

Christopher pulled on a cotta over his head.

"It's all right. I know what to do. You just miss out the bits that only a priest does. I'll explain it to the congregation."

"Have you told Mark yet?" asked Simon. "He'll be cross if he only hears at the last minute. You should have told him first, so he knows what to play. And what about the choir? And anyway, you're not allowed to preach a sermon."

Christopher ignored him.

"We'd better get started. You all get into position and I will tell the congregation what to expect. They'll have to lump it. It's impossible to find another celebrant at such short notice. Bob can be a let-down at times."

"It's that potty wife of his," muttered Simon. "He should have told her to get lost. Oh well, here goes. Lambs to the slaughter."

As soon as he began to address the congregation, Christopher knew, in a deep level of his consciousness, that he had made a mistake in not asking for Caroline's help. But, in the upper level, he would not admit it to himself. He had been a churchwarden longer than Caroline and it was his duty to see it through. But it was not easy. Not remotely easy. The congregation stared at him in a slightly hostile way and would not stand up and kneel down in the usual places. Mark was also hostile, as Christopher could tell from the unsympathetic organ playing. Only Justin seemed to have any fellow-feeling with him, but he was nervous and did not know what to do with the thurible when there was no priest. By the time Christopher reached the sermon, his mouth was dry and he was hating every minute of the service. He had no idea what he was going to say but, as one of the readings had been from the Book of Revelation, he tried to describe St John the Divine writing it on the island of Patmos. His words sounded silly. But he had not gotten far before there was an interruption.

"He wouldn't even give me a train fare," said a belligerent voice from the back row. "That was all I wanted. A train fare. He thinks he can stand up there, all high and mighty, like a vicar. But he wouldn't help a poor guy like me."

Christopher tried to ignore the outburst, but members of the congregation could not resist turning their heads to see where the voice was coming from. The man, encouraged by the interest that was being shown, stood up and spoke conversationally to the occupants of the pews, taking on the role of preacher.

"I came in here this morning, thinking that churches were places where you could tell your troubles, and I found him up there, cleaning the brass. I didn't get a polite word from him. He told me to clear out. I only wanted the price of a train ticket so that I could go and see my sick father. I work hard but train fares are expensive for folks like me."

Christopher saw, with rising exasperation, one or two of the more simple-minded members of the congregation getting their wallets and purses out. Why did people have to be so stupid? He decided to try to take control of the situation.

"All right, all right," he said firmly. "All that can be settled after the service. If you would like to sit down – sir – we can get on with the sermon. I was talking about St John the Divine."

"Not Christopher the Divine," muttered Simon audibly behind him in the chancel.

The man, who had now warmed to his task, did not sit down.

"I can see that some of you folk are more generous than him up there," he continued. Some of you are proper church-people, ready to help a chap like me that's a bit down on his luck. Just give me what you can afford. But I'd sack him, if I were you."

An angular, thin-lipped woman, who usually came to St Benet's without speaking to anyone, joined in.

"It's a shame," she called out, in a high-pitched, cracked tone. "It's a shame, that's what it is. If this church can't help this poor man, we ought to help him ourselves. I will give five pounds."

More purses were taken out and Christopher could hear notes rustling and coins jingling. The whole ridiculous affair was turning into a nightmare. He could hear Simon behind him making acid comments to Caroline and Justin.

"He should have had the help that we offered. Why does he have to behave like this? I warned him. If this all folds up, don't blame me. That man's making a laughing stock of him. We can't go on like this. The rest of us might as well go home."

To Christopher's horror – and before he could think of anything more to say – the angular woman had got out of her seat and was collecting money from the congregation. It was like watching a black comedy at the cinema. The homeless man, now grinning triumphantly, continued to address the congregation.

"God bless you, folks. I can see that there are some real Christians here. Real Christians, I say, not like the bloke up there. Your generosity really touches me. I can go and see my sick father, thanks to you. Thank you. Thank you."

The woman approached him and gave him a considerable sum of money, including five and ten pound notes. Christopher, reflecting bitterly that it was more than the congregation usually put in the collecting plate, tried once more to establish order.

"All right. Let's get on," he said loudly. "You can go and get your train ticket now, can't you? You won't want to be hanging around here any more."

The man had sat down again, still grinning, and looked as though he was not going to move.

"That's all right, mate," he replied genially. "I'm enjoying the service. I'll stay to the end. What was you saying about Patmos? I wouldn't mind a holiday there."

The angular woman looked over her shoulder at him and he composed his features into a comically serious expression. Christopher decided to ditch the sermon.

The service, although it was shorter than usual, seemed to last for hours. He gave out the consecrated Communion wafers from the aumbry, but about a quarter of the congregation declined to come forward to receive. Simon received his wafer with a very bad grace, Caroline looked anxious and unhappy, and Justin took his wafer awkwardly, nearly dropping it. At the end, Christopher invited the congregation to join him in saying the Grace, but only a few people joined in and most of them did not know the words. As soon as the service had finished, Caroline rushed to the back of the church to serve coffee, but the place was emptying rapidly. Christopher sat down in the chancel, expecting Simon to come and harangue him. But Simon officiously went and collected hymn books, pointedly ignoring him. Instead, the homeless man approached Christopher.

"Well?" said Christopher, wearily. "What do you want now? You've got your money."

The man grinned and slung his holdall over his shoulder.

"Yeah. I just noticed that you didn't contribute anything. You still can."

Christopher would have liked to have punched him, but he restrained himself.

"Just go, will you?" he replied, trying to keep his voice steady. "We've got the clearing up to do. And don't come back."

The man grinned again and swaggered off down the aisle and out of the church.

Caroline was the next person to approach Christopher. He saw that she was wearing her 'concerned but sympathetic' expression. He could have written her speech for her.

"Yes?" enquired Christopher in a flat voice. Caroline coughed slightly as though she were bothered by the smell of incense.

"Christopher," she began and then paused, seeing his familiar defiant expression. "Christopher, I know that the homeless man was a bit of a pain. But you could have handled the situation differently. Simon says..."

"Simon says, put your hands in the air," interrupted Christopher. Caroline tried to ignore him.

"Simon says that, if you try to take a service again, he'll walk out."

"Let him."

"It's not just that. Betty has had to dash home today and can't count the collection."

"There's not much to count."

"And I need to get home as well. Adrian and Aidan are both having lunch with us."

"All right. I'll tidy up. There's not a lot to do."

Caroline glanced down at the chancel floor and then looked at Christopher with a look almost of desperation in her eyes.

"Please, Chris. Don't be so stubborn. We're all trying to keep St Benet's going but you make things so awkward for me. I've tried so hard to work with you. I thought that we could have been good colleagues, despite what everyone says about you. I know that you really care about the place. Why can't you co-operate with the rest of us? You should hear the things Simon says about you."

"I don't want to hear them, thank you,' replied Christopher coldly. "Simon ought to keep his opinions to himself. If he wants to address me personally, let him. I don't see why you should be his messenger. In any case, I know what he thinks."

Caroline coughed again.

"Chris. There's something else. I've heard a rumour that the Archdeacon wants one of the curates from Christ Church to take our services. There might not be any truth in it, but..."

Christopher sat up straight.

"That's crazy," he replied. "Where did you hear that? Bob Bodkin is fine. It's just unlucky that he was ill today."

"Well, I was in the diocesan office buying a new yearbook and Fr Smith came in. You know, the vicar of Holy Trinity. Anyway, I said that we enjoyed having Bob taking our services and he said that it might not be for much longer because the Archdeacon was thinking of asking Christ Church to send someone. I asked him if he was sure it was Christ Church because the churchmanship is so different and he said that he was a bit surprised, as well. I don't suppose that anything will come of it."

Christopher wrinkled his brow.

"No," he responded, slowly. "Probably not. Although I wouldn't put it past the Archdeacon. Hadn't you better get along?"

Caroline hesitated for a moment as though she were thinking of something else to say. Then she turned and walked quickly to the back of the church. Christopher put his head in his hands and tried to think rational thoughts, but he felt numb. Christ Church! It could not be true. Caroline must have misheard. Nobody at Christ Church would want to take services at St Benet's. It was so different.

After a few minutes, another voice broke into Christopher's brain. This time, it was Mark's.

"Christopher," he said in a petulant voice. "I don't think you behaved very well today. You should have told me what to expect before you started the service. Don't you think that Caroline would have made a better job of it? The organist plays a key part in the liturgy and it simply isn't possible to conduct a service without prior consultation. I do have to organise the choir, as well. If this happens again, I might have to look around for another post."

Christopher removed his hands from his face and looked at Mark's peeved expression.

"That's your decision," he said. "If you will excuse me, I need to answer the call of nature."

Without another word, he got up and walked down the aisle to the room under the tower. Once inside and with the door closed, he stood still and tried to think coherently.

"Caroline must have got it wrong," he thought, "Nobody in their right mind would link St Benet's with Christ Church. We don't go in for all that stuff about being saved and having a personal saviour. I don't even know what it means. Why do I have to be troubled with all this? Why are they doing this to me?"

For several minutes, he lacked the energy or resolution to return to the body of the church. Then, making an effort, he pulled open the door and walked out, finding, with some relief, that the church was empty and that the lights were off. He could hear Caroline, Simon and Mark talking in the vestry. Not until he heard all three of them leave and the door slam shut did he go into the vestry. The lights were turned off in there as well – probably by the careful Caroline – and, as the day had become cloudy, the room was comparatively gloomy. Christopher had a sudden feeling of exhaustion and sat down limply on the chair by the table. Looking around the room, he realised that he knew exactly where everything was – the boxes of incense and charcoal, the wafers, – priest's and people's – the church registers, even the paper clips and scrap paper. He knew it all as well as he knew his own home. After a few moments of contemplation, he let his eyes rest on the bottom drawer of the vestment chest. He knew every stitch on that chasuble.

Although something inside him tried to persuade him not to open that drawer, he got up from the chair and, stooping down, pulled it open. With his hands shaking a little, he drew out the chasuble and carried it tenderly to the table, where he unfolded it and revealed the beautiful blue silk panel, with its glowing picture of St Benedict. But, today, there was little comfort, even from this.

Chapter six

'It was a sunny day in June.'

Christopher found himself composing this line in his head and then wondered why he had done so. It was actually a sunny day in June, but why should he say so? It felt as though he were detached from his real self. Mystified, he shook his head slightly and then tried to concentrate on a review of his immediate situation.

He had taken the Northern Line to Finchley Central and was now walking towards Max's home near Holders Hill. Max and Jenny had invited him to lunch and, although he had suspected that this was intended to cheer him up, he had accepted willingly enough. It would be something of a relief to chat to Max about his work at the Institute, or even about the weather. Anything to get away from church business. On the previous Sunday, Caroline had taken him to one side in that irritatingly confidential way that she had and had talked at him for twenty minutes. The gist of this was that Simon was offering to replace him as churchwarden, not by waiting for the parish elections next April, but now. Immediately. She had suggested that he should offer his resignation to the Bishop 'for personal reasons' and that Simon should be elected to take his place. At the time, Christopher had listened to her in silence, resenting what she was saying and even that she was talking to him at all. He had acknowledged to himself then, and still acknowledged, that Caroline, as his fellow churchwarden, had every right to discuss church business with him. But he had felt, and still felt, that she did not have any right to put forward the claims of her own husband. This was surely a conflict of interest. Had Caroline meant well? Christopher could not see any way in which this could be the case. Simon had long wanted to be churchwarden and presumably he was now using his wife to engineer Christopher's removal. So much for equal opportunities! In spite of the mild and pleasant air, Christopher shuddered.

He recalled Caroline's face at the end of that conversation – or rather, monologue. She had looked slightly embarrassed, slightly ashamed of herself, as though she had known that she was doing her husband's dirty work. Well, Caroline was not at all bad. He remembered being quite pleased when she had been first elected churchwarden. She was sensible and methodical and had some appreciation of the aesthetics of the church building and the traditional liturgy. But she was married to Simon and presumably loved him. Surely that showed a deep flaw in her character? From the beginning, it had placed an invisible barrier between the two churchwardens and, since Julian had left, the barrier had been strengthened and extended. Simon did not hide his hostility towards Christopher in public and probably made Caroline's life a misery over it in private.

Well, he certainly did not like Simon. Caroline was being pretty dumb if she thought that Christopher would agree to her suggestion. But Caroline surely did not think that. She was only carrying out her husband's wishes in order to prevent a row. Marriage seemed very unattractive at times and Christopher felt relieved that he was still single. But was that sour grapes? He remembered again the fair-haired girl at the conference a month or so back. He had dreamt about her one night recently. She had looked different, of course, but somehow he had known who it was. She had been in church, sitting in the congregation, while he had been in the chancel, wearing his cassock and cotta. She had suddenly gotten up, walked silently into the chancel, rearranged the vessels on the credence table and then given him a penetrating look before going back to her seat. Christopher remembered this because he had woken up at that point, in a panic because he thought that it must be Sunday and that he had overslept.

He quickly stepped out of the way of a car as he crossed a road. Max's house was only a couple of streets away now and he tried to turn his thoughts to the lunch ahead. Max was a good chap, totally unlike Simon. As he thought about Max, words from Corinthians chapter thirteen suddenly occurred to him.

'Charity suffereth long, and is kind; charity envieth not; charity vaunteth not itself, is not puffed up...'

He could not go on. He was being stupidly emotional about what was, after all, a businesslike friendship. Max was just a professional colleague who happened to be nicer than most. He and Christopher had met at many conferences and receptions and Max had appeared to enjoy his company. Christopher mentally reviewed the people at his office, thinking of them sitting at their desks on a typical day, and then shook his head firmly, causing a passing middle-aged woman to look at him suspiciously.

"They're boring, mostly," he said under his breath. "Why did God have to make so many dull people in the world?"

He opened the low metal gate which led into Max's front garden. It was the usual small suburban square patch but, at this time of year, it almost overflowed with flowers. On both sides of the narrow path were lobelia and alyssum, blue and white. In the same beds were big scarlet salvias, slightly floppy but handsome and imposing. On the right was a miniature lawn with a round bed in the middle, almost completely occupied by a sprawling rose bush covered in pink roses. Christopher paused. The blue of the lobelia reminded him of the blue silk on the St Benedict chasuble.

The front door opened and Max came striding out, beaming.

"Christopher!" he exclaimed. "How good to see you! I happened to glance out of the sitting room window to see if you were coming, and there you were in our garden. Good show of flowers this year, don't you think? I pruned that rose bush last autumn and look what has happened. Jenny says she has never seen it so covered in roses."

Christopher shook hands with him.

"Hello, Max," he replied. "It's good to see you again. I haven't got a garden at my flat – only a sort of prison yard. I have two shrubs and some concrete pots. I meant to plant bulbs in the tubs this year but I never got round to it. So they look uglier than usual."

"You should ask Jenny round," responded Max, turning back towards the front door. "She's got green fingers. She'd soon sort you out. Anyway, here she is."

His wife appeared in the doorway and greeted Christopher with a calm smile. She was dressed in a pink checked blouse and denim skirt and looked wholesome.

"Did you come on the Underground, Christopher?" she asked as all three entered the house.

"Yes, on the Northern Line. It's an easy journey."

"Well, come along into the sitting room and sit down. Or would you like to use the bathroom?"

Christopher followed Max and Jenny into the tidy front room and sat on one of the two armchairs. Max sat on the matching sofa, but Jenny remained standing.

"No, I'm fine," replied Christopher. "It didn't take very long to get here."

"Now," continued Jenny, while Max looked up at her affectionately. "Would you like a cup of coffee after your journey or would you prefer sherry?"

"We've got plenty of other things," added Max, "but I know that you like to be traditional."

Christopher smiled faintly.

"Sherry would be good," he answered. "I don't often drink it." In his mind, he saw a brief picture of his parents opening a bottle of 'British sherry' at Christmas.

Jenny pulled down the front of a cabinet, revealing a few bottles of assorted alcohol and some blue glasses with gold decoration on them.

"What would you like? We have dry, medium-dry or sweet. While you're thinking, I'll just pop into the kitchen to get some glasses."

She disappeared and Max took up the conversation.

"I can recommend the dry," he remarked. "My chief gave it to me when I produced a devastatingly clever report. It's good stuff – the sherry, that is. He knew that I had got him out of a hole and wanted to reward me. He knows his wines, all right, although I was surprised he gave me sherry. It's usually port. You see, I'm always doing clever reports."

Jenny reappeared, carrying three sherry glasses, which she placed on the flap of the cabinet. Christopher looked across at her.

"Dry, please," he said politely. "Max tells me it's rather special."

Jenny carefully poured out three glasses of sherry and handed one to Christopher, who immediately sipped it and then regretted doing so as he realised that he should have waited for his hosts to begin. Max did not appear to notice and took his own glass. Jenny sat down with hers on the sofa beside Max. They all sipped their drinks. Looking across at Max and Jenny, Christopher felt strangely lonely, even though they were smiling at him in the friendliest way possible.

"And where are the, er, kids?" he asked, taking another sip of sherry.

"They're busy doing a teenage show," replied Jenny, "so they won't be joining us for lunch. We might drop in on them later, if you don't mind."

Christopher privately thought that this might involve the sort of music he hated.

"Not at all," he said brightly. "Is it a Gang Show sort of thing? Your two seem to have plenty of talent."

Max butted in before Jenny could respond.

"Well, they have plenty of energy when it suits them," he said, deprecatingly, "and, no doubt, a certain amount of talent. They've been going off every Saturday afternoon to rehearse, so it's kept them out of trouble. Today, it's the dress rehearsal and parents and friends have been invited to take a look. It's probably not your sort of thing, Chris, but it won't take long. We won't stay for the whole time."

"I don't mind, really," urged Christopher, doing his utmost to seem interested. "It will be a change for me. I never did anything like that when I was a boy, you know. I was what used to be called a square. I'm afraid that I liked Latin verbs and making models of churches."

Jenny looked at him a little pityingly and then glanced at her husband.

"I suppose that was because you were an only," she said in a sympathetic voice. "It's very difficult for a child who has no brothers and sisters. I've got two sisters and Max has a brother and a sister. We were all Brownies and Guides and went off to camp and things. I've still got all my badges. And you were a Cub, weren't you, darling?"

Max made a comical face.

"Yes," he replied, "although my biggest memory of it is having to share a tent in a rainstorm with a boy who suffered from body odour. I felt absolutely trapped – the storm raging outside and the niff inside. I think that was why I didn't progress to the Scouts. And then there were all those knots. I can't think why we had to learn them. I've never used any of them since..."

"Yes, you have," Jenny contradicted him laughingly. "Don't you remember when we had that holiday in Devon – when Andrew was nine – and he had that big kite?"

She turned to address Christopher.

"Max got fed up with holding it in a gale, so he tied the string to a bush using one of his famous knots. He told Andrew that the knot was a special one which didn't ever come undone. We just stepped back to watch for a minute or two and the string undid itself. We never saw the kite again. The children were broken-hearted."

Max looked penitent but there was a cheerful note in his voice.

"Well, I just made a slight mistake over which knot I was using. I thought it was a clove hitch but it must have been something else. I do remember that I had to buy you all ice creams with double chocolate flakes to make up for it. You see, Chris, what dads have to put up with."

Christopher did not quite know what to say and sipped his sherry again. His family holidays had been nothing at all like that. Usually, his father had planned tedious walks, like route marches, and then, halfway through, when they were usually miles from a bus stop, his mother had started complaining about being tired. The last few miles had usually been a miserable trudge on a hard road, with both parents in a bad mood and Christopher striding along in front, occupied with his own thoughts.

Max seemed to guess something of what he was thinking.

"Well now," he said, draining his own glass. "Isn't it about time we thought about lunch? Shall I go and check the potatoes, love, or will you?"

Jenny finished her sherry and stood up briskly.

"I'll go," she replied. "There isn't much to do. You talk to Chris for a few more minutes and then come through. You're happy with salmon, Chris, I hope?"

Christopher nodded.

"Wonderful. It's my favourite fish. It's very good of you to invite me."

"Nonsense," responded Max, as Jenny left the room. "It's a pleasure. Jenny loves having friends to lunch and, you know, she felt so sorry for you that night you were sick."

"That was kind of her," replied Christopher.

"Well, that's Jenny for you," smiled Max. "I know I'm a lucky man. Hey, I hope you don't mind about this teenage concert thing. We won't stay long. Jenny thought that it might take your mind off things for a bit. You know, a bit of escapism."

Christopher stared at his glass, fearing that the conversation was going in a direction that he didn't like.

"What things?" he replied, bleakly. Max looked apologetic.

"Well, you know. That church of yours. I told Jenny all about it. But I won't mention it if you don't want me to."

Christopher finished his sherry and placed the empty glass on a convenient side table, where there was a small vase containing pink roses. For a moment or two, there was silence and Max looked across at his friend questioningly. Eventually, Christopher met his gaze.

"Oh, it's all right," he said, reluctantly and with a faint sigh. "Yes, the blasted church is getting me down. Well, not the church itself but some of the people in it. My fellow churchwarden's husband wants me to resign as churchwarden – for personal reasons allegedly – and then get himself elected to take my place. And Caroline, who is usually fairly decent, is acting as his mouthpiece."

Max looked puzzled.

"But surely," he replied, wrinkling his brow, "if it's getting you down, wouldn't you prefer someone to take your place? I'm not sure what the personal reasons are, but Caroline might really care about you – as a friend, I mean."

Christopher began to feel irritated but, seeing Max look anxious, tried to control the tone of his voice.

"You haven't met Simon! But, seriously, this is just a power-seeking attempt by a rather unpleasant individual. And having the churchwardens married to each other would be far from ideal. Simon apparently has his wife under his thumb, so there wouldn't be much hope for St Benet's. But let's talk about something else. How's the office?"

Max looked relieved.

"Oh, the office! I must tell you about the mysterious paper clip shortage while we have our lunch. Let's go through. Knowing Jenny, everything will be hunky-dory by now."

The two men made their way to the small but bright dining room at the back of the house. The oval table was set for three, with crimson table mats and napkins and stainless steel cutlery. On the plain wooden sideboard was another vase of pink roses together with a cheese board displaying a selection of five cheeses and a bottle of Australian dessert wine. A square table in a corner of the room held a neat pile of board games and some assorted stationery. Max indicated a seat to Christopher, who sat down slightly stiffly and gazed out of the window facing him. The garden was a reasonable size for a town garden, with a lawn and flower beds, all beautifully kept and very bright in the June sunshine. There was an old but short tree at the far end and a few shrubs strategically placed at intervals down each side. On the paved area outside the window was a garden seat and several tubs full of strawberry plants. Max took his seat opposite Christopher, but first glanced over his shoulder at the view.

"Lovely, isn't it?" he enthused. "The beds are especially good this year. Jenny put some geraniums in and they've really started to get going. They're bright red, all down both sides. There are perennials mixed up with them. And then we've got a few vegetables and herbs down the end. Kate is supposed to look after the vegetables and Andrew says he will keep the lawn in order. We have to chivvy them up, of course, but Jenny thinks that it's good for young people to learn about gardening. On the whole, they're pretty good. Oh, here's the lunch."

Jenny entered the room carrying two plates of sliced tomatoes and mozzarella cheese and placed them in front of Max and Christopher. She then returned to the kitchen and came back with her own plate. When she had seated herself at the table, there was an awkward pause. Max gave a sidelong glance at Christopher.

"We don't, er, normally say Grace or anything. Is that all right?" Christopher managed to smile.

"No, that's fine. I don't normally say it myself."

His companions looked relieved and picked up their knives and forks, Christopher following suit. But Max immediately put his down again.

"Gosh!" he exclaimed, in mock dismay. "I've forgotten the wine. It's in the fridge. I'll just get it."

While he disappeared to the kitchen, Jenny looked at Christopher seriously.

"I'm sorry you've been having a hard time recently," she said gently. "Max has told me that you have problems at the church you attend. If there is any way in which we can help, do let us know. I'm usually at work on weekdays but I can give you my mobile number. I don't know a lot about churches but you might just want a sympathetic ear. I took a counselling course once. Not that it's made me an expert or anything. I just mean to say that we're your friends. Sorry, that sounds daft."

Christopher felt his face turning slightly pink. He wished that women would not turn on this sympathy tap.

"Thank you," he replied, "that's generous of you. But it isn't really anything to write home about. Max is exaggerating."

Jenny looked as though she did not quite believe him, but admired his bravery. Luckily, Max returned then, carrying a bottle of white wine, which he had opened in the kitchen.

"Here it is!" he exclaimed. "Now we can have lunch properly. It's a Chilean Sauvignon, Chris. I hope that suits you. Some of these New World wines are knocking the old ones for six. Shall I pour?"

Max poured the wine for himself and Christopher but Jenny, who said that she would be driving later on, declined the wine and poured herself some water from a glass jug. All three started eating and Max succeeded in keeping up a conversation about paper clips, Human Resources departments and office gossip. Jenny put in the odd comment and sometimes asked Christopher for his opinion. Christopher ate the excellent meal mechanically and tried to keep up his end of the discussion, but the attentive hosts, inoffensive conversation, neat lunch-table, clean and tidy room and view of a bright, well-tended garden all contributed to his strange feeling of detachment. He knew that his would-be friends were doing all they could to make him feel welcome and he tried to act the part of a happy and grateful guest. But he also knew, not only that he was failing, but that his hosts knew that he was failing. Their reaction was to become more and more kindly – 'a drop more wine, Christopher?' 'have some more potatoes,' 'there are seconds of fruit fool,' 'I'm sure you could do with a top up of coffee.'

At one point, when he was staring at the garden, having forgotten what was last said to him, Jenny touched him lightly on the forearm.

"I can guess what you're thinking, Chris," she said. "You're wondering how old that tree is at the bottom. We're actually not quite sure. It was obviously here when we bought the house, but we've never decided whether it was here before these houses were built. I suppose it was country, then. It's funny to think of all this as fields. I love the countryside, but we have to live in London because of Max's job and the kids' school. My job, too. Do you ever get out into the country? I'm sure you could do with a break sometimes."

"How can I get a break?" he replied, still gazing at the garden and unable to disguise a hard edge to his voice. "I have to be in church every Sunday. There's so much to do. And if I didn't turn up, Simon would take charge."

"But, surely," reasoned Jenny, "you have your fellow churchwarden to help. From what I've heard of her, Caroline is a good-hearted person and would not begrudge you the odd Sunday off. I do think that everybody ought to have a holiday sometimes. Caroline must go on holiday herself. Hasn't she got children?"

Christopher glanced at Jenny reluctantly and then looked back at the garden.

"Yes, two grown-up sons. Or, almost grown up. It's typical of Simon to have called them Adrian and Aidan," he responded as Max smothered a grin. "And I admit that they do have holidays. But, you see, I'm always there to make sure everything goes properly. And, anyway, it's always a relief not to have Simon around, with his barbed comments and complaints. He's worse than ever now. And the organist is no better."

There was silence for a moment or two while Christopher continued to contemplate the garden. But he saw out of the corner of his eye an exchanged look between Jenny and Max. Then Jenny spoke.

"Chris, Max and I have been wondering – just this last day or two, actually – we've, um, booked a cottage for a week in Wales – Snowdonia – and we thought it was a one-bedroomed place. But it turns out to have a single bedroom, as well. It's in August and the kids will be on an orienteering course in the Yorkshire Dales. We just wondered whether you might like to come with us. We'll be driving and there's plenty of room in the car. We can easily pick you up."

Max, seeing his friend look unresponsive, took over from his wife.

"I know you hate giving other people trouble, Chris, but it would be a real pleasure to have you with us. You could go off on your own, you know, and explore churches – well, I'm not sure if there are many – or just go walking and things. Or come around with us. We'd love it. Don't imagine that we only want each other all the time. Come on. You don't have to decide now. The cottage is booked in any case."

Christopher bit his lip and turned to respond to Jenny.

"Thank you. I don't really know what to say. It's terribly kind of you both, but..."

"No buts," chipped in Max, cheerfully. "I know you, Chris. You'll always find an objection to something if you can. Especially anything that concerns you personally. This attitude might be good in your work at the Institute, but it won't wash here. We only want you to go away and think about it. For heaven's sake, anybody would think that we were handing you a dagger. For use in emergencies."

Christopher managed to smile. He knew that it was impossible to be angry with Max. Meanwhile, Jenny leaned across with the cafetière and poured more coffee into his cup. He felt that he was almost being killed with kindness.

"All right," he said, after another brief pause. "I'll have a think. Tell me what week it is and I'll go away and consult my diary. But you really don't have to, I'm a miserable old sod to have around. You'd regret it the moment we got there."

"Rubbish!" exclaimed Max. "It would be great to have you there. Jenny always loves having extra people to cook for – don't you, darling? – and she'd find jobs for you to do around the place. Keep you busy. Making packed lunches and things. It would give you a holiday and be a treat for us as well. What could be better?"

After the meal, Christopher helped Max and Jenny to load the dishwasher. Then Jenny looked up at the plate-shaped clock on the kitchen wall.

"It's time we went to the show," she said briskly to the other two. "The kids will be wondering where we are."

Max rinsed his hands in the sink and wiped them on a small towel which hung from a hook.

"We'll be OK. It won't take long to get there. And, afterwards, Chris will be within walking distance of home."

"Where is this place, then?" asked Christopher conversationally. "Is it a hall?"

"Sort of," replied Jenny, taking the car keys from a drawer. "It's a church hall actually, but you wouldn't think so. They've done it up amazingly and it's like being in a professional theatre. They get loads of people there and it's so friendly! You'll probably know it, as you're a church person. I've never seen anything like it before. The minister is a super chap. Max met him at a conference."

Max looked slightly self-conscious.

"Yes, do you remember that conference we went to the other week? Well, there was a talk from this vicar chap about ethics in the workplace, d'you remember? And it was surprisingly good. I don't think you managed to get to it. But the kids didn't get involved through me. All their friends were going to this church hall every week for a club or something and they joined in."

Christopher said nothing.

"Well, you know what youngsters are," added Max lamely. "They have to do what their friends are doing. I sort of had a feeling that you had something to do with this church. I know it's not your own one."

Christopher turned his face away.

"Not if I can help it," he muttered. Jenny had gone into the hall to fetch a jacket and did not hear what he said. But Max looked crestfallen.

"Sorry, Chris, I would never have let Jenny suggest it if I'd known that you wouldn't be keen. We thought you would enjoy going to a church. Is there something wrong with this one?"

"Bloody hell! Wrong?" exclaimed Christopher, still looking away. He struggled to find words to continue, but some sense of Max's disappointment dawned on him and he turned back to glance at his friend.

"Oh, don't worry, Max," he managed to say, although it was with an effort. "It's nothing whatsoever to do with you. Just church politics which are best left alone. Of course I'll come and watch the show. You and Jenny will want to see Andrew and Kate doing their stuff. Is it singing?"

Max's look of concern melted and his face relaxed into its usual cheerful state.

"Not sure, actually. They've been keeping it all very secret, but I think there's singing and dancing and things. This afternoon is very informal. Parents and friends have been invited to call in any time between two and five. There's a cup of tea as well. Anyway, Jenny's gone out to the car, so shall we get on?"

The drive to Christ Church did not take long, but Jenny had trouble in finding a parking space. All the roads around the church seemed to be packed with parked cars and, after driving around for about ten minutes, Jenny decided to park in a supermarket car park a short distance away.

"I'll have to pay when we leave," she remarked to Max and Christopher as she locked the car, but at least we've found somewhere. If I know Andrew and Kate, they'll be getting impatient to see us."

The three of them walked briskly out of the car park and along three or four streets until they reached the church. As they approached it, Christopher hung back and looked, with unwilling eyes, at the scene. As before, there seemed to be people everywhere, some emerging from the doorway of the extension and more going in. Several had children with them and there appeared to be whole families, including well-dressed and sprightly grandparents. The banner on the front fence had been replaced with a new one, even brighter than its predecessor. This one proclaimed:

'Half a million have visited our mission website. Have you? Go to www.christchurchmission.org.'

Christopher grimaced and followed Max and Jenny into the extension. He found himself in a smart entrance hall, carpeted with a new-looking red carpet and with modern religious art displayed on the walls. One showed Christ standing on a green hillside with a crowd of people standing or sitting in front of him. The listeners wore business suits, fashionable casual wear or sports clothing. On the right-hand side of the entrance was a hatch with a sleek kitchen behind, shiny with stainless steel. Smiling young people in their twenties and thirties were handing out cups of tea and urging the visitors to help themselves to biscuits. In front of him, Max and Jenny exchanged impressed glances and Jenny looked over her shoulder to see Christopher's reaction, clearly expecting him to look equally impressed. He attempted to smile back reassuringly but did not fail to notice a slight shadow pass across Max's face.

'Poor old Max,' he thought bitterly. 'Why does he have to be taken in by these awful people?'

Max and Jenny guided him to the hatch and handed him a cup of tea and oat cookie.

"They say we can take these into the hall," shouted Jenny over the hubbub. "Are you OK, Chris? Mind someone doesn't knock your tea over. Let's go in."

The three of them, carefully holding their cups and saucers, went through a pair of swing doors opposite the entrance and into the main hall. They were greeted by a young man in a red polo shirt and beige trousers who guided them to seats in the middle of the hall. In front of them was a stage with proper stage lighting and scenery showing a desert landscape. On the stage, children and young people wearing vaguely Arab costumes were engaged in lively choreography which was intended to convey an impression of the Exodus. Jenny nearly spilt her tea as she recognised Kate at the front of the stage and Andrew at the back, both singing and dancing with infectious energy and enthusiasm. Max grinned as he took his seat between Jenny and Christopher.

"Typical of our kids!" he exclaimed affectionately. "Right in the thick of it as usual! Well, I never. Are they doing the whole Bible?"

Jenny pointed to a white screen just above the proscenium arch and they all read:

'The Old Testament in Dance. The Exodus. For the cloud of the Lord was upon the tabernacle by day, and fire was on it by night, in the sight of all the house of Israel, throughout all their journeys.'

While Max and Jenny gazed lovingly at their children, Christopher covertly looked around the hall. It was true what Jenny had said. The hall did look like a professional theatre. The comfortable, upholstered seats, the smooth floor, the stage, the blacked-out windows, all declared the management to be efficient and well-resourced. Most of the seats were occupied by the relations and friends of the children on the stage and these people, like Max and Jenny, were intent on watching the performance and following every move of their own children.

"Corporate happiness," he thought.

Moving around the hall discreetly were four or five young adults wearing red polo shirts and beige trousers, showing people to their seats, removing used cups and saucers and generally making sure that everything ran smoothly. Christopher reflected grimly that the whole outfit was a good deal more effective than most of the conferences which he attended. Nothing had been forgotten. There were fire exit signs, signs to lavatories, emergency lighting installations and wide gangways for wheelchairs.

For about forty minutes, Christopher endured the loud singing and athletic dancing which was taking place on the stage. While Moses was talking to God on top of a mountain (a ramp on the stage), he glanced at his watch as secretly as possible, hoping that Max would not notice. But Max had not forgotten his friend, despite his adulation of his offspring.

"It's all right, Chris," he whispered, leaning across. "We don't mind if you slip out. You've done very well. See you soon."

"Thanks, Max," replied Christopher gratefully. "Your two children are really good. I'll be in touch soon. Thank Jenny for me."

As he eased himself out of his seat, Jenny turned her head and smiled her goodbye warmly and confidentially.

Within a minute, Christopher was on the pavement outside the church. The sun had gone behind a bank of colourless cloud and there was a late afternoon feeling about the atmosphere, although it was not so very late. People were still going into the hall and a few were trickling out. Christopher took his handkerchief out of his pocket and wiped his face, feeling as though he had just recovered from a fever. The light seemed strange and the air felt heavy. For a second, he hesitated about which way to turn to head for home. Then, stuffing his handkerchief back in his pocket, he set off by one of his usual routes, trying to restore normality to his life. He had not enjoyed the day and the fact that his friends had been overwhelmingly kind and sympathetic only made him feel wretched. But, at present, there were no rational thoughts in his head, only a paralysing dullness. A closing sentence offered itself.

'The June day, which had started brightly, ended under a cloud.'

Chapter seven

Christopher lolled back moodily in his leather office chair. The day was hot and he had a headache. Two of the usual occupants of his room were on holiday, leaving him and Rebecca Court, a junior member of staff who had the distinction of being the 'Conference and Events Co-ordinator.' When she had been appointed, Christopher had asked the Human Resources department, 'Why only one conference?' but he had got blank looks in reply. Rebecca usually did her work reasonably well, but in a cool and detached way, as though she were dealing with business which was essentially an insult to her intelligence. Christopher did not care very much what she thought about the work, as long as she did it. But she nevertheless irritated him. She lived with her boyfriend in Lewisham and, when not at work, they went clubbing and did other things which Christopher had no interest in. Consequently, he only ever talked to her about the Institute's work.

Looking across the dusty hot air of the room, he noticed that she was playing a computer game.

"Haven't you got any work to do, Rebecca?" he asked sharply. She glanced at him and then back at the screen.

"Sorry, Chris, but it's July and we don't have any events or conferences. I finished that set of minutes that you asked me to do. Anyway, Paul and I are going on holiday on Saturday."

For a few moments, she carried on playing the computer game. Christopher brooded. He hated being called 'Chris' by people like Rebecca, but that sort of thing was normal in his office. When she had first come, he had tried calling her 'Miss Court', but she had laughed and the joke had been taken up by other junior staff. He had even overheard two of them mimicking him. He coughed slightly.

"Rebecca, there are one or two things that you could do before you go on leave. For a start, could you make a list of the autumn conferences, matched up with their venues and giving estimates of numbers attending and the dimensions of the main meeting rooms? You could also give an idea of the seminar rooms and how many delegates they hold."

Rebecca twitched her shoulders and carried on staring at the screen.

"OK, I'll do that. I just need to finish this level," she replied absentmindedly.

Christopher picked up a letter that was lying on his desk and which he had brought to work with him. It was from Mark Evans and he had found it lying on his doormat when he had arrived home from work the previous evening. He had felt too tired to read it then. It was printed on one side of A4 and was a general moan about the parsimonious amounts being paid to choir members and, by implication, to Mark himself. He stared blindly at it for several seconds and then put it back on his teak-veneered desk, pushing back his keyboard to make more room for it. After a quick look at Rebecca, who was still absorbed in her game, he took a pen from his pen tray and proceeded to draw daggers in the margins of the letter, with their tips pointing at the text. When he had drawn six, three on each side, he added dripping blood and carefully drew a little pool beneath each dagger. That relieved his feelings somewhat, but he had no idea how to answer the letter. The parish was struggling financially and he was still contemplating the possibility of doing without a choir altogether. Caroline had, of course, counselled against this, saying that the services were dreary enough already and that the loss of the choir would kill them off completely. Well, it had to be admitted that she had a point. But where did Caroline think the money was coming from? He knitted his brows and then drew another two daggers on the letter.

After another ten minutes of inertia, Christopher looked at his watch and switched off his computer. He had arranged to take flexi-leave so that he could go to the church. Before this hot spell, there had been torrential rain and he had noticed water spilling over the parapet on the roof, an indication of problems – possibly a blocked gutter. He wanted to go up on the roof when Caroline and the others were not around to question and criticise.

"I've got flexi-leave this afternoon, Rebecca," he said loudly, standing up and taking his jacket off the back of his chair. "Don't forget to do that piece of work I mentioned. If anyone phones, tell them I'm on leave and will be back tomorrow."

"OK Chris," replied Rebecca, still concentrating on the game. "Going anywhere nice?"

He put his jacket on and straightened his tie.

"Nice? Not really. See you tomorrow."

When Christopher arrived at the church, he found Justin explaining the finer points of Georgian church architecture to a group of Spanish tourists. As most of them did not understand English, their leader – a smartly-dressed woman in a red blouse and black trousers – was repeating the talk to them in Spanish. Christopher smiled encouragingly at Justin, but he noticed that Justin's words were being only approximately translated, if that. He heard the guide telling the group that the church was medieval, that the Royal Arms dated from the sixteenth century and that the church had been taken over by the Protestants. He decided not to interfere. His own Spanish was fairly limited and he would not have attempted to deliver a talk in it.

Justin loved neo-classical architecture and it was best to let him rattle on. Christopher went into the vestry and found two letters waiting for him on the table. He ripped open the envelopes. One of them contained an invoice for electricity and he shuddered when he looked at the amount of money being demanded. The other was a letter from a homelessness charity, asking for funding.

'Dear vicar', it began. 'Have you ever known what it is like to sleep in a doorway on a cold night, lying on cardboard? Have you ever had to beg for food? Shaun discovered what it was like when his abusive father threw him out of his home when he was only 16. Sleeping in doorways by night and tramping the streets by day, he soon got drawn into a life of cheap alcohol and drugs, relying on soup runs and hand-outs for food. Then, one day, he turned up at our centre near Victoria.'

Christopher's face hardened.

"Bloody nuisances," he muttered as he tore the letter into tiny pieces and let them fall into the bin. "I hate these emotive case studies. Why can't they just ask for your cash straight off?"

He placed the invoice in a tray marked 'Treasurer' and then moved towards the door. But a thought struck him and he turned back and opened a cupboard which stood against the wall opposite the vestment chest. This was where the altar supplies were kept. Kneeling down, he peered into it and mentally ticked off the various contents.

"Yes, plenty of charcoal," he murmured, "exactly as Justin said. And what about incense? Hm, yes, two boxes of *Glastonbury*, unopened, plus half a box. Wafers. Let me see. Nearly half a box of priest's wafers. That should be OK for a bit. And then people's wafers. Not too many left, but then we don't use as many these days."

He peered even further into the cupboard, which contained packages of various shapes and sizes, some of them wrapped up in paper with elastic bands round them, and some in grubby plastic bags.

"Now, candles. I can only see a couple of the big ones. That won't do. And only one box of the ones for the stands. I'll have to do an order. I won't bother telling Caroline. I'll pay for these myself. It shouldn't come to too much."

Drawing his head out of the cupboard, he clambered to his feet and brushed the dust carefully from his trouser knees. Nobody had done any cleaning for a while and he thought that he had better do some once he had come down from the roof. As he carefully closed the cupboard doors, he thought briefly of asking Justin to clean the vestry floor, but almost as quickly dismissed the thought. He listened for a moment with his head inclined in the direction of the church. There was no sound, so Justin had evidently finished with the Spanish tourists. Christopher felt in his pocket for the bunch of keys which usually lived there and went back into the church, where Justin was standing in the chancel, staring at the brass plaque commemorating Charles Aitchison. He turned his head quickly to greet Christopher and then looked back at the plaque.

"I love this one," he said thoughtfully. "It's almost Arts and Crafts in style. Well, 1920, so sort-of late Arts and Crafts. Not Art-Deco. I suppose that we have to thank him for us being Anglo-Catholic. What was he like, Christopher? Do we know much about him?"

Christopher joined him and gazed affectionately at the brass tablet which he had recently polished up again.

"We don't know much about his private life but he must have had tremendous courage and a huge belief in the Catholic Movement. You know, when there were ritualism riots outside the church – when he put six candles on the altar – he apparently went out into the street, stood on an orange box or something and started shouting prayers at the crowd. Some yob pulled him down and took his biretta off his head, holding it up like a trophy, with Fr Aitchison pressed up against the wall of the church by the rioting crowd. He could have been killed, or badly hurt anyway, but some policemen came along and rescued him. I've read the account of it in 'The Times'. But what's really odd is that nobody ever took him to court and, in the end, this church had full Catholic ritual and people seemed to accept it."

Justin looked at the tablet with reverence. After a while, he remarked,

"He must have had good artistic taste as well. Didn't he buy the big candlesticks and the aumbry? They're very fine. It must have been fascinating to have been here in his time. I wonder how big the congregation was."

Christopher smiled sadly.

"It was completely different then. There were still slums around the place and Fr Aitchison used to draw huge congregations of poor people. He seems to have been an impressive preacher and packed them in. There's an old book of his sermons somewhere but they're not like modern sermons. I think that we would probably be embarrassed by them – all about the sacraments, living the Christian life and making your confession. He also had loads of organisations in the parish and arranged trips to the seaside for slum children and women's sewing groups and stuff like that. We wouldn't recognise it now."

Justin grinned.

"You sound just like a teacher, Chris. You've got it all off pat. Did you ever think about going into teaching? I think you'd be terribly good at it."

Christopher bent down to brush his trousers again.

"I did think about it a bit when I left university. But I didn't want to have to do a teaching course for another year. I didn't want to be dependent on my parents but, as I had no money of my own, I had to get a job. I joined the civil service for a bit and then went to the Institute. It's all boring, really. Are you thinking of teaching? You're very good with the tourists."

Justin smiled self-consciously.

"I wouldn't mind. But I've got a while to go yet. I do sort-of like telling people things, but I don't think I'd be very good with the discipline side. Not in a school, at least. I suppose that I might think about college teaching. I actually had another idea, although I don't know what you'd think of it, Chris."

Christopher straightened up and glanced at him curiously.

"Oh, what's that? You don't have to tell me, Justin, if you'd prefer not."

Justin took a look around the church before speaking, to check that they were alone.

"Well," he said quietly, "I 've been thinking about the ministry."

"Ministry?" echoed Christopher. "Do you mean a government department?"

Justin looked embarrassed.

"No, the Christian ministry. I've been wondering whether I would be accepted for ordination training when I've graduated. I don't think it's a stupid idea. I really enjoy helping at the services and I seem to get on with everyone. What do you think?"

Christopher could not trust himself to reply, so Justin continued.

"I've been looking at the diocesan website and it says there are conferences and things where people can learn more about it. And then you can go through a discernment process while you explore your vocation. I think I should really enjoy that. And then you can choose whether to go to theological college or whether to do the diocesan ministerial training scheme. That takes longer and, anyway, I would prefer theological college. The trouble is -" he paused and Christopher made an effort to say something.

"I see. This is very unexpected. I'm sorry I can't take it in all at once. What is the trouble?"

Justin looked wistful.

"The trouble is that the website advises you to talk to your vicar in the first place. Only we don't have one. I'm not sure what to do, Chris. Can I talk to you about it or should I go and see the Archdeacon or someone? I'm not sure I like the Archdeacon very much."

Christopher grimaced.

"The Archdeacon is a bastard," he replied. "But, Justin, are you sure? The ministry isn't for everyone. You're quite young still and you might change your mind. What do your parents say?"

Justin ran his hand through his hair.

"I haven't exactly told them yet. You're the first person I've mentioned it to. But I've been thinking about it a lot over the past few months and it really does appeal to me. Oh, I know it's early stages and people might think I'm being an idiot, but I don't see why I shouldn't at least consider it. You don't think I'm being mad, do you, Chris? It's partly because of you that I got the idea."

Christopher began to feel that he was having one of his bad dreams.

"Because of me?" he managed to say. "I can't believe it. I seem to have rows with half the clergy."

Justin smiled and looked around the church with affection.

"Well, St Benet's, anyway. It sounds a bit mawkish, but it's here that I've learned about the beauty of worship. There's a perfect blend here of the classical and the spiritual. I'd quite like to do a thesis on it if I ever get the chance. And the Prayer Book liturgy seems to complement it – with the incense, of course. Can you imagine what it would be like if we went all happy-clappy? I'd run a mile, for a start. But, what do you think, Chris?"

Christopher could not find the right words for a few seconds and a shade of disappointment began to pass over Justin's face. Then, knowing that he was being ungracious, he made another effort.

"Look, Justin. I don't feel that I'm the right person to advise you on this. I have very mixed feelings about the priesthood just at present. But why don't you have a word with Bob Bodkin? He's a decent chap and might have some good advice for you. I'm sorry to be a wet blanket. I've got a bit of a headache today."

Justin's face brightened.

"Of course! Fr Bob! I don't know why I didn't think of him. He's a bit scatty at times but he's very pastoral. Yes, that's a very good idea. And he will know who else I ought to speak to. Of course! Sorry about your headache, Chris."

Christopher jingled his church keys in his jacket pocket and started to move off, leaving Justin with a satisfied look on his face.

"It's nothing, really, Justin. I think it's called the Church of England. Look, I have to go up on the roof to see what's causing that overflow. Don't come with me. I'll be OK. You stay down here and do your stuff with the visitors."

Frowning, Christopher went to the back of the church and let himself into the small room under the tower which contained the circular staircase leading to the roof. As he ascended the steps, which were broad and comfortable at first, but got narrower after a landing, he thought about what Justin had said to him. It was unwelcome news and he did not feel like analysing his thoughts any further to find out why it was unwelcome. It was irritating. It was disturbing. Justin would surely have second thoughts. A lot of impressionable young people toyed with the idea of entering the Church, but very few of them ever ended up doing so. Justin would feel differently after a week or two. Surely Bob would warn him against it. It was just annoying. Why did Justin have to think of it? Irritating. Disturbing. Annoying. Annoying. The steps seemed to echo his words as he went up and up.

He reached the door which led onto the roof and reached mechanically into his jacket pocket for his keys. There was a sign fixed to the wooden door which said 'Hard hat area' but Christopher could never remember anyone wearing a hard hat. If they did, it wouldn't save them if they fell off the roof. He was almost the only person who ever went up there. The inspecting architect went on the roof every five years and Caroline went up there about once a year, partly to prove to herself that she could do it and partly to fulfil all the duties of a churchwarden as she understood them. When she went up, she would tread very gingerly on the leads, keeping well away from the parapet and trying not to look down. The view was not very good, in any case, because the church was largely surrounded by office buildings, but she still preferred not to look at it. Christopher had no similar qualms and quite enjoyed going up on the roof because he could be on his own there and not be bothered by people like Simon or Mark.

He pushed open the door and saw immediately the cause of the overflowing gutter. The gully around the sides of the roof was full of dirty-looking water, and five plastic balls of the sort used by young children were bobbing about in it. In the right-hand corner nearest to where Christopher was perched at the top of a short set of steps, a tennis ball could just be seen in the murk, blocking the downpipe. Christopher stared thoughtfully at it for a few moments, trying to decide whether to remove his shoes and socks in order to wade through the water. He knew that, if he kept them on, he would get them very wet, but the prospect of slithering through the grey water in bare feet was not appetising. After gazing hesitatingly for a few more seconds, he lifted his head and looked around at the office blocks which clustered around, trying to see into their windows. Who had thrown those balls onto the church roof? He could imagine that it must have become a game – a rather stupid and irresponsible one – designed to add variety and laughter to a boring office routine. Bright, young, upwardly-mobile executives, no doubt. Were those people looking at him now and enjoying his discomfiture?

The building far over on his left-hand side, which faced the vestry door in the alley, was an early twentieth century one of some distinction. Built of narrow red bricks with stone facings, it had made some attempt to complement the eighteenth century architecture of the church. Mercifully, it had escaped both the Blitz and subsequent attempts to redevelop the area. Glancing sideways at it and trying to measure the distance from the higher windows to the gully on the other side of the church roof, Christopher decided that the culprits could not possibly work there. Apart from the fact that he did not want to blame that particular building, he felt that some of the balls would have landed in the gully nearer to that side, had they been thrown from there. He shifted his gaze to the blocks more directly in front of him and on his right-hand side. There were three modern office blocks, apparently made mostly of tinted glass, quite close to the church, with others visible through gaps between the buildings. He peered at the top floors, screwing up his eyes in the bright sunlight, and wondered if those sightless windows even opened. The balls must have come from somewhere. With his head tilted backwards, he looked from building to building, almost trying to force an answer from them. But, as he shifted his precarious position in to see round to the other side of the tower, he started to feel slightly dizzy and spots and flashes appeared in front of his eyes. Deep inside his brain, he told himself off for wasting his own time in such a fruitless exercise. But still he looked up, almost mesmerised by the view. Odd thoughts came into his mind, such as the possibility of falling off the roof, and he remembered a dream which he had had, weeks ago, about falling off Beachy Head. The blocks grew larger and more threatening. They were now the mythological Cyclops and he was a tiny mortal, about to be caught up and tossed around as a primordial giant's plaything. Tossed around, like one of these coloured balls. And, when the giants had finished with him, would he be thrown casually back onto the church roof? They now loomed over him, blocking out the sky. Perspiration broke out on his forehead and trickled slowly over his temples.

It was a spell he had to break. Sitting down heavily on the top step and looking down at his feet, he started to take his shoes and socks off. The job would have to be done. It was a simple one and would prevent damage to the stonework. He placed a sock in each shoe and arranged them tidily on the step beside him before balancing carefully on the other two steps, down to the roof. As he stepped into the tepid water, he found that it was slightly deeper than he had thought and hastily rolled up his trouser bottoms until they reached to just below his knees. Moving carefully, he waded to the downpipe and tried to shift the tennis ball with his foot. It did not budge. Sighing, he rolled up his shirt sleeves and plunged his right hand into the water, taking hold of the ball with his fingers and pulling firmly. The first attempt failed. He tried again and, this time, the ball came out of the downpipe so suddenly that Christopher staggered and nearly fell over backwards. He saved himself by clutching at the side of the tower but the splash soaked the front of his trousers.

"Hell!"

But the water was disappearing down the pipe and the coloured balls were now moving towards it. Christopher recovered himself and waited to catch them as they arrived, forcing himself to concentrate on the task and not look either up at the office blocks or down at the street. One, two, three, four, five. As they came, he plucked them out of the water and placed them on the central raised area of the roof. Standing there, with wet clothing and a tight chest, high above the street, Christopher suddenly and irrationally thought about the Odyssey and its hero, Odysseus, who had tackled everything that came his way. Were tragic heroes born or made?

After the first rush of water had gone, the flow diminished to a trickle and then stopped. There were still puddles in the gullies but the worst of the flood was gone and Christopher breathed more easily again. He raised himself to his full height and, using the tower wall as a support, looked at the main roof. Opposite the set of steps was a door leading into the area above the church ceiling. Nobody ever went in there but it occurred to him that water might have seeped around the door and flowed into the space beyond, possibly damaging the ceiling. He frowned. It was probably filthy in there but hadn't he better take a look, just in case? He moved cautiously back to the steps and put his shoes and socks on. His feet felt damp and clammy but he supposed that they would get dry somehow. He got his keys out of his jacket pocket and selected the one that he thought would fit the keyhole in the little door opposite to where he was perched, choosing it because it was the one key which he had hardly ever used. When he had first become churchwarden, years ago, he had unlocked that door and peered into the gloom beyond, but the prospect had been so uninviting that he had backed away and locked the door again. Well, he would have to face going in there now. Thinking about future dry cleaning bills, he took his jacket off and folded it neatly, placing it on the lead roof, well away from any water or dirt. He then unlocked the door and put his head inside the space. It was dark and stuffy and he realised that he should have brought a torch up with him. However, as his eyes began to get accustomed to the darkness, he could see further in and, with relief, saw enough to know that the floor of the space was not under water. The area immediately next to the entrance looked a little damp but there was no sign of any huge puddles.

He knelt down carefully and looked further in. The cavernous space stretched back further than he could see, over most of the church ceiling. It was roughly boarded, with gaps between the planks, and the flooring looked thick with grime and dust. He started to see more. A few feet in from the entrance there appeared to be a large bundle of something. He was curious and, despite the absolute certainty of getting his already-crumpled and wet trousers in a terrible state, he decided to crawl in and investigate. The space was too low to permit his standing upright but there was plenty of room for crawling or shuffling. Once he was properly inside, he noticed that light was coming in from sources other than the doorway. Along the sides of the roof space, a dim light was coming up from the church interior, where the ceiling had been inserted in sections, and this light enabled him to see quite a long way ahead. He could see the outlines of some boxes piled up quite a long way inside and it was evident that, at times in the past, the roof had been regarded as a useful place for storage.

He stopped to listen. The sound of muffled conversation was coming from the narrow gap on his left-hand side and he steered himself across the boards to listen. He could distinguish Justin's voice and also an unfamiliar one, probably a tourist's. Justin was speaking loudly and Christopher, interested to hear what he was saying, stretched himself at full length on the boards and tried to peer through the narrow gap to the church below. The view was restricted but he could see most of Justin, who was standing next to the pews on the north side of the church, and also two men, who were sitting on a pew beside Justin. The latter was clearly having a good time, describing the church and its activities to the two tourists, who were smartly dressed in suits.

"We have a Sunday Eucharist, of course," announced Justin, "with full ritual. And then there's a weekday Eucharist as well which the college chaplain usually takes."

One of the men said something which Christopher could not catch and then Justin spoke again.

"Yes, that's taken by Fr Bodkin from Holy Trinity. We've not had a rector of our own since Epiphany, when Fr Abbotsford left to go to Chichester. The congregation's gone down a bit since then."

The other man said something, which, again, Christopher could not quite hear. He could see Justin bending over the man to hear what he said and then answering him, pointing towards the chancel, but his reply could not be heard either. The first man seemed to join in and all three of them pointed and gesticulated for a few moments. Most of their words did not reach the listener in the roof but Christopher caught the odd word, mostly from Justin – 'reserve the sacrament', 'cottas', 'use wafers' and 'communicants.' Christopher smiled. Justin was obviously in his element and had found a willing audience. The three men in the church disappeared in the direction of the chancel, out of Christopher's field of vision, and the conversation became faint and disjointed. Christopher continued to peer through the crack, although the draught was starting to make his right eye water. It was odd to look directly down into the church, where everything was looking tiny, like furniture in a doll's house. The sunshine coming in through the church windows illuminated the dust in the air, so that, from Christopher's vantage point, there seemed to be a fog or mist in the building. After a while, the voices became louder again and appeared to be directly below where Christopher was lying, although he could not see anyone.

"I hope you will visit St Benet's again," said Justin's voice, loudly and cheerfully. "It's been really interesting showing you the church."

"I will, at least,' replied another voice. 'It's been terribly good of you to show us round. Are you studying at the college?"

Justin answered the question in a softer voice and Christopher could not quite hear what he said. Then the other visitor said quite a lot, also in a softer voice and indistinctly. Then, all three men came into view, moving towards the west end of the church, and quickly disappeared out of view again. The second man spoke again, this time much more loudly.

"Well, thank you again, Justin. Don't forget to come and see us at Christ Church. We'll give you a tour in return for the one you've given us. Goodbye."

"Goodbye!" called out Justin.

There was nothing more to see or hear. Christopher scrambled back into a crouching position and frowned. Christ Church? Which Christ Church? Was it a church at all? Could it be the town in Dorset? No, that would be silly. Well, he would ask Justin for an explanation when he went down again. He would just finish what he was doing.

Christopher had been so distracted by the episode below him that he had to think for a second or two in order to remember what he had been doing before he had started peering through the gap. He then continued his crawling progress towards the bundle ahead of him. It was not very far in and he could now see fairly well, at least for several feet in front. Reaching the package, he found that it consisted of a huge roll of polythene, black with the dirt of years, and seemingly tied up with string. With a rueful reflection that he could hardly get dirtier and more disreputable than he was already, he took hold of a large knot in the string and dragged the whole affair towards the entrance, disturbing layers of dust as he did so. Backing himself up against the set of steps, and blinking in the bright sunshine, he manhandled the bundle into the dip between the steps and the doorway which led into the roof space. There was something about grubby polythene which was particularly dreary and depressing. This specimen was completely horrible, dark grey or black all over, with lighter grey smears where he had touched or brushed against it.

As he contemplated it with distaste, it began to be apparent that it was not so much a bundle of polythene as something wrapped up in polythene and tied with string. It was impossible to see what, and he shifted his attention to the big knot and a consideration of whether it could be untied. The string was the old-fashioned, frayed sort and the knot looked formidable. Christopher leaned across and took his bunch of keys from the little door in front of him, thinking that one of them might have an edge sharp enough to cut through the string. He chose one and started to saw a section of the string. It was no good. His second choice was more effective, however, and for a couple of minutes he scraped away at the string, gradually weakening it until it broke and fell apart, disturbing more of the dust. With hands that were already completely filthy, he slowly unfolded the large sheet of polythene, drawing himself back slightly to avoid breathing in too much dust. When he had unfolded the right and left hand sides of the polythene, he could just see that the object inside was made of some kind of fabric. For no particular reason, his heart started to pound and he felt his hands trembling as he peeled back the remaining sides of polythene.

"Why am I shaking?" he pondered. "This is stupid. I start undoing this ridiculous great bundle of old rubbish and I tremble like an idiot. The sun is making me dizzy. I ought to go back down again and leave this to another time."

But he carried on unwrapping the package and finally exposed a folded piece of thick material. He knew why he was shaking. It was an altar frontal, folded up in a large rectangle, with the decorated surface on the inside of each fold.

He paused. At the edges of his vision, the office blocks appeared to be moving, shimmering in the unfriendly sunshine. He felt sick. He wished himself elsewhere and yet he wished to unfold this frontal. He wanted to look at it and yet he didn't want to look at it. He longed to be at home instead of being perched on the church roof. He wanted to be clean and dry and comfortable, like a small child. But, first, he would unfold the frontal. A police siren screamed past in the street below. For a moment, Christopher thought that his eardrums would burst.

Touching the cloth with only his fingertips, in order to preserve it from most of the dirt on his hands, he gently unfolded some of it, so that he could see what it looked like. There was no room in the cramped space where he was crouching to open it up completely and he had to rearrange it in order to get a good view of one section. It was creamy-white and made of stamped velvet. A blue silk border, embroidered in gold, ran round the edge and another length of it ran down the front, about a third in from the side. Christopher guessed that there was another strip further along, making three sections on the front, each with an embroidered figure in it. The figure he could see was an angel, dressed in gold with a green cloak and red and gold wings, facing inwards and standing under a canopy of elaborate gold tracery. The embroidery was exquisite and, despite its age, brilliant in the hot sunshine.

"Wonderful. Beautiful," he gasped. "Wonderful or rué work. Just wonderful."

He stared and stared, consuming the feast with his eyes until they felt strained and weary. It was too much to take in. He knew that he should not be exposing any of the altar frontal to the sunlight and yet he could not immediately bear to fold it up again. It was the missing frontal. Not lost, but here all the time, over his head, keeping watch. It seemed a miracle.

There was suddenly a noise behind him, coming from the tower staircase, and he hastily folded back the cloth and pulled a piece of the polythene over it. Justin's voice sounded from over his head.

"Hey, Chris! You all right? I was just going to leave."

Christopher twisted himself round.

"Oh, hello, Justin. Yes, I'm fine. I've cleared the blockage."

Justin looked at the plastic balls which were still sitting on the top section of the roof and grinned.

"What you might call a balls up!" he commented. "Anyway, Chris, you've done the trick. Hadn't you better come down? You've been up here for ages. You've got black all down you."

Christopher scrambled to his feet in the confined space, trying to hide the bundle from view, but Justin looked past him with curiosity.

"What you got there? Was that stuff blocking the gully, as well?"

"No, this is just some rubbish I found in the roof space. I'll have to clear it up another time. You get on, Justin. You've done a good stint in the church. I really am grateful. You don't have to, you know. Go on. It's time you went home. I'll be down in a minute. But lock up, would you?"

Justin turned to go.

"All right. I'll be off then. Mind how you go coming down, Chris. You look in a bit of a state. Bye."

He turned to go and Christopher turned back to look at the bundle. But a thought suddenly occurred to him and he twisted himself back and called out harshly,

"Oh, Justin! Just a minute! Can you just come up here a sec. I just wanted to ask you something."

There was a scraping sound in the tower and then Justin appeared again in the doorway,

"Hello. Yes, what is it?"

Christopher turned his face away.

"Oh, nothing much. I just noticed that you were talking to some visitors in the church a while ago. They mentioned Christ Church, I think. Were they visiting from Dorset?"

"Dorset?" Justin looked blank. "No, they were local, I think. They were telling me about their church. It was really interesting. They were great blokes. The church was Christ Church. Anyway, I'll get off. I'm meeting up with a friend for a drink. Bye, Chris."

He was gone and Christopher did not call him back a second time. Christ Church. Christ Church. Which Christ Church? For the time being, the magic of the missing altar frontal was broken.

Chapter eight

"Have some more toast, Christopher. And here's the honey. Mind, the jar's sticky."

Christopher passed his plate across to Jenny with an unaccustomed feeling of wellbeing, while Max sat on the opposite side of the table, beaming at him. The sunshine was pouring in through the kitchen window of the small stone cottage where they were staying, near Bala in Wales. The breakfast table had an old-fashioned red checked tablecloth on it and there was a cheerful display of crusty bread, jam, honey and the remains of boiled eggs. He started to spread butter and honey thickly on his toast.

"Thanks, Jenny. This is really good honey from that farm shop. If I am walking past there, shall I get another jar?"

He could hardly believe the sound of his own voice. He seemed to be in a dream or had become somebody else. He had never intended to come on this August holiday and yet, here he was, tucking into breakfast in the most happy and sociable way possible and looking forward to another day's walking. He had not intended to come, but a concatenation of circumstances had changed his mind. In the first place, he had been getting a lot of headaches recently. He had diagnosed himself as suffering from stress but had no idea how to tackle it, other than taking lots of aspirins and other painkillers. The stress was mostly emanating from the church, where the situation seemed to be getting increasingly bleak, with no suggestions for a new parish priest coming from 'authority', and people like Simon and Mark becoming more unpleasant by the day. But a holiday for Christopher had seemed impossible, because he would have had to leave Caroline and Simon to look after things in his absence. He would not have minded Caroline doing that but he knew that Simon would have attempted to dominate. But then had come the news that Simon was going on some sort of training course, probably to train him up in even more pedantic minor legislation than usual. And the best news was that the course clashed with the holiday being organised by Max and Jenny. When Christopher had subsequently discovered that the Archdeacon would also be away and that Justin was free to help out at St Benet's, he had considered the idea of the Welsh holiday with tentative interest. And then had come the telephone call from Max. Max, at his most considerate and heartening, had rung at the crucial moment 'just to check' and to say how much he and Jenny were looking forward to having Christopher's company. At the time of the call, Christopher was resting his aching head on his hand and staring at an invoice from Mark.

"Sod it!" he had blurted out, somewhat to Max's surprise. "I'll come. I've had enough of the whole tribe of them."

So here he was, eating toast and honey in the sunny cottage kitchen. But last minute doubts had almost caused him to withdraw. Did Max and Jenny really want him? Could Caroline and Justin really manage the parish? Would Simon cancel his training course? Would Bob Bodkin get sick again? Even on the morning of his departure, he had seriously thought about ringing Max and Jenny to tell them that he wasn't coming. Before he could do so, they had arrived in their car and carried Christopher off with them. He had sat in the back of the car, brooding, while they had chatted away about the route, the weather, where they might get lunch and what they were going to do on the holiday, sometimes disagreeing with each other but then changing the subject as though they were trying to put on a good act. It had seemed to Christopher that they were treating him as though he were a favourite child who had been ill, checking that he was comfortable, offering him drinks and encouraging him to eat at lunch. He slightly resented this, but it seemed so ludicrous that he could not help also feeling amused. It was impossible to feel resentful with Max. When, at lunch in a pub in the Cotswolds, Max had urged him to finish his chips, Christopher had burst out laughing.

"Honestly, Max, anyone would think that I was about six, the way you go on. I've had enough chips, really! I don't need building up."

Max had grinned but Christopher also noticed that he exchanged a look with his wife.

"Sorry, Chris. It comes from being a dad. We usually have the sprogs with us and I try to make them eat their lunch if they're being picky. Andrew likes his grub but Kate has reached the age when she thinks she ought to be dieting or going vegetarian or something. I tell her that's all nonsense."

Jenny had calmly laid down her knife and fork with a smile in Max's direction.

"Yes, darling, and you tell her in such a way that she'll decide to go off and be vegan or naturist. Don't you believe him, Chris, when he acts as though he knows all about fatherhood. He doesn't understand that, if you want teenagers to do anything, you tell them the opposite. The other day, Kate put on a ridiculously short skirt for the school end-of-term party. Max would have blown his top and told her that he would disown her if she wore such a thing. But, luckily, he was at work. So I said that she looked lovely and that it reminded me of my own schooldays. You can guess what she did. She promptly went back to her bedroom and put on a different one. It's just psychology."

That first day had been spent driving and shopping for provisions. At about tea time, they had reached the holiday cottage and found it to be very acceptable, with a large kitchen and small sitting room downstairs and a large bedroom, small bedroom and bathroom upstairs. Christopher's room had in it a single bed, chest of drawers, a rail with some hangers and a shelf of mouldering books, including a few classics like *Great Expectations* and *Swallows and Amazons*. After a sort of high tea, consisting of pasta with bottled tomato sauce, bread and cheese and yogurt, he had pleaded tiredness and retreated to his bedroom, thinking that Max and Jenny would wish to be on their own. Sitting on his bed, under a low ceiling, he had felt very lonely and half wished that he had not agreed to come. It had seemed rather like the first evening at a boarding school – or, at least, the sort of boarding school that he had read about when young - with him as a little boy feeling homesick and not knowing anyone. He could hear Max and Jenny talking downstairs, with the occasional laugh from Max, but could not pick out any words. Outside the cottage, crows could be heard croaking and sheep bleating, while the bright daylight faded and turned into dusk and then darkness. Eventually, Christopher had taken *Great Expectations* off the shelf and, sitting huddled next to the bedside lamp, he had immersed himself in the troubles and aspirations of little Pip.

But, the next morning, a change had started to come over him. Max and Jenny had greeted him at breakfast time with looks of genuine pleasure and they had all enjoyed opening the cupboards and drawers in the kitchen to find where things lived. The breakfast itself had been pleasantly chaotic and there had been a delicious moment of farce when, having searched the entire kitchen for egg cups, they had found them artistically displayed in the china cabinet in the sitting room. The conversation had been about Welsh history, footpaths, maps, local food, farming and the weather. Christopher strongly suspected that Max and Jenny had formed a pact not to mention either St Benet's or Christ Church, and he had noticed, or thought that he had noticed, a few fleeting but meaningful glances between them. Despite feeling that he was being patronised slightly, he was nevertheless grateful for their kindness and sympathy. In some ways, it was a pleasant novelty to be treated like a delicate but much-loved six year old. With some bitterness, he thought back to his childhood, when nobody had ever treated him like that. And, when his parents had become elderly, they had expected more solicitous care from him than he could ever remember receiving from them. Why did the miseries of his childhood keep intruding like this? It seemed sometimes that they had become so woven into his being that it would be impossible to unpick them without destroying the rest of him.

On the first two proper days of the holiday, Christopher had gone out walking on his own and had explored the area to the north of Bala Lake. The exercise and fresh air had soothed his soul and, in the evenings, he had gathered round the table with his friends to eat lavish and informal dinners and then to play the well-used board games which they had found in a drawer in the sitting room. On the second of those evenings, they had played *Monopoly* until after midnight, pretending to be unscrupulous property developers and indulging in hilarious role play. Christopher had amused his friends by buying up all the posh areas like Mayfair and Park Lane and building hotels on them – only to have to mortgage everything shortly afterwards. Christopher was beginning to feel that St Benet's was only a bad dream and that reality was here, in this cottage in Wales.

He crammed the last piece of toast in his mouth and wiped his sticky hands on the piece of kitchen roll that was doing service as a table napkin. Max looked across at him indulgently and then, with half a glance at Jenny, said brightly,

"Well, what has everyone got planned for today? Even Jenny must admit that we've done enough shopping for stores. Subject to your approval, Chris, I wondered if we might all go for a walk together today. I feel like some proper exercise and, if I just have Jenny with me, I'm likely to get lazy."

"Go on! Blame me!" exclaimed Jenny with indignation. "The fact of the matter is that you slow me down, with all your anecdotes and stories which I've heard thousands of times. The kids found you out long ago and they have all your funny stories numbered. They say things like, 'Dad's telling number twenty-six.' But, I agree it'd be good to have a decent long walk. Come on, Chris. You're the great walker. Didn't you reckon that going up Aran Benllyn would make a good walk? That's the mountain just above here, isn't it?"

"Mountain!" broke in Max. "Hill, more like. These aren't the Alps, you know."

"I'm sticking with mountain," responded Jenny, firmly. "What do you think, Chris?"

"I'm with you, Jenny, on this," he replied with a faint smile. "I agree that they're not on the scale of the Alps or the Himalayas, but they have mountain shapes and characteristics, so let's call them mountains."

Max pretended to look crestfallen.

"Vanquished again!" he said sadly and then grinned. "But let's get back to our mutton – or rather, our walk. How about if we make up some sandwiches and things and all go up this mountain-hill, with a picnic at the top? Chris can be our Sherpa. What do you chaps think?"

Christopher did not answer at once, not because he disliked the idea but because going out for a long walk with other people seemed a novel proposition. He nearly always went walking on his own and yet the thought of pleasant company and a picnic on a brilliant sunny day was deeply attractive. He looked down at his plate and scraped up a crumb or two, which he ate.

"Yes, let's," he said, after a moment or two. "That'd be good. You'll need to wear your boots, though. We'll walk into Llanuwchllyn from here and then there's a good path up from there. At least, according to the OS map. I'll show you after we've done the washing up. There should be plenty of time for us to get to the top, have our lunch and come down again."

Max drank the last of his tea and started to stack the crockery.

"Great. That's agreed, then. It shouldn't take us too long to wash up if we all muck in. Then Jenny can make the sandwiches."

A piece of crust thrown by Jenny caught him on the ear and he made a face at her.

"What was that for?" he enquired. Jenny smiled complacently.

"That's for being a male chauvinist pig," she replied, "or whatever they call it these days. You can make the sandwiches and Chris and I will wash up. Only don't get in our way. We'll wash up while you tidy our bedroom and then you can make the sandwiches while we look at the map and plan the route. I'm sure that Chris has already tidied his bedroom."

"Yes, dear," Max said meekly, but with a glint in his eyes. "Can I go to the toilet, please?"

"You should have gone at playtime," replied Jenny. "Run along now. And don't forget to dust under the ornaments."

Christopher helped Jenny to clear the table and carry things across to the sink. Max and Jenny seemed to him a very strange married couple, always teasing each other and saying things that they didn't mean. It was completely unlike the prim conversations which his parents had had when he was a boy. In fact, they had not tended to have conversations at all in his hearing – not, at least, any that concerned him. They had said things like, 'We'll talk about this later' or 'wait till Christopher's in bed.' Christopher could remember lying in bed and straining his ears in order to hear what his parents were saying about him downstairs. Thinking about it now, he suspected that the conversations had been very dull but, at the time, he had felt desperate to know what they were saying. Much of it had concerned his school work which, in his opinion, had been none of their business.

Jenny put on a pair of rubber gloves and handed Christopher a tea towel.

"That's the only thing wrong with this cottage," she commented, as she turned the hot tap on. "No dishwasher. But, never mind, it won't take us long. I'll wash and you dry, Chris."

Christopher obediently took the tea towel and stood ready to take the first item. It was very soothing to be doing washing up in this way, with the sunshine lighting up the rustic cottage kitchen and a geranium plant on the windowsill scenting the air. And there was a companionable walk to look forward to and Max's doorstep sandwiches. The holiday was so far exceeding all his expectations. Jenny turned her head and smiled at him.

"Now we're on our own, Chris, I want to tell you how much we're enjoying having you with us. It's doing Max no end of good. You know, he's very fond of you."

Christopher stiffened slightly.

"Well, same here," he replied awkwardly.

"Yes, I'm sure of that," continued Jenny, putting a handful of cutlery on the draining board. "It's good to see the two of you getting on so well. I know that you've been business colleagues for quite a while, but I do think that you are proper friends now. Max loves being with me and the kids but friends are important too, and I know that he respects you enormously. He always says that you have interesting ideas about everything. Oh, when you've dried them, could you put them in the tray in the drawer?"

Christopher carefully dried three knives and placed them in the correct drawer. He did not quite know what to say. He wished that Jenny had not started this conversation, which was creeping into personal territory where he did not want to go. Why did women always feel obliged to do this? Jenny had been fine up until now, but she clearly felt it her womanly duty to investigate his mental state. Why did she want to know? She darted another look at him.

"I could see that Max really wanted to go on this walk today. He was getting restless yesterday and kept wondering where you were and how far you'd walked. He seemed almost jealous. When you said that we ought to go out together today, he positively glowed. If you two want to go ahead and chat, I shan't mind."

Christopher felt that it was his turn to say something, so he cleared his throat politely.

"Thank you. But we can all chat together. Anyway, some of the walk'll be a bit steep and it's probably stony near the top. I'll show you the map after this."

Jenny placed some soapy mugs on the draining board.

"That's good," she replied. "I always like to know where I'm going. But I also wanted to say how well you're looking now, Chris. We thought you looked a little peaky when we came away. The fresh air must be doing you good. I expect you're glad to be away from your office – and your church, as well. I know that you care about it a lot."

Christopher turned away to put some more cutlery in the drawer. The cheerfulness of his earlier mood was evaporating rapidly now.

"Yes," he said flatly. "It's always good to be out in the fresh air. And we've been very lucky with the weather. Do the scissors go in this drawer?"

"Yes, that's right," she nodded. "And these mugs go in the cupboard on the wall. But what was I saying? Oh yes, that church must be getting you down. Have you got a vicar yet?"

He dried a mug and opened the cupboard door before replying.

"No, not yet. But someone comes and helps us. Two actually."

"That's good," she said reassuringly. "I thought that all the work fell on you. And isn't there another churchwarden, as well? I think you've mentioned Caroline? She must be a good help. I've heard Max say that you like her. She's married, isn't she? And with two sons, I seem to remember. With funny names. You mentioned her when you had lunch with us."

Christopher dried another mug and put it in the cupboard. He was wondering how he could change the subject.

"Yes, Caroline's married," he responded, trying to sound brisk. "I say, Jenny, d'you think Max needs any help? He seems to be taking a long time. It only took me a few minutes to do my room."

Jenny gave a rueful smile.

"He'll be fine. He's probably dusted a book and then picked it up to read it. Housework isn't really his thing, although I suppose that I shouldn't say that. Equal rights and all that. But he's always been a dear with the children. I always think children make people a bit more human."

Christopher noticed the unconscious insult and felt his cheeks turning slightly pink. He tried again to turn the conversation.

"Jenny, have you visited this area before? You've chosen a very nice cottage."

Jenny did not want the conversation turned.

"Yes, it's a lovely cottage. We found it on the internet. But weren't we talking about your Caroline? You were going to tell me more about her sons. What sort of ages are they?"

He rummaged in the cutlery drawer before replying, attempting to steady his voice.

"I've hardly met them. They're grown up. Adrian and Aidan. Her husband is vile and he's called Simon. They may have a cat but I'm afraid I don't know its name or age. Shall I dry those plates now?"

Jenny handed him a plate but was evidently surprised by his brusque reply. Her cheeks reddened.

"Don't get shirty, Chris love. I was only interested. You ought to be getting to know me by now. Don't imagine that all women are the same. I'm certainly not Caroline, and Simon sounds as though he's the exact opposite of Max. I really wanted to let you know that we're always here for you, whatever happens. But we're worried about you. That church of yours seems to be getting you down. It seems to be on your mind the whole time. That isn't healthy for anyone."

"Jenny, please!"

"But it does. We've noticed it. I expect it's because you haven't got a vicar and the extra work is too much, especially as you have a full-time job. I've been thinking and I wonder whether you wouldn't be happier going to a different church and not doing so much. I'm not suggesting that you give up church altogether because I know that you take your religion seriously. But there are lots of other churches in London to choose from. I expect there are some near your office. You could be more content at one of them. And what about that nice church our kids go to..."

Crash! A plate had slipped from Christopher's hand and smashed to pieces on the stone floor. Christopher stood frozen for a second, tea towel in hand. Then he threw the tea towel on the draining board.

"Sorry, you'll have to clear that up yourself. I can't stand any more of your blasted preaching. What right do you have to lecture me like this about my private life? Where and how I go to church is my business." His mouth was going dry but he started to shout more loudly.

"I was enjoying this holiday until you started going on at me! I kept trying to tell you that I didn't want to discuss it but you would go on. Why couldn't you just talk about the weather or something? Why?"

Jenny had stared at him at first, completely taken aback, but now tears started trickling down her cheeks.

"Chris, don't! I meant well..."

"I'm fed up with people meaning well! Fed up to the back teeth. You can go on your own walk today. I'm going on my own!"

He turned, almost choked by his own outburst and collided with an astonished-looking Max, who was just entering the room, having heard the noise of the plate breaking and then the argument. Max, quickly glancing past him and seeing Jenny's face, turned back to him with a look of angry reproach. Christopher brushed past him and rushed upstairs to his bedroom. He banged the door shut behind him and sat on the bed. He could feel his heart thumping in his chest. What should he do? Where should he go? Could he get back to London from here without asking Max and Jenny for a lift? His brain refused to work. It felt as though the machinery had jammed. His walking boots were on the floor beside him. With shaking hands, he started to put them on, fumbling clumsily with the laces as he threaded them round the hooks and through the holes, and having to redo them twice. He would go on his walk up Aran Benllyn and try to clear his mind. He took his rucksack from the corner of the room and his waterproof jacket from the back of the door. The rucksack contained his empty water bottle and he took it out and held it for a moment. How could he get some water without going into the kitchen? The bathroom, of course. Trying to be as silent as he could, he opened his door and edged across the landing, regretting that he had put on his boots. There was a muffled sound of sobbing from downstairs and some soothing noises from Max. He did not want to hear. In the bathroom, he filled his bottle from the cold water tap. A few minutes later, he crept down the stairs and let himself out by the front door.

The cottage was a short distance from the village of Llanuwchllyn and Christopher set out along the narrow road that led to it, walking rapidly and with slightly irregular steps. As he stuffed his waterproof jacket into his rucksack, he realised that he had left the map behind. He could not face going back for it and making a sheepish entry into the cottage, so he decided to press on without it. The lack of the map was unlikely to prove a drawback because he had studied it thoroughly the day before and almost memorised the route from Llanuwchllyn. The weather was dry and sunny, with very few clouds in the sky, and, had Jenny and Max been walking with him, they would no doubt have looked forward to a happy and energetic day. Christopher was not happy. His chest was still pounding uncomfortably and his stomach felt upset. He tried to concentrate on the walk ahead, struggling to remember distances and gradients, the terrain and the likely lack of shelter. But mental pictures of Max, Jenny and the cottage kept intruding.

He saw Jenny starting to cry, and then blamed himself for being a beast. But, immediately after, he saw Jenny persistently bothering him when he did not want to be bothered. And then he felt resentful and angry about Jenny's attitude and thought that she had been hypocritical about him. Then he saw the happy breakfast scene, with himself eating toast and Max and Jenny smiling, and despaired of ever being able to recapture such happiness or such friendship. But he also remembered – or thought he remembered – conspiratorial glances being exchanged between Max and Jenny, and then he felt that he had been patronised and humiliated. Anger, regret, self-blame, self-pity – these circulated in his mind, but all were painful. Finally, he saw pictures of Max's angry face.

He soon reached the small village and, after a short search, found a likely-looking path heading in the direction of Aran Benllyn. Despite the tussocky grass underfoot at the beginning of the path, he hardly slowed down but walked with almost mechanical speed and determination. The ground rose in front of him almost immediately and the path followed it upwards, sometimes skirting the edge of stony humps and outcrops on his left. The sky was still blue above his head, the grassy hill was intensely green and Christopher could see the darker green of trees below him on his right. A few sheep wandered about, nibbling the grass here and there and following their own zig-zagging tracks. But Christopher was not in the mood for nature or for anything else. As he strode along, he tried to clear his mind of the unwelcome pictures that kept appearing, like miniature nightmares that were bent upon destroying his rest.

By lunch time, he had clambered up the rocky summit of Aran Benllyn and perfunctorily looked at the view. On any normal day, he would have perched there and gazed out over the surrounding fields and hills with deep appreciation, noting the underlying geology which gave the landscape its form. Today, he glanced around grimly and then slipped and slithered down the rock and scree to a grassy slope, where he found a level area on which to sit. The sun was almost unmerciful now and Christopher had not brought a sun hat or anything to shield his face from the glare. His shirt was soaked in sweat and sweat was rolling down the sides of his face and dripping off his chin. As he sat awkwardly on the grass, a bored-looking sheep drifted up to him, stared him in the face, and drifted away down the slope to join its companions. Christopher watched it go.

"Goodbye, sheep," he murmured. "A stranger will they not follow; but will flee from him; for they know not the voice of strangers. That's that, I suppose."

Shrugging off his rucksack and opening it, he took out his water bottle and gulped down about half of its contents. It was lunch time but he had no lunch. He was not hungry, in any case. But, as he sat there, it suddenly occurred to him that he was in a slightly difficult position. There was still most of the afternoon ahead of him but what should he do? If he carried on walking in the same direction, he would get further and further into the Arans, where the paths were notoriously tough and he had neither map nor food. A better idea would be to retrace his steps to Llanuwchllyn and then walk into Bala along the road. He could get some food there and even find a bed for the night. But the thought of doing that brought a lump to his throat. What would Max and Jenny think of him? And was it fair to them to reject their hospitality and stay in a hotel?

He looked down at Bala Lake spread out beneath him like an ornamental pond in an eighteenth century garden and saw tiny figures at the far end. He guessed they were families enjoying the fine weather, sunbathing and eating ice creams beside the blue, sparkling water. They looked like insects. Around him, the hills and mountains seemed completely empty, with him as the only living creature in a great expanse of green and grey. He knew that he was being indecisive but he still could not seem to cudgel his brain into any kind of rational thought. Wearily, he lay back in the grass and closed his eyes.

"Mind if I join you?"

Christopher woke out of a doze with a start and heaved himself into a sitting position. An athletic looking man of about his own age was standing over him, blocking out the sun. He was dressed for serious walking, with a check shirt, long khaki shorts, thick, hairy socks and boots. As he spoke, he shuffled a rucksack from his back and threw it down on to the grass.

"Of course," Christopher responded automatically. "Help yourself. I was just resting for a minute."

The stranger sat down beside him, exposing the sun once more. He had short fair hair and tanned skin and exuded good health and energy.

"Great view, this," he commented in friendly tones. "I never tire of it. Which way are you going? Have you come down from Aran Fawddwy?"

Christopher ran his tongue over his dry lips and glanced sideways at the man.

"No, just from Benllyn. I – I stupidly left the map behind so I didn't want to go too far. Have you come from over there?"

The man was rummaging in his rucksack and did not reply for a moment. Then, with a grin, he pulled out a plastic sandwich box.

"Yes, I have. It's a favourite route of mine but I don't often get such good weather. I got stuck in a tremendous storm up there once. Had to shelter under a rock for about two hours while the thunder and lightning raged around me. Totally atmospheric but I did wonder if I was going to have to spend the night up there. Sandwich?"

He offered his box and Christopher politely extracted a thick cheese and pickle sandwich. The man continued speaking.

"Anyhow, the weather cleared up eventually and I got home soaked through and in the dark. You on holiday?"

"Yes," replied Christopher, with his sandwich halfway to his mouth. "Just a week, unfortunately. Do you live here?"

His companion swallowed a large mouthful of sandwich and nodded.

"Not quite here. Llanfair Caereinion. A few miles off. I work from home."

Christopher looked at him curiously.

"You don't sound very Welsh," he said, almost accusingly. The man laughed.

"I'm about as Welsh as Big Ben. No, I moved here a few years ago because I wanted to get out of the rat race. I used to work in the City but I got sick of it. The pay was good but you had to sell your soul. I think I was drunk half the time. Wine bars and all that. Anyway, I found that I could make a good living as a self-employed consultant. And then it occurred to me that I could work from my computer and iPhone anywhere. Property was dirt cheap here and I picked up an eighteenth-century cottage in Llanfair for hardly anything. So, I spend a good deal of my time walking in these hills and still manage to make a living. I can recommend it. My partner's with me."

Christopher could not think of much to say but he wanted to seem pleasant.

"Oh, and does she like it here?"

The stranger smiled.

"It's a he," he replied, cheerfully. "Yes, Brian loves it. He's not so keen on the walking as I am, so he sort of keeps house while I'm out. He drives around quite a bit. He's a psychiatrist. What do you do?"

Christopher looked down at the lake and licked traces of pickle from his fingers.

"Oh, just a boring job in London. I work for an organisation which promotes good administration. There's not a lot I can say about it, really. It pays the bills."

The man looked sympathetic.

"Bad luck! But why don't you chuck it in and do what I've done? Or are you married or something?"

Christopher shook his head.

"No, I'm not married. I live on my own. But I'm not sure how I would earn a living here."

"It's easier than you think," the man responded. "Look, you could, say, set up your own business training other businesses to do their admin better. You could do most of that via the computer – with training packs and things – and travel around a bit, as well. You'd never regret it. My life has been transformed since I came here. I feel fitter than I've ever done. Why don't you?"

Christopher stared down at the lake through the hot brightness.

"I can't. I've got other responsibilities," he said. "I just can't."

The man inclined his head towards him and gave a knowing look.

"Ah, is it a kid or something?"

Christopher tried to smile but suspected that he looked more like some ghastly death's-head.

"Much worse than that. A church. I'm a churchwarden."

The stranger grinned.

"Churchwarden! I thought they'd been abolished in the Middle Ages. You surely don't believe in God? Sorry. That's hackneyed. I suppose you must."

"Yes – no! It's not like that. I have to look after the parish. We haven't got a rector. It's a sort of duty. There are the services to organise and the repairs. And, well, other things. Vestments and stuff."

He knew that his explanation was lame and that the man was unimpressed, but he was at a loss over what else to say. The man turned slightly to look at him with curiosity.

"It does sound a bit mad to me, although I have to admit I'm an agnostic. You seem to be saying that, although you don't believe in God, you have to spend most of your time looking after a mouldering old medieval building full of hymn books and things for people who do. Or do they? Does anyone really believe in God these days?"

There was a brief silence. Christopher took another gulp of water from his bottle before replying.

"It's not like that. The building is classical, anyhow. And I suppose I'm a Christian. I just don't think of it like that. I've always assumed that the people who go to church do believe in God. We're not fundamentalist at my church. Some places are. We don't really talk too much about faith, as such. At least, not amongst ourselves. Clergy preach about it. But it's assumed. It's sort of part of the liturgy. At my church, we believe in the beauty of worship."

The stranger stared blankly at him and then glanced away.

"Go on." he said. "Tell me more.'"

Christopher undid the laces on his boots and did them up again before continuing. Then, still looking at his boots, he spoke slowly and seriously.

"It's probably hard for you to understand, if you weren't brought up in the Church. There's probably not a lot more I can say. The liturgy is, like, well, the words of the service. We use the Book of Common Prayer, mostly - that's Cranmer, you know - and the language is the language of Shakespeare. It's glorious. And then there's the building: Georgian and one of the best of its kind in the country, especially the interior. At least, I think so. And we have some wonderful vestments - chasubles and altar frontals, embroidered in gold thread and a hundred years old. We don't use those ones very often. They're so fragile. But I suppose that it all somehow helps you to think and contemplate. Me, at any rate. Sorry."

The moment he stopped speaking, he felt that it had been a strange, or even a silly, speech. The man must be thinking that he was slightly crazy. It seemed weird to be sitting on this Welsh mountain talking about vestments, and yet the conversation had mysteriously led in that direction. Christopher adjusted his boot laces again and looked his companion covertly. The man was now looking down at the lake thoughtfully, with his chin on his knees, evidently wondering how to respond politely. After a few seconds, he lifted his head and smiled faintly.

"I do, sort of, understand what you are saying. I think that Brian would have a better idea and probably have a technical name for it. You'd like Brian. He's very perceptive. It's not my scene. The scientific view is compelling, and getting more so. But I can see that there is a painful sense of loss for a lot of people. For them, the old world is much more safe and appealing. But we face a brave new world that has no place for – what d'you call them? – vestments. We grow up but we want to cling to our favourite teddy bears for comfort. Next time I'm in London, I'll try to drop in to your church. It sounds magnificent. You must tell me where it is."

Looking at his watch, he started to repack his rucksack.

"Well, I suppose I'd better make tracks. Look here. Can I offer you dinner or something? Brian has promised to pick me up near Lake Vyrnwy. It's not that far. You'd enjoy meeting him and he'd know more about what you're saying than I do. You could even kip at our place afterwards. If you wanted to come back over this way tomorrow, he'd be happy to drive you across. How about it?"

Christopher scrambled to his feet politely but shook his head.

"That's very kind. But I should be OK for tonight. Thanks for the sandwich, by the way. I would have starved, otherwise."

The stranger stood up and shrugged on his rucksack.

"I really mean it," he said, pleasantly. "It'd be good to have some company, for a change. Brian's only fault is that he doesn't like hill-walking. But he's a great cook and we'll have a tremendous supper tonight, with wine. Why not come?"

Christopher straightened up. Why shouldn't he go? He could ring Max and Jenny and probably get home fairly easily from Llanfair Caereinion, especially if this Brian could give him a lift somewhere. Meeting the man's enquiring gaze, he nodded.

"Well, if you're really serious… Thank you. I'll come. It's jolly decent of you. I'm afraid I haven't got any kit with me."

"No problem," his companion replied. "We've loads of stuff at the cottage and you're about Brian's size. He won't mind at all. He loves having visitors and showing off his culinary skills. Ready?"

Christopher tightened the straps on his rucksack and prepared to follow the stranger down the track. The thought of having a convivial supper and spending the night with these two friendly men was attractive, but also unnerving. He felt that he was straying out of his depth, first by coming to Wales in the first place and then by going off with this person who had appeared out of nowhere, decent though he seemed.

As they walked down the slope, the man pointed out a red kite circling above them in the sky and then started talking about kites and how they had spread from Wales into the Home Counties. From kites, he went on to talk about ravens and then about the other birds that could be seen in the locality. Christopher half-listened, admiring his knowledge and the ease in which he fitted into this rugged landscape, but also wrestled mentally with his own predicament. Was he doing the right thing? Had he made a mistake in agreeing to the man's invitation? Hadn't he better back out? There was still time. After about a mile of walking, he stopped and took off his rucksack. He had decided not to go to Llanfair after all.

"I'm sorry," he declared, not hiding his profound embarrassment. "I'm afraid I can't come. This is terribly awkward for me. It's not fair to you and Brian. I'm not good company and it would ruin your evening. You go on."

He looked up to find the man gazing at him with a look of pity in his eyes. The sunshine poured over both of them.

"Are you sure?" replied the man, not coaxingly but with open friendliness. "It really is no trouble. I was looking forward to it. Don't worry about Brian, he's the nicest person in the world."

Christopher shook his head. The temptation to change his mind again was almost overwhelming but something deeply embedded in his head told him not to.

"No. I'm really sorry. I shouldn't have said I would. I'll stay here."

The man extended a hand and Christopher took it reluctantly.

"No problem. You do what suits you. Perhaps we'll bump into each other again. And think about what I said about the rat race. It's not worth it. Bye."

Christopher stood and watched the man walking briskly down the path with a confident, loping stride. He covered the bumpy ground with surprising speed and was soon a small figure against the green grass. At the bottom of an intermediate hillock, he turned and gave Christopher a cheerful wave before disappearing from view. As though on cue, the sun ducked behind a wispy cloud and the surrounding hillsides, with the almost-rectangular lake at the bottom, became unnaturally dull and colourless. The water looked like a sheet of lead. Feeling suddenly weary and heavy-hearted, Christopher sat down listlessly on a grassy rock and dragged his rucksack from his back. But the landscape was not, after all, in tune with him. After a few minutes, the sun reappeared, the water sparkled, the little creatures at the Bala end of the lake moved around excitedly and the hills regained their colours. Looking pensively at the sparkling water, he remembered something else that had sparkled: the gold embroidery on the altar frontal that he had found in the roof space. In his mind, he relived the finding of it and his intense excitement when he had exposed the angel under its golden canopy. Since then, he had twice gone to the church after work and taken the frontal out of its hiding place, carrying it down the tower steps as a mother would carry a child; gently guarding it from brushing against the walls. In the church, he had placed it over the altar and knelt down before it to study its workmanship. There were three golden canopies, separated by bands of blue silk, embroidered in gold. Under the central canopy was a swooping dove, surrounded by stylised roses and leaves on curling, thorny stems. On the right was an angel and, on the left, a figure of St Benedict which matched the one on the chasuble. Although the blue silk had faded and several threads had come adrift, the brown, gold, red and green embroidery was still vibrant and glorious and the craftsmanship was of awe-inspiring quality.

Christopher had worshipped at the altar for a long time on those two occasions, but it was the discovery on the roof that filled his memory now. His hands had shaken then and they shook now.

The afternoon slowly wore on. Christopher stayed in the same place, sometimes sitting and thinking, and sometimes getting up and walking around to stretch his legs. The sheep seemed to have moved away in search of sweeter grass. The sun eventually disappeared gracefully behind the high mountains on his right and a greyness spread across the countryside. The families enjoying themselves at the far end of the lake packed up their things and went home to tea. A cool breeze ruffled Christopher's sweaty hair. At about six o'clock, he drank the last dregs of his water and considered his situation with a mixture of anxiety and depression. Several times during his lonely vigil, he had regretted not accompanying the friendly walker to a supper with wine and a comfortable lodging for the night. But the regret had been tempered by a feeling that, not only would he not have enjoyed himself, he would have spoilt his new friends' evening, as well. Looking down at Bala in the distance, he tried to steel himself to seek a hotel room for the night, perhaps at that ugly, sprawling Victorian hotel in the main street. But a picture of Max and Jenny kept obscuring his thoughts: Max and Jenny sitting sadly in their cottage, looking at their watches, with the kitchen table set for three. Then he forced himself to be angry, blaming Jenny for treating him badly and ruining his much-needed holiday.

While he was abstractedly looking down the grassy hillside, a slight movement caught his eye. A small figure was picking his way over the tussocks, sometimes stopping and looking up towards the summit of Aran Benllyn. Christopher wondered idly whether the man was returning to urge him to come to Llanfair Caereinion for the night. He half-wished that he was. But it became apparent that this figure was not as athletic as him. As he came closer, Christopher could see that he was shorter than the man and much less used to hill-walking. He stumbled frequently. Could this be Brian? Again, the new stranger stopped and, with his arm held up to shield his eyes, stared upwards to where Christopher was sitting. The pose was familiar. It was Max. Christopher could feel his mouth going dry and his heart pounding. At the same moment that he recognised Max, Max recognised him. He waved, moving his right arm in a half-circular sweep. Christopher stood up and waved back.

Twenty minutes later, Max stood beside him, out of breath and perspiring.

"That's great!" he gasped. "I've found you. Dinner's cooking and we've got a bottle of wine."

When Max had recovered his breath, the two men plodded down the rough path together, not saying much, but both understanding that there was a truce. Only once did their eyes meet. In Max's eyes, Christopher saw bewilderment mixed with compassion. He had no idea what Max saw in his.

Chapter nine

Christopher carefully broke the foil bubble encasing a paracetamol tablet and slid the tablet into his mouth. He had woken up on this September morning with a throbbing headache and swallowed several tablets since breakfast time, apparently with little effect. Bob Bodkin was droning on in the pulpit about the Blessed Virgin Mary and her various feast days, struggling to give equal weight to both the Catholic and Protestant traditions, but sounding unconvincing about both.

"And then we come to the doctrine of the Immaculate Conception, which was a matter that was disputed in the Middle Ages – about whether it was immaculate, that is, because, of course, we naturally believe that Mary must have been conceived. Tradition has it that her parents were St Anne and St Joachim, who do not actually appear in the Bible. They are traditional, along with so much else, some of it important, some trivial. Anyway, in the Roman Catholic Church – which, of course, only really became the Roman Catholic Church after the Reformation – it was defined as a dogma by Pope Pius the Ninth in 1854. Anglicans hold differing views on the subject,"

"And about most things," muttered Christopher.

"although the Book of Common Prayer refers to it only as the Conception. And then we turn to the Nativity of St Mary, which we are celebrating round about this time. As you might expect, there is no dispute about whether Mary was born and it might be said that this is the most uncontroversial of her feast days. We know very little about her birth and early childhood other than what has been handed down to us by tradition. Nobody knows where she was born, although there are many traditions. There was even a medieval Gospel of the Birth of Mary, which I imagine is completely spurious."

Christopher shifted his gaze to the chancel and smiled slightly at the sight of Justin listening to the sermon with rapt attention, his mouth half open and his left hand resting on the brass thurible stand beside him. Only Justin could find Bob's sermons interesting. The smile weakened as Christopher thought of Justin's new 'vocation' and the deep interest in all Church matters that he was now exhibiting, as though to justify his wish to be a priest. Justin had not confided very much in him since the conversation in front of the brass tablets in the chancel, but Christopher knew that he had been busy in diocesan circles, making appointments to see people and attend meetings. He felt a private agony over the whole business and knew that he was not being rational in wanting both to know what Justin was thinking and doing. It was almost a physical pain. He remembered the silly little girls at his primary school, who were always falling in and out of obsessive friendships with each other. No, it was not like that.

Almost reluctantly, he continued to look at Justin. The young man had tidied up his appearance recently and had a haircut, presumably in readiness for the interviews he was hoping to attend. He looked neat in his black cassock and white cotta, despite their shabbiness, and Christopher thought that he detected a new button at the bottom of the cassock, where one had been missing for ages. Justin's shoes were black and clean. This was unusual. Although Christopher had always insisted that servers should wear black shoes, Justin had often turned up in brown ones or trainers and then been very apologetic. He was clearly making a big effort to turn over a new leaf. Well, it wouldn't last. Justin would find himself mixing with horribly enthusiastic ordination candidates who had 'got

God', all wanting Bible classes, house groups and mission services. He would then come to his senses again and consider careers that were appropriate to his talents.

While Bob continued to find things to say about the Blessed Virgin Mary and her birth, Christopher shifted his attention to the other occupant of the chancel, Simon, who was acting as the sole acolyte. Caroline, who usually sat in the congregation these days to boost the numbers in the pews, was sitting bolt upright in the third pew from the front. Simon, looking slightly impatient and restless, was leafing through his hymn book, looking up the hymns for the rest of the service. He was usually contemptuous of Bob's abilities as a preacher and was conspicuously not listening to him now. Although Christopher was not finding the sermon riveting himself, he nevertheless resented Simon's attitude and behaviour in the chancel. Servers should never draw attention to themselves. This was what all new servers were taught. They should be invisible, merely moving things around for the convenience of the priest and never becoming the centre of attention. This was why black shoes were important. Christopher shuddered slightly as he thought of churches where the servers wore dirty white trainers.

As he looked meditatively at Simon, a feeling of intense dislike came over him, causing him to narrow his eyes and press his lips together. Yes, he really, seriously, wholeheartedly hated Simon. He hated his threadbare, moany voice, his gloomy face, his pedantic attitude towards everything and his boring, useless profession. There was no point in trying to concoct a spirit of Christian love towards Simon; it was impossible to love him in any sense of the word. He knew, of course, that Simon hated him back. Caroline probably reasoned with him and begged him to understand Christopher's good points, but he transparently detested him. This seemed to Christopher to be slightly unreasonable, because he regarded himself as a nicer person than Simon, but it did not really matter. There was jagged enmity between them.

But should he try to love Simon, despite everything? Christian teaching was clear on the subject. You should love your enemies. He remembered hearing a sermon about Christ's teaching on the Mount, in particular the verse, 'For if ye love them which love you, what reward have ye?' So there was little merit in loving someone who loved you, because that didn't require any effort. The important thing was to love people who didn't love you, because that was difficult. Christopher wrinkled his brow. He couldn't remember anybody loving him, least of all his parents. They might have persuaded themselves that they loved him, but he had always felt that they hadn't. At any rate, they had never shown it. As a little boy, he had often lain awake at night wondering what he could do to please his mother and father, to put them in a good mood and stop them nagging him. He had decided very early on that he was not an appealing child, not lovable and not deserving of any spontaneous affection. When little, he had, almost daily, stared at his reflection in the mirror in his bedroom, not liking what he saw and wishing that he could be a different person. Eventually, when in his teens, he had found his way into churches and discovered some solace in the liturgy, the architecture, the vestments, the silence.

Simon was continuing to irritate him. He seemed to have discovered that they were going to sing the hymn, 'Her Virgin eyes saw God Incarnate born,' and looked decidedly peeved. Simon disapproved of the Virgin Mary because she had become identified with 'Romish' practices and was not, therefore, properly Anglican. Christopher remembered a conversation that he had had with Max some months previously about the ethics of making people redundant for the wrong reasons. Well, he would have made Simon redundant without a qualm.

But what was love, anyway? Parents were supposed to love their children and children their parents. But did they? Christians were supposed to love their enemies, but would the enemies still be enemies if you loved them? And, if all enemies became loved ones, there wouldn't be any enemies left to love. And what was hatred? Was it only the absence of love or a fighting force in its own right? Christopher frowned. His head ached still and he was not having a good day. He looked away from Simon to the east window of the church, a beautiful, plain eighteenth century window with a neat pediment over it. Its serenity and elegant proportions soothed him, as they had done so many times before, and he felt his face muscles relax. Here, at least, there was no threat, no animosity. And, in his mind, he saw the wonderful colours and workmanship of his secret altar frontal and chasuble, displayed against the east window, the simplicity of the latter acting as a foil for the rich needlework.

The sermon ended and everybody stood up with a creaking and clatter to sing the Nicene Creed. Christopher stood up wearily and joined in.

'I believe in one God the Father Almighty,
Maker of heaven and earth,
And of all things visible and invisible.'

He looked across to the choir, which seemed to be singing very badly, and realised that there were only three members present. Mark was playing the organ in what Christopher suspected was a deliberately glum and gloomy way, as a protest against Christopher's threatened budget cuts. The choir members, two women and a man, who were dressed in jeans and sweatshirts, with blue choir gowns dragged over them, were singing the Creed in a completely nerveless and mechanical way, not even quite hitting the right notes. Christopher felt loathing towards them and made up his mind to axe the choir, despite Mark's bitter opposition. If Mark were to leave as a result of that, so be it. He was not a brilliant organist anyway and there were always hard-up musicians out there looking for positions. In fact, when St Benet's got its new rector, it would be a good idea to make a fresh start, in any case. Get rid of some of this dead wood and start again. Hilda and Betty and all the rest of them. Even Caroline, perhaps. For a few moments, Christopher cheered up at these heartening thoughts. Then his brow darkened again. What new rector? Nothing had been heard from the Archdeacon for quite a while now. Nothing about curates from Christ Church. In fact, he had heard vague rumours, via Justin mostly, of a possible amalgamation with St Andrew's, where the Reverend Jill Johnson muddled her way through the liturgy. Perhaps that could be borne. Jill would need another priest to take care of St Benet's and the other priest could be an Anglo-Catholic who liked the Book of Common Prayer. It was not a stupid idea. But was there any foundation in the rumours?

Christopher hardly noticed the rest of the service. At the end, he supposed that he had gone up to receive communion but he could not remember doing so. His head continued to throb and, when Caroline served the coffee, he took his cup to a pew near the pulpit, as far away from the milling group at the west end as possible, and sat down heavily. At the moment, he could not face making conversation with anybody. But he was not left in peace for long. Bob Bodkin, also holding a cup of coffee, sat down next to him.

"You all right, Chris?" he enquired sympathetically. "You look a bit pale."

Christopher mustered a weak smile.

"Hello, Bob. Yes, I suppose so. I've just got a bit of a headache. The choir didn't help."

Bob looked puzzled.

"Choir? What have they been up to?"

Christopher stirred his coffee, looking dubiously at the globules of milk which floated on the surface.

"Well, nothing. That's the problem. There were only three of them today and they sang as though the service were a criminal's funeral. Mark's playing was awful, too."

Bob shrugged his shoulders slightly.

"Oh! I'm afraid I didn't really notice. Sorry about that."

"Don't apologise. You're not a churchwarden."

"I really wanted to suggest that we went and had a bit of lunch together. You can tell me what you did on your hols, Chris, and we can have a chat. Isn't there a good little pizza place near here?"

Christopher tentatively sipped his coffee and then grimaced.

"This milk's going off. I suspected as much. I hate off milk. I wouldn't drink it if I were you, Bob. And, yes, I suppose that lunch might be a good idea. I didn't really have any breakfast."

Bob looked across at him kindly.

"I can drink coffee whatever it's like. I expect that's one of the qualities of a priest. It's funny, but I can never taste whether the milk is off or not. But, look here, I'll just circulate a bit and do my clergyman thing and then we'll go and have a pizza together. My wife's gone out with a friend today. They're going to talk about cats."

Christopher watched him amble away, cup in hand, and attach himself to a group of elderly women at the back. It was obvious why he had suggested lunch: his wife was out and therefore not going to cook for him. He would expect Christopher to foot the bill for the meal, as well. Clergy always expected the laity to pay for them. But perhaps his company would be a pleasant change. Christopher had spent the last couple of Sunday afternoons mooching around the church, tidying up books, polishing the pews with best quality furniture polish and having brief glances at the chasuble and altar frontal. He had invented rules for himself – one glimpse of the chasuble for six polished pews, a look at the altar frontal (brought down carefully from the roof) for three tidied cupboards. His rules were probably completely weird, but there was nobody to know or care. The previous Sunday night he had lain awake, wondering what jobs he could give himself to do in order to earn more time with the embroidery. Only Caroline had noticed that the church was looking tidier, but she had assumed that Justin had been doing the extra work.

"I do think Justin has improved," she had said to Christopher before this morning's service. "He's really starting to grow up. He looks much smarter in the sanctuary and have you noticed how tidy the church is looking? You can smell the polish."

Christopher had changed the subject straight away and talked about the parish finances. These were so precarious at the moment that Caroline had felt constrained to pursue the topic with him and discuss electricity bills, diocesan payments and choir costs for about ten minutes. She had worn her 'concerned look' and he had taken malicious pleasure in piling on the agony, even going so far as to exaggerate the likely size of the winter fuel bills.

Christopher remained in his place until Bob came to collect him. He did not have the energy today to help tidy the church or watch over Betty while she counted the collection. No doubt his absence would make everyone feel happier. Waving casually to the small knot of people at the back of the church, he and Bob wandered out into the street and then paused.

"Which way?" enquired Bob, looking around him. "I'm sure I know the place. I mean, it's Italian and does pizza and pasta and things."

Christopher smiled slightly.

"That doesn't exactly narrow our search. But I think I know the one. If we cross the road and take that turning over there, there's a little restaurant called *Bella Roma*. Does that sound familiar?"

Bob wrinkled his brow thoughtfully.

"Hm, yes. I think so. I got taken there once by Fr Smith in one of his rare generous moods. I think it was when he wanted me to cover for him for the whole of August. I do remember that the food was good."

Christopher led him across the road and into the restaurant, which had pictures of Italy on the walls and plastic-coated tablecloths. A slim waitress approached them and asked, "How many?" in a Polish accent. On Christopher convincing her that there were two of them, she led them to a table on the left-hand side, against the wall, and handed them copies of the menu. About half the tables in the restaurant were occupied, mainly by youngish couples who seemed, reassuringly, to be tucking into large amounts of food. The waitress disappeared and Christopher, after a brief glance around the room, turned his attention to the menu. It consisted of fairly typical lists of types of pizza and pasta and a much shorter list of puddings. On the back was a list of wines and other drinks.

Curiously, he did not feel particularly hungry, even though he had eaten only a stale currant bun for breakfast, and it took him only a moment to decide on a cheese and tomato pizza. He looked across at Bob to see how he was getting on and found him earnestly studying the menu, like a little boy who had been taken out for a treat by a doting uncle or aunt.

"Well, Bob," he said. "Have you made your mind up?"

Bob looked slightly flustered.

"There's so much choice," he replied anxiously. "I don't know what to have. Are you having pizza or pasta, Chris?"

"I'm having pizza."

"Right. Ought I to have pizza, as well? On the other hand, the pasta looks good. There's a girl over there – please don't look – who has a huge plate of pasta in front of her. I can even smell it. No, I think I'll have pizza. What are you having?"

"Cheese and tomato."

"Hm. There's one here that has chicken, mushrooms, peppers and sun-dried tomatoes on it."

"Well, have that, then."

"Yes, OK. But I quite fancy the garlic and seafood one. Oh dear. And what about drink? Are we having wine?"

"Yes, if you like. White or red?"

At this point, the waitress glided up to them, with her order pad and pen poised. She glanced at Bob first and then shifted her gaze to Christopher.

"You are ready to order?"

Christopher spread the menu out in front of him in a business-like way.

"Yes. I'll have a cheese and tomato pizza, please."

Murmuring 'Margarita', the waitress wrote something on her pad. Christopher continued.

"And my friend will have… Bob, what are you having?"

Bob looked down at his menu.

"Oh, I'll have a ham, cheese and forest mushroom one, please."

The waitress wrote again on her pad. She then looked back at Christopher.

"And what would you like to drink?"

Christopher turned his menu over and looked at the list of wines. They all looked rather expensive. Bob spoke up.

"Could we have the Tuscan Vermentino, please?"

The waitress wrote the name down and slid away before Christopher could countermand the order. The wine was one of the most pricey ones. Bob looked apologetic.

"Sorry, I just fancied it. I hope that's all right?"

Christopher nodded, trying not to let Bob see his slight feeling of irritation.

"No problem," he managed to say. "It's good to have lunch out for a change. It'll save me cooking much this evening. Thank you for your sermon, by the way. Most interesting. The BVM does excite the most polarised opinions. I liked the way you went through all the Mary days."

He glanced at Bob to see if he suspected any mendacity but the latter looked pleased and flattered.

"Thank you," he replied warmly. "I'm so glad you enjoyed it. I did try to deal fairly with the dormition-assumption issue. Of course, St Benet's with its Prayer Book tradition must come down on the side of the dormition, but one still ought to mention the Roman position. Similarly, the Immaculate Conception can't be ignored, even though you and I hold an Anglican view on the matter. However, we are on much safer ground with the nativity…"

Christopher noticed with relief that the waitress was approaching them with a bottle of wine in her hand.

"I'm sorry, Bob, I'll have to stop you there for a sec. Our wine's arriving. This should be good."

The waitress poured a small quantity of wine in Christopher's glass and stood back politely while he sipped it. Bob looked at him expectantly.

"Yes, that's fine. Thank you."

Christopher nodded to the waitress and she filled up both their glasses. As soon as she had gone, Bob seized his glass and drank about half the contents. After he had done so, he caught Christopher's eye.

"I was just ready for that," he declared. "Preaching does take it out of you. The wine's very good, by the way. Perhaps just a little too cold. I wonder when our pizzas will arrive. Nice little place, this, isn't it? Now, where was I over the sermon?"

"I think we covered it pretty well," replied Christopher, hastily. "Tell me about your holiday."

Bob pulled a face and spread his table napkin on his knees before replying.

"Oh, well. It wasn't quite what we'd hoped for. We had to leave the cats, you see, and Susan asked her sister Sharon to come and stay so that we could get away. It was very decent of Sharon, actually, because she's not particularly a cat-lover. Anyhow, we went to a very nice guest house in Norfolk, near Walsingham, and had a pleasant week, even though it rained quite a lot. There are some wonderful churches round there, Chris. You ought to go."

Christopher nodded.

"Yes, I should. I've been to Norwich itself, but not Walsingham. I don't think I'd fancy the National Pilgrimage much. But what was the problem? You said it wasn't what you'd wanted."

Bob nervously drank some more wine.

"Oh, the holiday itself was fine. It wasn't that. It was when we got home. Cranmer was missing."

"Cranmer?" replied Christopher in a puzzled tone. "His biography?"

"No, no, I shouldn't mind losing that. It was our black and white cat. Apparently, he'd gone off the day after we left but my silly sister in law decided not to tell us in case it ruined our holiday. It was such a shock for Susan. Cranmer was her favourite."

Christopher did a passable imitation of Caroline's concerned look.

"That's bad. And did Cranmer turn up again?"

Bob shook his head.

"No, worst luck. No sign of him. We're going to get a new kitten. Susan's gone off to talk about it today. But it won't be the same as Cranmer. He was so affectionate. Parker has had to take his place."

"Parker?" queried Christopher.

"Parker's the fluffy one. Half Persian, I'm told."

Christopher noticed the waitress approaching them with their pizzas and shook out his own napkin with a slight sense of relief.

"Well, here's our lunch," he said brightly.

Bob's expression changed from one of mournful resignation to one of eager expectation.

"My word, they smell good. If the food's as good as the last time I was here, we'll be all right. Thank you, my dear. That looks very good."

The last two sentences were addressed to the waitress and she smiled perfunctorily as she placed their pizzas in front of them. Christopher did not feel very hungry but he tried to survey his pizza appreciatively while Bob almost drooled over his. The waitress went away but returned almost immediately with a large pepper mill in one hand

and a dish of grated cheese in the other. She placed the dish on the table and held the pepper mill poised over Christopher's pizza.

"Black pepper?"

Christopher nodded and she scattered pepper liberally over his lunch.

"Parmesan cheese?"

Again, he nodded and she spooned the cheese over it.

The same procedure was followed with Bob's pizza and then she left them, saying finally,

"Enjoy your meal."

With a beaming face, Bob picked up his knife and fork and started to attack the pizza, tearing about a quarter of it into bite-sized pieces and then eating them one by one before moving on to the next quarter. Conversation lapsed. Christopher drank a mouthful of wine and then cut a small portion of pizza. As he raised it to his lips, the pepper irritated his nose and caused him to sneeze violently.

"Too much pepper," observed Bob, with his mouth full. "I thought that she had overdone it. Nice girl, though. And very polite."

Christopher wiped his nose with his handkerchief before finally eating the piece of pizza. He hardly noticed the taste and mechanically cut and ate the next piece while Bob launched himself voraciously at the second half of his own pizza. Christopher wondered vaguely whether he ought to talk about something, but Bob seemed happily occupied with his meal for the time being. The scrape of metal on china and the chatter and laughter from the other customers made the restaurant seem noisy. Christopher's head ached still.

Bob made short work of his pizza and looked across in an apparently predatory way at Christopher's plate, which still held about half a pizza.

Christopher raised his head and looked at him in surprise.

"Can you manage some?" he replied. "I seem to have got quite a lot left. The pizzas are very large here."

Bob held out his plate and Christopher shifted about half the remaining portion on to it. He was not sorry to get rid of it and succeeded in eating the last bit without too much trouble. He washed it down with a gulp of wine and thought about reviving the conversation. Suddenly, Bob put his knife and fork down on his empty plate with a clatter and looked across at Christopher with a serious expression.

"I hear your holiday was a bit of a disaster, Chris."

Christopher, thrown completely off his guard, went on the defensive.

"Where did you hear that, Bob?" he replied in a stilted voice. "I don't remember mentioning anything to you."

Bob straightened his knife and fork clumsily and seemed flustered by Christopher's tone.

"Oh, sorry, Chris. I expect I've got it all wrong. But Justin said that you were down in the mouth when you got back, so I assumed you hadn't enjoyed yourself. Wales, wasn't it?"

Christopher found that his mouth had gone dry and that a lump had mysteriously arrived in the back of his throat. He knew that Bob meant no harm and yet he resented being asked about his holiday. When he spoke, his voice did not seem to be part of him. It sounded harsh and strained.

"Justin should mind his own business. The holiday was fine. I just came back with a virus or something. I don't think I've shaken it off yet. Yes, I went to Wales."

There was silence for a few seconds. Then Bob tried again, this time very gently and solicitously, as though Christopher were a sick child.

"I'm sorry about the virus, Chris. You should take care of yourself more. I hope you don't skip meals or anything. But didn't you go with that nice friend of yours and his wife? I'm sure they would have looked after you. Did you stay in a cottage?"

Christopher clenched his fists under the table and looked past Bob at the side wall of the restaurant. When he replied, his voice still sounded detached.

"Yes, that's right. They rented a cottage near Bala. It was very decent of them to invite me. I went walking and things. Good scenery."

There was another brief silence, this time mercifully broken by the reappearance of the waitress, who skilfully removed their used plates.

"Would you like to see the dessert menu?" she enquired briskly.

"Yes, please," replied Bob before Christopher could say the opposite.

A moment or two later, they each held a menu card. Christopher looked at his with complete indifference while Bob announced the various dishes with relish. The waitress stood beside them, patiently waiting to take their orders.

"What d'you fancy, Chris? We can have peach ice cream with chocolate sauce and chopped hazelnuts. Or Italian trifle. Or chocolate sponge with whipped vanilla cream. Or..."

"I'm sorry, Bob," Christopher broke in. "I've really had enough. I'll just have a coffee. Black, please."

Bob looked disappointed but continued to study his menu with attention. After a few more moments, he smiled up at the waitress.

"The trifle, please. And I'll have coffee, too. Cappuccino for me, please."

After the waitress had left them, Bob looked across at Chris with a kind expression.

"You've done a good job with young Justin, you know. He's probably going to be recommended for theological college after all the usual processes. A thoroughly nice, sincere young man. He speaks highly of you.'

Christopher shook his head slightly.

"Nothing to do with me. I imagine he got the idea from Julian. Isn't he a bit immature to be going down that road? He might change his mind."

Bob took a sip of wine.

"He's young, it's true. But he knows his own mind and I think he'll impress the selectors. At least St Benet's will have produced a potential ordinand before the changes."

Christopher felt a shudder run through him, but he instantly tried to recover himself.

"What changes? I suppose you mean a link with St Andrew's. Justin has been talking about that. It might not be too bad."

There was profound silence for five seconds. Even the other customers seemed to have stopped talking. Bob glanced awkwardly towards the kitchen area and spotted their waitress collecting his trifle from the hatch.

"I can see my pudding coming," he commented with affected cheerfulness. "They're very efficient here. I'm glad it hasn't gone downhill since the last time I came. We must do this again. It makes a very nice change and gives us both a bit of a break."

He seized his glass to drink more wine, but there was hardly any left. Christopher, mechanically pouring some into it from the bottle, noticed his own hand trembling.

The waitress arrived and placed a dish of trifle in front of Bob.

"Would you like your coffee now or later?" she enquired.

Bob, with a covert glance at Christopher, smiled at her fussily.

"Oh, straight away, please, if you would be so kind."

She detached herself from them and returned to the service area of the restaurant. Christopher watched her go before repeating his question.

"What changes? What are you talking about?"

Bob put a large spoonful of trifle in his mouth and ate it slowly with a slightly guilty expression, much to Christopher's irritation. When he had swallowed enough of it to be able to speak, he inclined his head towards the back of the restaurant.

"I really shouldn't be eating so much cream but this is delicious. That sweet girl will be bringing our coffees in a minute. I suppose you don't fancy trifle, yourself? Ah, I remember you said you weren't hungry. She's just coming."

They both watched silently as the waitress approached their table with two cups of coffee on a tray. She carefully placed a cup of black coffee in front of Christopher, put the other coffee next to Bob's dish of trifle and walked away. Christopher waited until she had reached the other side of the restaurant and then resumed.

"What changes?"

Bob squared his slumped shoulders and looked directly at him.

"Look, Chris, you mayn't like this but it's probably for the best. I gather that the Bishop and Archdeacon have decided that a curate from Christ Church should come to St Benet's as priest in charge, with a view to a formal link. A church plant, I think they call it. The chap they have in mind is a smart young man, with lots of energy and, er, vision. Apparently, he's already called into the church on a couple of occasions and loves it. He thinks he can bring the place alive. It's what it needs."

Christopher felt as though someone had hit him hard on the back of the head.

"Christ Church? But Justin said St Andrew's. Has he been telling me lies?"

The words sounded limp and inadequate. Bob shook his head firmly.

"No, no. Justin really thinks that it is St Andrew's. He told me so himself. Don't blame the lad. He thought it would please you, even though I gather that you don't think much of Jill. According to Justin, you think she's a bit mumsy."

He smiled but there was no returning gleam from Christopher. He was trying to clear the fog in his brain.

"I don't understand, Bob. Where did Justin get it from? He's been going to all these diocesan meetings and things. I thought that he would have got it right."

Bob coughed slightly and then drank some wine so clumsily that a splash landed on the tablecloth.

"I suppose I shouldn't really say this, but I have a hunch the Archdeacon deliberately misled him. Oh, for good pastoral reasons, I'm sure. He probably didn't want unhelpful rumours to spread and he would have known that Justin would report things back to you and Caroline. You can sort of see what he meant. Making you think St Andrew's would be the link parish was breaking the news gently. And, Chris, you must look at this positively. It's not your tradition, I know, but Christ Church know how to get bums on seats and a take-over by them could save St Benet's from redundancy. This curate might not be quite so fundamentalist as the others. We all know how hard you've worked to keep things going, but..."

"Bloody bastard!"

Christopher shook with pent up anger and his voice seemed to fill the restaurant. Bob looked surreptitiously at the other customers, who were merely exchanging amused looks with each other before going on with their eating and drinking.

"Chris, please. I can understand your feelings, but perhaps this isn't the place."

"Damn the place. The Archdeacon is a bastard of the first water. It's despicable to tell a load of lies and guff to a lad like – like Justin..."

His voice cracked on a sob but he stifled it and went on.

"He's got it in for us because we're traditionalist. And parishes like us don't bring in money. And he hates me personally. This is just vindictive. He knows quite well that Christ Church is anathema to me. I'd like to wrap his guts round his stupid fat neck."

Bob was suffering agonies of embarrassment. He tried eating another spoonful of trifle while he thought about what to say next. Before he could speak again, Christopher rose to his feet.

"I'm going to the bog," he said quietly. "Help yourself to the rest of the wine. I won't want any more."

In the cubicle, Christopher put down the lid of the lavatory pan and sat on it, trying to collect his thoughts. His head, which had ached all morning, now felt numb and he could not think with any clarity. Was it true about Christ Church? Had Bob got it right? Bob was vague at times and it would not be surprising if he had got this all wrong. Had Caroline been right, then? Was Justin mixed up in it? And, if so, how? And what about the Archdeacon? Christopher could well believe that he was going around telling everyone a string of malicious lies, but had anyone really approached Christ Church? And where was the Bishop in all this? Could he be appealed to over the head of the Archdeacon? Would he be a sympathiser? And what about the church fittings and vestments? What would happen to them? This last thought made him feel bloated and sick and he tried to blot the question out of his mind.

For several moments he sat there, asking silent, unanswered questions and wondering if he could find the strength to return to the table, where Bob would, no doubt, be anxiously awaiting him. A few beads of sweat trickled down his forehead. He pulled his handkerchief out of his pocket and wiped his face and neck with it, feeling as though he had just run five miles or scaled a cliff face. He studied the cubicle door and carefully read some graffiti which had been scrawled in thick pencil and black marker pen, almost by way of a dialogue:

'Nicola is a tart.
Ha ha. Jam tarts.
I luv Nicola.
Who luvs u?
Ha ha.'

He tried to focus on the words, almost as though they offered the means of escape, but they spoke of another world where he would be an alien.

After five long minutes, he pulled himself to his feet and walked unsteadily back into the restaurant. Bob was sitting meekly at their table with a little saucer in front of him, containing the bill. As Christopher approached, he half rose and then sank down again, eyeing his friend questioningly.

"All right now, Chris?" he mumbled.

Christopher resumed his own seat and leaned across to take the bill.

"I see the waitress has been," he responded briefly. Bob gave a gentle cough.

"Yes, she brought the bill a moment ago. You just missed her. She said she'd be back in a minute. Thank you for an excellent lunch, Chris. I'm sorry that I mentioned the Christ Church thing. It might come to nothing."

Christopher bent his head and stared at the bill, but the print was blurred.

"Not your fault, Bob. Don't feel that you must apologise and all that. I've been struggling with a headache today."

He drew out his credit card wallet just as the waitress silently materialised beside him. A machine was placed on the table and he dutifully inserted his card into it while she stood over him. As he tried to take in the words and figures that appeared on the little screen, the waitress said in an encouraging tone,

"There is a space for you to add a tip – if you wish."

He continued to stare helplessly at the screen until a slender and well-manicured hand descended on to it, the forefinger pointing at a space between the cost of the meal and a box labelled 'total'. He looked at the hand with a flicker of interest. The pointing finger stirred a memory of a poem he had once learnt at school.

"The moving finger writes," he muttered under his breath and then, with a deep sigh, he added a ten pound tip and completed the transaction.

Chapter ten

Christopher looked gloomily out of the coach window. It was a cloudy October day with the first chill of winter in the air. The autumn countryside, with its copper trees and damp green grass would have glowed and sparkled had the sun been shining. But it was not. A ceiling of mottled cloud in various shades of grey extended over everything.

The coach was on its way to Wendover in Buckinghamshire but had stopped in Great Missenden because somebody had wanted a lavatory. It was the autumn office awayday and the staff were going on a country walk in the Chilterns, beginning in Wendover and ending in Chesham. To encourage teambuilding, lunch was going to be prepared by staff working in groups. And, after lunch, team games were to be the order of the day. Christopher had opposed the whole business from the start, on the grounds that the staff would miss a day's work, that the event was unlikely to improve staff relations, that it would encourage a lot of unnecessary clothes-buying and that the weather would almost certainly be wet. But his boss had overruled him. The only good thing about the day so far was that he had managed to get a double coach seat all to himself. As he huddled into it, he reflected sourly that none of the staff had actually wanted to sit next to him. Glancing down at his corduroy trousers and then at the tweed jacket reposing on the seat beside him, he supposed that he must seem like a boring old fogey to some of them. Everybody except him was kitted out in special hiking clothing and gear – walking trousers, base layers, microfleece mid-layers, windproof anoraks, anti-blister socks, waterproof boots and even walking poles. All these just for a stroll in the Home Counties. His face hardened in contempt.

But his fellow workers and their vanities did not occupy much space in his mind today. In the first place, he had an uncomfortable feeling that he was not behaving at all properly towards Max. Max had left messages recently on both his home and office telephones, as well as his mobile, suggesting meeting for a drink or a meal, but Christopher had ignored them. Max's voice had sounded warm and kindly, as usual, but with a deeper note of persuasion in it. There had been a conference the week before, the sort of conference which both Max and Christopher usually attended, but Christopher had opted not to go, claiming to himself that he could not spare the time. It was after the conference that Max's messages had started to arrive. Almost mechanically, he now took his mobile phone out of the jacket pocket beside him and switched it on. A buzz proclaimed that a new message had arrived. Guiltily, he looked at the message. It was from Max. 'Let's meet for a drink. Long time no see.' He quickly switched the phone off and replaced it in his pocket. He could hardly bear to think of poor old Max.

But there was a bigger issue troubling him. Two weeks ago, not long after his lunch with Bob Bodkin, he and Caroline had received emails from the Bishop's secretary, inviting them both to visit the Bishop and have a glass of wine with him. The emails had been courteous and had gone on to say that the Bishop wished to thank the churchwardens for all the sterling work that they were doing during the current vacancy. Caroline had immediately sent an artless reply, saying that she would accept with pleasure and hoped that the date would also suit Christopher. He had taken longer to respond, wishing to review in his mind the situation at St Benet's and the possible reasons for the Bishop's invitation. The real ones.

The piece of information – or was it a rumour? – which Bob had let drop was a likely candidate, but he struggled even to think about it. It was the dark shadow that fell across his bed in the hours before dawn, that lurked in every doorway in the dusk and that seemed to smother part of his brain. He had tried to avoid it by considering other possibilities, such as a link with St Andrew's, which he had decided to accept with a semblance of equanimity, or even some new, previously unmentioned solution. Eventually, he had sent back an email, merely saying that he would attend on the evening specified. That evening had been the previous one.

He peered through the coach window at the inoffensive little car park. There was no sign of the staff member, who had probably had to search the small town for a public lavatory. Without meaning to or wanting to, he relived the meeting at the Bishop's house.

He and Caroline met at a café before they went to the appointment. This had been her idea and he had not been able to find a good reason for refusing. He bought the coffees and they found a corner table and two armchairs, Caroline remarking awkwardly that they could have a cosy chat together before facing the Bishop. In practice, it felt like a blind date, with neither of them knowing what to say. Christopher was determined not to mention Simon in any context whatever and she seemed determined not to say anything which could annoy Christopher.

"You look smart, Christopher," she said, stirring her coffee far more than was necessary. "That's a nice tie you're wearing. I suppose you've come straight from work."

He stirred his own coffee.

"Yes. I always wear a suit and tie for work, but you'd think it was a gorilla suit the way everyone else looks at it. They all wear unsmart casual."

She smiled weakly.

"Yes, I can imagine. Our boys always tease Simon over the way he dresses."

There was silence for a few moments and the stirring continued. Caroline then made another effort.

"I suppose we ought to agree on our response to the Bishop. Do you think that he really just wants to thank us? It seems a very nice gesture. I wonder if other churchwardens get invited for a drink like this. I – I'm not very good with wine. If I drink too much my cheeks go all red."

"Why don't you ask for water, then?"

She wrinkled her brow.

"Yes, I expect I could. But it might be a bit rude, considering that he has mentioned a glass of wine. I'll be all right if I just stick to one glass. Simon sometimes calls me the one glass wonder."

Christopher privately marvelled that Simon had even that much of a sense of humour. But he merely nodded and then nearly burnt his mouth with a gulp of the coffee.

"I wish they wouldn't serve the coffee so bloody hot that it skins your mouth," he grumbled, placing his cup back in the saucer. Caroline looked concerned.

"I hope it really hasn't done," she replied.

He took out his handkerchief and wiped the froth from his lips.

"I expect I'll survive. But, Caroline, don't you think this is more than just a social call with the Bishop? I mean, isn't he going to talk about our future – the parish's future, that is? I can't believe he's going to give up half an evening to drink third rate wine with a couple of obscure churchwardens just for the fun of it. Surely not."

Caroline tentatively licked up some of her own coffee froth, looking thoughtful.

"Well, who's to say it'll be third rate wine? It might be second rate. But I see what you're getting at. The idea about Christ Church seems to have gone away. The only plan I've heard about recently is some sort of link with St Andrew's. Perhaps a plurality or something like that. I know that you wouldn't like it, Chris, but I really don't think it's too bad an idea. Their tradition isn't terribly different from ours and they're very nice at St Andrew's. I'm not quite sure how it'd work because I suppose they'd need a curate or assistant priest, but it could all be worked out. We can't go on like we are. The congregation seems to be melting away like dew in summer. Wouldn't you consider it?"

Christopher turned his face away and looked across the coffee shop, where a dozen or so smartly-dressed young executives and lawyers, spread out in ones and twos, were enjoying a few moments of peace at the end of the working day.

"I might. But I doubt whether that's going to be on the cards. Where did you hear it?"

"Well, from Justin, I think. But he seemed pretty sure about it. Is there some problem?"

He turned slowly back and looked her in the face.

"Justin's been a victim of the diocesan mafia. He's been duped."

She started to laugh and then stopped abruptly.

"Diocesan mafia? That's a bit melodramatic, Chris. It's what Simon would call a pathological over-reaction. I'm not sure what you're getting at. Are you saying that someone has told Justin fibs? Why should they?"

He drank some coffee, which had now cooled slightly, and paused before replying, wishing that he did not have to explain himself to Caroline. And why did she keep having to mention bloody Simon?

"At any rate, he's been led astray. Bob Bodkin said as much. Caroline, what would you say about a church plant from Christ Church?"

Well, he had said it. Caroline looked startled.

"Christ Church? I thought it had come to nothing. Are you sure? Christ Church?"

He looked at her attentively.

"Christ Church. The evangelical one. What do you think?"

Her face cleared and she almost smiled.

"Of course! The Christ Church Mission! Win a million souls for Christ! That must include us, but they'll have to work hard for a million at St Benet's. Gosh, that would be interesting. We'd have a packed church. Justin never mentioned that, which is odd, but... Actually, he did mention it. I seem to remember him saying that one of their curates had called in. A terribly nice young man. And beautifully dressed. Wouldn't that really be better than St Andrew's? You've got a thing about Christ Church, Chris."

Christopher wondered whether he was having another nightmare. He almost wanted to hit Caroline. At this moment, she looked like an imbecile. But before he could form even the ghost of a reply, she repeated her question.

"Chris, listen to me. Wouldn't that be better than St Andrew's? The Christ Church people are hugely successful. They would lavish care and attention on dear old St Benet's and really wake the place up. They've got pots of money and volunteers galore. Not to mention paid staff. I know it's not your sort of churchmanship but it may be the future of the Church of England. The Archdeacon loves them and besides..."

"The Archdeacon can go to hell and stay there. He only loves them because they pay a fortune to the diocese. He sold out to mammon years ago. Caroline, you must be mad! They're fundamentalist. They brainwash people."

Her cheeks flushed up as she looked at Christopher.

"It's you that's going mad, Chris! I hate to say this, but these days you try to run St Benet's like a little Hitler, bossing us all about. You should hear what Simon says about you. If you really, truly cared about our church you would welcome Christ Church with open arms."

She grabbed her cup of coffee and took a hasty gulp. He glared at her.

"You can't be serious! Caroline, just think for a change. They would fillet the place, take out all the historic fittings, remove the altar, put in shiny floors and mezzanine levels, have a worship space with a screen and drum kit, get rid of the…"

He paused suddenly, unable to go on with the list of crimes. Caroline, with bright red cheeks, was gazing into her coffee cup as though a spider lurked at the bottom. With an exasperated sigh, he picked up his own cup and drank the rest of the contents. There was a painful silence. Then Caroline raised her head and looked him in the face.

"Chris, I don't want a row with you. I know you care about St Benet's. But something has got to happen and it might be that Christ Church would be the best solution for us. The people there are probably very decent. They can't bite you. Why don't you try to see things differently? You're making yourself ill for no good reason. Let's make it up and go and enjoy a drink with the Bishop. We've always been good friends, haven't we?"

Christopher rummaged in his brief case, wondering what he could say to her. He felt prickly and not at all inclined to 'make it up'. Caroline was being weak and compliant over the future St Benet's, possibly because of Simon. That she did not seem to appreciate the implications of a takeover by Christ Church astonished him and he could hardly face having any conversation with her ever again. Yet she had been some sort of a friend in the past. They had worked together amicably and he had even enjoyed her company at times. He now felt a faint and annoying sense of bereavement. Closing his briefcase, he stood up and looked at his watch.

"Yes, we ought to be going. Are you ready?"

A few minutes later they were standing on the Bishop's front door step. Caroline had rung the bell and inclined her ear to the intercom, but nothing had happened so far.

"Shall I try again?" she enquired, giving Christopher a worried glance.

"You might as well," he replied. "I suppose we're going to be interviewed by Mr Slope instead of the Bishop."

She looked uncomprehending and, with a sigh, he explained briefly.

"You know. In *Barchester Towers*. Mr Slope, Bishop Proudie's chaplain."

She looked apologetic.

"Oh dear. I'm so sorry. That's Trollope, isn't it? I'm afraid I've never read it. Do you want to tell me about it?"

"Just ring the bell again."

This time, a friendly voice greeted them.

"So sorry. Did you ring before? Just push the door, it'll open."

Christopher pushed and he and Caroline found themselves in a spacious hallway, with a large reception desk on the right. A pleasant-looking man in early middle age stood on a circular rug in the middle of the floor, extending his arms in a welcoming gesture. Although he was wearing an open necked shirt, with a pullover and corduroy trousers, Christopher knew that he was a priest.

This was the Reverend Jack Lambert, the Bishop's senior chaplain and assistant.

"Caroline! Christopher! Welcome! It's so good of you to come. You found your way here all right? How do you do? How do you do? Come along in. The Bishop has had to go to the cathedral for a drinks reception, but he should be back soon. I'm afraid he'd forgotten about it, but he can't let them down. There's a disabled group there, so it's especially important. Any coats? No, well come along in here."

He led them to a short corridor straight ahead and into a room on the left, which was comfortably furnished and looked like a study or small sitting room. On a low table were a bottle of wine, three glasses and a plate of assorted cookies. Three armchairs were drawn up around the table and the chaplain indicated them expansively.

"Now do sit down both of you and let me pour you a drink. Well, this is nice."

Christopher and Caroline clambered awkwardly into the chairs and watched the chaplain pour three glasses of red wine. Neither was able to reciprocate his cheery manner. Caroline shyly took a chocolate cookie and nibbled it, sitting hunched up and holding her left hand carefully underneath to catch the crumbs. Christopher looked around the room for signs of the Bishop's paperwork but saw nothing. The desk on one side, behind an armchair, supported a computer, a pot full of pens and pencils, a small stack of brand-new religious paperbacks and a framed photograph of the Bishop's children. On the other side of the room was a small sideboard, on which was a vase of white chrysanthemums, a few uninteresting ornaments and a decanter of wine.

When the chaplain had passed the drinks around, he smiled broadly at them and offered them the cookies.

Caroline, in taking another, seemed to be wondering if she had been rude in taking the first without being asked. Christopher took two and placed them on the table beside his glass, wondering why biscuits were being served with wine. Was this some mysterious social custom known only to the chaplain? Or was it designed to catch them out? He could not think of anything to say but the chaplain apparently did not notice.

"I say, I'm really sorry. I didn't even introduce myself. I'm Jack – Jack Lambert, senior chaplain here. The Bishop asked me to welcome you and get started. He mostly wanted to thank you for the sterling work you're both doing at St Benet's. It's not easy to run a parish in a vacancy and we don't want you to think that your efforts go unnoticed. How are things going, by the way?"

Christopher decided that Caroline could have the trouble of replying and looked pointedly at her. She was engaged in nibbling her cookie and coughing slightly over a crumb lodged in her throat, but she rose to the challenge.

"Fine, thank you." [cough] That is, the congregation has gone down a bit [cough] but nothing to worry about. [cough] Fr Bodkin has been [cough] wonderful. [prolonged coughing] I'm so sorry but I've got a crumb stuck. Perhaps Chris…"

The chaplain gave her a kindly glance and looked expectantly at Christopher.

"Christopher, while Caroline recovers her equilibrium, perhaps you could enlarge on what she says."

Christopher shrugged his shoulders.

"It's as Caroline says. We're OK generally. You can't really expect a parish to show growth in a vacancy. Bob Bodkin does his best but he'll never set the Thames on fire. The arts college chaplain is doing the weekday services and they're going all right, I think. I do have a full-time job, you know."

The chaplain looked thoughtful and sipped his wine.

"I know what you mean about Fr Bob, but he's a decent bloke. I hear you've produced a possible ordinand."

Christopher could see that the chaplain expected him to say something, but he did not want to talk about Justin.

"Yes, apparently."

Caroline, who had recovered from her coughing fit, decided to chip in.

"That'll be our Justin," she replied, brightly. "He's a lovely young man. Very sincere. We think he'd make a very good priest but he's dreading the selection process. They do make some odd decisions sometimes, don't they? D'you think he'll get through?"

The chaplain drank some more wine before replying.

"Well, of course, I can't possibly say," he replied airily. "Naturally his vocation needs to be tested. But I've heard very good reports of him. And I think I've seen him at some of the meetings. A tall, neatly-dressed young man?"

Caroline grinned.

"Well, neatly-dressed these days, at any rate. Ever since he got the idea about the priesthood, he's become very tidy."

Christopher finished his wine and put the glass down firmly on the table in front of him.

"I'm not sure I believe in vocations," he stated bluntly. "I've always suspected they don't really exist."

Caroline looked shocked but the chaplain smiled blandly.

"That's an odd view for a Christian. But never mind. We're here to talk about St Benet's. We were discussing the congregation just now, weren't we? How many would you say you had on a Sunday? And what about the weekday service? D'you get many at that?"

Caroline looked to Christopher for guidance but he turned his face away.

"Oh, well, it varies, you know," she replied, hesitantly. "Sometimes we get as many as thirty or forty on a Sunday and about ten on a weekday. Or thereabouts."

Christopher noticed the chaplain writing in a small notebook which he had produced from nowhere.

"I see," he replied. "That's not at all bad, is it? For example, how many did you get last Sunday? I'm sure you wrote it in the register."

Caroline directed an agonised look at Christopher but he continued to look away.

"Mm, last Sunday? Let me see. It was a bit difficult because a lot of the tube lines weren't running because of engineering work, so some of our regulars couldn't get in. I think we had, er, fifteen communicants and three choir members who didn't communicate. I think that's right."

The chaplain again wrote surreptitiously in his book and then refilled Christopher's glass. Caroline looked anxiously at her own glass and made a move with her hand to cover it, but the chaplain did not attempt to fill it. Putting down the bottle, he smiled at them both conspiratorially.

"Look, guys, I'll come clean with you. The Bishop has an idea for St Benet's which you might not like straight away, but which has a lot of mileage in it. He thought he would confide in you this evening but, unfortunately, he's been delayed. I know he won't mind my mentioning it before he arrives. He wants you two to be the first to know."

Christopher stiffened but bit back a sarcastic reply. The chaplain continued.

"We care a great deal about St Benet's. It has a long history of service to the community and Julian's ministry was universally admired. Unfortunately, good priests always get snapped up. I have no doubt that you're doing wonders during the vacancy but we can't allow this to go on. That's what the Bishop thinks."

Caroline opened her mouth to say something but thought better of it.

"We've naturally considered a raft of options but the one that seems best is a link with Christ Church. It's a vibrant church, stunningly so, with a large staff and an exciting mission programme. They have an enviable list of activities and cater for all ages. I cannot speak highly enough of them. I wish my own ministry were as successful. I realise this will have taken you by surprise, but what is your first reaction?"

"What sort of a link?" muttered Christopher, finding that his mouth had gone dry.

The chaplain sipped his wine fastidiously.

"Naturally, that will have to be worked out in due course," he replied, carelessly, "but Mr Newton – James – is keen to expand their ministry into neighbouring areas, including yours. They have a very successful model which can be reproduced in other settings, even where, as in your case, there's no church hall. I believe this may be an exciting opportunity for St Benet's. Caroline, what is your impression?"

Caroline shifted her position in her armchair and glanced uneasily at Christopher.

"Oh, um, yes. Christ Church is amazing. I don't know how they do it. But, er, what about parish boundaries and all that? Can they legally expand into other areas? I always thought that in the Church of England..."

"Absolutely!" broke in the chaplain. "But I fear that you and I still think along old-fashioned lines. We must grasp the opportunity to explore new ways of being church.

Parish boundaries don't really come into it. If we were to have a church plant at St Benet's, we could easily square it with any legal requirements. The Bishop is easy-going on those aspects. The important thing is to bring the good news of Jesus Christ into people's lives, wherever they may be, and to draw them into a welcoming church. I'm afraid that BCP worship doesn't really work these days, if it ever did. It's a shame, because I'm quite fond of the dear old Prayer Book, but we have to face the facts. Churches like Christ Church are five hundred per cent more successful in attracting new people into the church, especially young people, than parishes with traditional styles of liturgy and worship. I'm sorry, but there it is. We mustn't bury our heads in the sand. I propose, therefore, to tell the Bishop that you are content for Christ Church to move in by Christmas."

Christopher felt as though he had been stabbed in the stomach.

"Christmas?" he gasped. The chaplain nodded and placed his wine glass firmly on the table.

"Yes, these things are best done quickly. There should be no problem. Caroline, you're happy with that?"

She looked anything but happy.

"Christmas! It seems so soon. How will we get everything ready in time? There's so much to do at that time of year. Carols and things. Could it be a bit later, do you think?"

The chaplain's expression was open and reassuring.

"Oh don't worry, Caroline. Richard Anthony – one of the associate clergy at Christ Church – will initially come to help you by conducting the services. A group will inevitably come with him – he's a popular young man – and things will move on from there. Richard has already been along to take a look and I believe he had a warm welcome from your Justin. He's quite capable of sorting out carol services and so on. I'm sure you will support him. He looks forward to working with you both. Now, have you two had a holiday this summer? It's so important to take a break. I must tell you about my trip to Crete."

The meeting lasted exactly an hour. After that time, Christopher and Caroline were ushered out of the house in the most friendly way imaginable. The Bishop had not appeared but, as they walked away from the house, he strode past without noticing them.

Christopher had been so absorbed in his recollection of the previous evening that he had not noticed the coach moving again. It now seemed to have left the main road and was approaching the little town of Wendover, with its studiously picturesque little cottages and stylish restaurants. Gazing miserably out of the window, he saw the entrance to a car park and felt the coach lumbering inelegantly into a space. As the driver put the brake on, the Chairman's PA, Susie, leapt to her feet at the front of the coach and stridently addressed the occupants.

"Hi, everyone!" she shrieked. "I hope you've enjoyed the ride. I'm sorry about the dismal weather but I know you'll all agree that the countryside's very pretty. Shall we give our lovely driver, Stan, a round of applause for getting us here?"

The staff dutifully clapped. Susie raised her voice again.

"OK. Well. We start our walk from just along the road from here. There are loos across the way and I advise everyone to make use of them. Otherwise, you'll have to find a hedge. All right for you guys but not so good for us girls."

A titter ran round the coach.

"Now, listen. We're going to stop halfway along the route and make our very own cooked lunch. I want some strong fellas to carry the cooking things and the rest of us will carry the food. When you leave the coach, don't forget to collect your food package. Also, there are maps for team leaders. No satnav allowed!"

There were cries of 'shame' from some of the male staff. Laughing, she raised a hand.

"No, I mean it! Anyone found using satnav will have to do the washing up. That's by order of the Chairman. Any questions?"

An athletic-looking young man put his hand up.

"Please, Miss! Are vegans catered for?"

The young man's friends laughed loudly but a few staff members looked disapprovingly at them. Susie waited until the noise had died down and then continued.

"I was not notified of any vegans. We have three vegetarians and one gluten-free person and they are all provided for. Now, if there are no more questions, we'll get on. Stan will collect us from Chesham and, if we get there in good time, we can find some tea shops. Let's go."

Still wrapped up in thought, Christopher trailed behind the group as it plodded slowly along a track which led into woodland. Normally, he would have overtaken everybody with ease, but he wanted to avoid having to hold any conversation with the participants. The scene from the previous evening kept running through his mind like a film, interspersed with pictures of the church interior, the wall plaques, the vestments and that secret, wonderful altar frontal. He felt sick and out of sorts and, as usual, his head ached. In a deeper level of his mind, he knew that he was ashamed of his own apparent inability to take action, to grip this hydra that was plaguing him and to overcome it, no matter how many heads it grew. He felt trapped but seemed to lack the energy, the sense of purpose even, to fight his way free. As the path entered the trees and the daylight dimmed, he suddenly had an overwhelming feeling that he could not face the rest of the walk or the jolly, teambuilding lunch. A short distance in front of him, Rebecca Court was walking with the athletic young man who had asked the question about vegans, her attitude suggesting light flirtation.

Christopher speeded up his own pace until he was just behind Rebecca and the young man.

"Oh, Rebecca!" he called.

There was no response. He tried again.

"Rebecca! Can you just stop for a second? I want a word."

She stopped with evident reluctance and looked round at him, while her companion loitered a little further on.

"Yes, Chris? What is it?"

Silently hating her, he explained the case as briefly as possible.

"Look, Rebecca, I've got a bad headache. I've decided to go back to Wendover and make my way back to London somehow from there. Could you please make sure you tell Susie? Otherwise, she'll think I've got lost or something and send out a search party. Will you do that?"

She nodded and shrugged her shoulders.

"OK. I'll tell her. See you tomorrow."

Christopher did not quite believe her but he saw no point in prolonging the discussion. Turning on his heel, he retraced his steps back to Wendover as quickly as possible, plodding along the track with no regard for wildlife or scenery. As he walked, he tried to stir his half-working brain into action, but he found only questions and not answers. The question that repeated itself most often was whether he was making a fuss about nothing. Why didn't he welcome the arrival of the Evangelicals, help them to settle in and then hand over the work to them? He could then have an easy life. Even take a proper holiday. Start living again. Perhaps enjoy his work. Go for long country walks. Forget about the church. But the part of his brain that was not functioning properly held the answer, clammed up and dark, but there all the same. And he really knew what that answer was.

It was a wearisome journey back to Islington. When he reached Wendover, he plodded up to the station at the end of the main street, only to find that he had just missed a train back to London. The following train had been cancelled, so he had no option but to hang around for nearly an hour. As there was not much to do in Wendover at that time of day or, as he thought, ever, he went into a café and ordered a cup of tea. But the café was full of chattering, well-dressed, middle-aged women who had come from a keep-fit class and were tucking into large pastries and buns. The only spare seat was at a table already occupied by three of these women and he had to endure their patronising glances, amused smiles and hearty conversation while he drank his tea. He wished he had gone without.

Eventually, a train took him back to London. It was late afternoon and drizzling when he turned into his own street, where a man holding an umbrella was walking up and down outside his flat. Max. Christopher hesitated, unsure whether to turn back and hide somewhere. But Max had spotted him and approached with a broad smile but troubled eyes.

"Chris! I hoped I'd catch you! I was just wondering how you were. My texts seem to have got lost in the ether or something. I thought we might go for a drink. It seems ages since we met up. How about it, old chap?"

Christopher tried to manage a smile.

"Max! Hello. I was meaning to get in touch. How – how's Jenny?"

Max took a further step towards Christopher and then stopped.

"Oh, she sends her love, of course. Actually, now I come to think of it, she asked me to ask you what you are doing for Christmas."

"Christmas?" replied Christopher, searching in his befogged brain for an answer. "I don't know. I'm not sure. I hadn't really thought about it yet. Stay here, I suppose."

'Don't do that. Jenny – I – would love you to come over for a few nights. We can easily fit you in. It'll only be family. We usually play games and go for walks and things. But you don't have to make your mind up yet. Let's go for a drink. I've discovered a great pub we haven't tried before. Good food, as well. Jenny's gone to some class or other this evening, so I thought we'd push the boat out and have dinner. It's all on me. I haven't told you about my promotion yet, have I?"

For a brief second, Christopher mentally accused Max of boasting. Yet, even in that second, he knew the thought was unworthy.

"Promotion?" he faltered.

Max looked smilingly modest.

"Oh, well. The same job really, but upgraded. I thought we'd celebrate. Do you remember that night on the tiles we had when you landed your present job? When Jenny was staying at her mother's with the kids? Still…"

Christopher pushed back his damp hair and avoided looking at the sympathy in Max's eyes.

"Max, I'm sorry. It's good of you, but… Well, actually, I've got a bad headache. I'm not fit company for anyone tonight."

"Chris." Max's voice had a note of urgency in it. "You really must go to the doctor's about these headaches. You shouldn't keep getting them like this. I don't need a drink right now. Let's go into your place and have a cup of tea. I don't mind making it."

Christopher felt panic rising in his chest. He wanted only to get into his flat and be alone. Before Max could continue trying to persuade him, he pushed past his friend brusquely and took out his door key.

"No, Max. Not this evening. Another time. I'm not in a fit state, I tell you. I need to lie down. Sorry you've had this trouble."

Leaving Max looking forlorn on the pavement, he got his front door open and almost fell into the hallway, slamming the door behind him. Then, leaning with his back to the door, he covered his face with his hands.

Chapter eleven

Christopher sat in the front pew of the empty church. Somewhere, the heating engineer was checking the controls and radiators, but Christopher felt disinclined to follow him around. He had slept very little during the previous night and now his face ached, his eyes were sore and his legs felt strangely heavy. Cold weather in October and early November had prompted another spate of complaints about the heating system and eventually, and with considerable reluctance, he had called out the engineer. As there was a PCC meeting this evening, Christopher, by leaving his office at 4.00pm, could combine the engineer's visit with the meeting. The Archdeacon was coming.

The sleepless night had felt like a journey to the back of the north wind, gusts of which had roared about his apartment building until early morning. Christopher had, before settling down, tried to read a book about the English Reformation, but the lines of print had blurred before his weary eyes and he had read the same page over and over again without having the faintest idea of its content. Yet, when he had put his head down on the pillow and closed his eyes, he had known that sleep would not come easily. After an hour of fidgeting, he had got up and drunk a glass of whisky, hoping that it would knock him out. But it had had the opposite effect.

First, he had had worrying thoughts about Max, whom he had not seen since that awkward encounter outside his flat a fortnight ago. On and off during the night, he had watched that encounter in his mind as though he had been a third party, looking on from the outside and watching his own and Max's expressions, but knowing all the time that he had been Christopher and not somebody else. Brief flashbacks of the summer holiday had also appeared, especially the row with Jenny, which seemed to have grown to monstrous proportions. And mixed up with them had been delicately-drawn miniatures of happier times with Max, joking at those awful conferences and sinking a few pints at the pub. Moving his head restlessly on his pillow, he had made a solemn pledge to make it up somehow – he hardly knew how – with his best and, possibly by now, his only friend.

The pledge, however, had not brought peace. Other thoughts had come into his mind, even more disturbing. He had relived the musical show at Christ Church, which, in his half-dream, had become more colourful and more raucous than the reality. As, once again, he had watched the children dancing, had seen the text above their heads grow larger and more threatening: 'For the cloud of the Lord was upon the tabernacle by day, and fire was on it by night, in the sight of all the house of Israel, throughout all their journeys.' Opening his eyes, he had seen only the darkness of his bedroom and heard the gentle ticking of his alarm clock.

And then he had dozed for a short time, only to wake suddenly, as though disturbed by something moving in the flat. But, as he had lain there listening fearfully, he had sensed only the ticking clock and the wind rushing around the angle of the building. And then had come more thoughts. This time, he had been in St Benet's, looking at the chasuble in the vestry and touching its embroidery reverently. And then, mentally, he had ascended to the roof and spread out the altar frontal in all its glory on the roof itself. These memories – or were they fantasies? - had calmed him a little and, again, he had dozed.

But the night had been of unusual length. Before dawn, discovering that he was awake, he had reached for the alarm clock and peered at its luminous dial. Five o'clock and still two hours to go before his usual time for getting up. He had felt tired out and wide awake, all at the same time. In those two hours, yet more lurid pictures had appeared before him, as semi-wakeful nightmares. This time, he had seen the Christ Church picture transferred to the St Benet's interior. But the St Benet's interior, known and loved by him so well, had seemed a travesty of its usual self. All the pews had gone. The altar had gone. The chancel had been turned into a stage, with a white screen hanging above it. The walls had been covered in garish murals and not a memorial tablet could be seen. And there had been people milling about, eating and drinking, wearing brightly-coloured tee shirts and jeans. Christopher had had the odd sensation of being present but ignored, moving amongst the occupants of the building like an invisible man.

When the thin November light had finally crawled into his bedroom, he had opened his eyes with a strange feeling of relief. Curiously, the worst night he could ever remember had brought neither fear nor self-pity, but strength. And now, as he sat calmly on the front pew in the gloomy church, he planned his course of action like a military commander planning a campaign. The engineer emerged from the vestry and approached him.

"Well, that's that. I've nailed the beggar. It was the thermostat, after all. You all right, sir? You look a bit pale to me."

Christopher looked up at him.

"Thank you. I'm fine. This place always makes people look sickly. And, anyway, I had a bad night. So, it was the thermostat?"

"That's right. I thought it was that to start with but then I started chasing air locks. This old system will need replacing one of these days. They don't make them like this any more. I'll just tidy my tools. The firm will send you the invoice."

"Thank you. So the heating system is now working normally? No sudden cut-outs?"

The engineer grinned.

"Well, I can't guarantee it, but it should all run properly now. Good job too, considering the weather. See you then. Have an early night tonight!"

The engineer returned to the vestry to collect his things and then walked through the church to the main entrance, giving Christopher a final wave and a murmured, "Cheers, mate." Christopher continued in his place for another half hour or so, looking around the quiet church, resting his tired eyes on cherished locations – the font, the pulpit, the windows, the altar with its emerald green frontal – and thinking strategically.

After that time, he heard the outer door of the vestry open and close, accompanied by a muffled conversation between Caroline and Simon. He could hear chatty conversation from Caroline followed by monosyllabic replies and grunts as chairs were scraped on the floor. Then more people entered – Betty and Hilda, also chatting and gossiping, although with nervous undertones to their voices. Mark arrived and made a few complaining remarks to Caroline, who answered reassuringly, although with a noticeable effort. He heard his own name mentioned once or twice, interrogatively. Had he arrived? Was he going to come? Who was chairing the meeting? Finally, the door slammed and he heard Justin's cheerful voice, apologising for being a bit late and asking everyone how they were. He also asked, loudly, if Christopher were coming to the meeting. Nobody thought of looking in the church until Justin put his face round the vestry doorway.

"Chris! Why didn't you say you were here? We were wondering when you were going to arrive. You all right? What you sitting there for?"

Christopher stood up stiffly and achieved a faint smile.

"Hello, Justin. I've had the heating engineer in, looking at the boiler controls. He's just this minute gone. Is everyone here?"

"Yes, except the Archdeacon. D'you think we ought to start without him – or will he blow a gasket? I suppose we could do the normal business without him. You're chairing the meeting, aren't you?"

Christopher beckoned to him silently with a forefinger in front of his lips. Justin slid from the doorway and joined him beside the front pew.

"Justin, can I consult you?" whispered Christopher. Justin's face took on an almost comical conspiratorial look.

"Of course, Chris. What is it?"

"I'm going to ask Caroline to chair this meeting because I don't want a row with the Archdeacon. When the old sod raises the matter of Christ Church, just say whatever you really feel about it. Don't take any notice of me. I promise to be on my best behaviour."

Justin looked puzzled.

"But Chris, I thought you hated the idea. I'll stick up for you, if you like. We could ask to be taken over by St Andrew's. I shan't mind. I don't see why the diocese should do the very thing you don't want. You are churchwarden, after all."

Christopher turned his face away and swallowed hard.

"It's no use, Justin," he replied in a cracked voice. "They've made their minds up. It's best to go along with it. You won't suffer. Come on. The others'll be waiting for us."

He almost put a hand on Justin's arm but thought better of it. Together, they went into the vestry where their colleagues were sitting around the table looking moody. Within a few minutes, Christopher had installed Caroline at one end of the table and taken a seat on the side, at the opposite end, with an empty seat beside him. The chair on his other side, at the end of the table, had been left for the Archdeacon. For a short time, there was virtual silence while Caroline shuffled her papers, looking for the agenda. But, before she could begin the meeting, there was the sound of the church door opening and closing, and heavy footsteps in the church.

"Good evening, everyone," announced the Archdeacon brusquely as he entered the vestry and started taking off his coat. Hilda got up and, un-thanked, received it from him and hung it on the coat stand. He took his place at the table and accepted a set of papers from Christopher.

"OK, OK. Let's get started. Caroline, are you chairing this? Come on. Let's start, shall we?"

Caroline looked nervously down the table at him.

"Would you like to lead us in prayer, Archdeacon?"

"Do you normally start with prayer? All right. Heavenly Father, guide us in all our doings so that we might please you. And send the Holy Spirit to guide this PCC meeting so that the right decisions will be made. We ask this in the name of our Saviour, Jesus Christ. Amen. Carry on, Caroline."

Caroline took a deep breath and glanced at Christopher nervously.

"Thank you. Item one. Apologies. Do we have any?"

There were a few grunts and murmurs. She continued.

"No apologies, then. I think we're all here. The next item on the agenda is the treasurer's report. Would you like to report, Betty, please?"

Betty drew herself up and referred to a well-fingered sheet of exercise book paper.

"Last month's income was seven hundred pounds and three pence, down three hundred and twenty two pounds from the previous month. Expenditure was, er, well, Common Fund two thousand pounds, sanctuary supplies thirteen pounds sixteen pence..."

The Archdeacon interrupted her.

"What's all this, Betty? Don't you have a print-out for us to see? We can't remember all these figures."

Betty turned pink but stood her ground.

"My apologies, Archdeacon, only my computer broke down last week and I haven't been able to print anything. My nephew, Jake, has promised to come and fix it."

He sighed and shook his head.

"All right, Mrs Cook. Never mind. I've heard all I need to. Caroline, would you like to proceed?"

Caroline looked down at her agenda.

"It's the churchwardens' report. Christopher, I wonder if you would like to say something."

Christopher leaned back in his chair and looked at the faces around the table. It struck him how pathetic and unattractive they looked – Caroline, Betty and Hilda looking nervous, Mark looking mutinous and Simon, cynical. The Archdeacon looked strained. Only Justin seemed friendly and encouraging.

"Not a lot to report," he said calmly. "But the heating engineer has been and he wasn't able to fix the problem. So, I am afraid that the heating might cut out again from time to time, or even do something much worse. He said that the system is getting old and needs replacing. We don't have the money, of course. Nothing else to report from me. What about you, Caroline?"

She looked at him in a pleading way, as though urging him to say something more, but he shook his head. Simon chipped in.

"What do you mean, he couldn't fix it?" he asked testily. "Is he going to do a written report? We can't be expected to freeze this winter."

Mark decided to join in.

"It's not fair on my singers," he complained. "The cold affects their voices. And what about me? Am I supposed to play the organ with blue fingers? We elect the churchwardens to deal with this sort of thing."

"Hold on," broke in Justin. "We all know the system's on its last legs. Why are you getting at Christopher? He's done his best. He called the engineer in, didn't he, and probably gave up an afternoon's work to be here. Nobody else ever volunteers to come in."

"It's his job to call the engineer. He's waited long enough. He never gives a toss for the music."

Caroline began to look flustered.

"I'm sorry, everyone, but I'm sure the Archdeacon doesn't want to hear us arguing. I do sympathise with you, Mark, because it must be difficult to produce such, er, such fine music in a cold church. But the parish can't afford a new heating system at the moment. It's not really Chris's fault. Shall we get on?"

The Archdeacon, with a sidelong glance at Christopher, who remained placid, looked at Caroline almost approvingly.

"Thank you, Caroline! Yes, do get on, please. The heating system doesn't matter very much, now. Is that the end of the churchwardens' report?"

Caroline hesitated, trying to avoid looking at her husband, who was fidgeting and mouthing words at her.

"I think so. Or, at least, the other things can wait till next time. The next item on the agenda is Ministry. You asked for that to be put on, Archdeacon. Would you like to speak to it, please?"

The Archdeacon drew himself up to his short height and cleared his throat importantly. Christopher settled himself more comfortably in his chair and hooked an arm over the back of it. Hilda took up her pen to write and the other members turned to look at the Archdeacon with interest and some curiosity.

"My friends," he began and then paused, as though waiting for Christopher to interrupt him. But Christopher said nothing.

"My friends, I wish to congratulate you all for keeping the show on the road at St Benet's during this relatively long interregnum. The Bishop and I know how hard you've all worked and we want you to know that it's appreciated in the deanery, and, indeed, in the diocese." He paused again, with another glance at Christopher, who met his eyes without expression.

"I know," he continued, "that the churchwardens have borne the heaviest burden, but the rest of you have done your share. The Bishop has particularly praised the work that Caroline has done. And Christopher, of course." He stopped again, clearly expecting an explosion from Christopher at this juncture. But no explosion came and the Archdeacon seemed unnerved by the absence of it. He coughed slightly and then resumed.

"So, it's now nearly a year and I am happy to tell you that your efforts are being rewarded. After much prayer and consultation, the Bishop and I have decided to progress a church plant by Christ Church. Christopher and Caroline have already been fully consulted about this. The Reverend Richard Anthony will take the services from the third

Sunday in December with a view to his being licensed as priest in charge next year."

He stopped and looked at the faces around the table. Nobody said a word. Caroline rearranged her papers. Hilda dropped her pen on the floor and scrabbled for it. Betty looked intently at the table. Simon and Mark exchanged significant glances. Justin looked at Christopher, who stared into space. The Archdeacon, finding that there was no verbal response, felt obliged to continue his monologue.

"You will, of course, need to expect changes. These are inevitable. But they will transform St Benet's from a tired parish that has slightly lost its way - through no fault of yours, of course - into a vibrant, modern church, full of life and with a mission to proclaim the good news of Jesus Christ to the world. Mr Anthony is deeply committed to his Christian vocation and will have the full support of Mr Newton and the team at Christ Church. It will be a new beginning for St Benet's. I'm sure you share my great excitement at the prospect."

Despite his confident words, the Archdeacon was beginning to look ill at ease with his unreceptive audience. Christopher sensed that his own silence was irritating the Archdeacon even more than an argument would have done and he privately started to enjoy the feeling of power which it was giving to him. He rearranged his arm over the back of his chair and looked intently at the Archdeacon's reddening face.

"Now, has anyone any questions? Christopher, you were about to say something, I think."

Christopher looked from side to side as though he were searching for the recipient of the Archdeacon's enquiry.

"Me? No, I don't think so, Archdeacon. You have made yourself quite clear."

The Archdeacon's cheeks took on a darker shade of red.

"I thought I saw your lips move," he replied accusingly. "But no matter. Has anyone else a question? Caroline?"

Caroline looked up, startled.

"Er, thank you," she faltered, glancing at her husband. "I just want to ask, er, what happens to the PCC and parish officers when Christ Church come?"

The Archdeacon tried to smile encouragingly, but failed and only succeeded in looking shifty. He then leaned back and clasped his hands on the table in an effort to look commanding, but his physique was against him and he looked only pompous.

"Thank you, Caroline. That's a very good question. Now, of course, when Mr Anthony comes, he will doubtless bring a large number of followers with him. His charismatic ministry and worship will rapidly attract others and you will find that new people will wish to join the PCC or be churchwarden. You and Christopher are legally churchwardens until next May, although I imagine that the Bishop would accept your resignations if you decided that you wanted to go early."

A stifled snort from Christopher caused him to stop and look round nervously before continuing.

"I naturally hope and expect that you will welcome these newcomers with open arms. It's a wonderful opportunity for this parish and will be its saviour. You have all worked hard but I'm sure you will take the opportunity to stand down and let others shoulder the burdens. Justin – for you, it is a godsend. You will be able to explore your vocation in the best possible environment. Any more questions?"

As his fellow members tried to think up questions to ask the Archdeacon, Christopher savoured his new power. He felt almost euphoric. It was clear that his silence and apparent acquiescence were annoying the Archdeacon far more than any shouting or bad temper would have done. The Archdeacon had, no doubt, prepared himself for a slanging match with Christopher and he wasn't getting one. As he grew more frustrated, puzzled and nervous, Christopher enjoyed a new sensation of confidence and control.

But, deeper down, Christopher felt a kind of horror. This scene through which he was living seemed unreal and dream-like. The changes that the Archdeacon was describing surely could not happen. The thought of St Benet's – quiet, classical, beautiful and soothing – full of loud and chattering people who were oblivious to its subtle influence, was preposterous. It could not happen. The church had not been built for that. Oh, for a return to Julian's lofty elegance and gracious liturgy! That would be a thousand times better than this. Christopher remembered the last time that he had received communion from Julian and the eerie feeling that perhaps God was there, after all. The memory caused a shiver to run down his back. Would God come to save him now?

The Archdeacon tapped his fingers on the table.

"Any more questions or comments?"

He seemed to be willing Christopher to speak. But it was Justin who spoke up.

"Could I just ask, please, Archdeacon, whether you think that the church building will be changed in any way?"

The question, mild though it sounded, sent a shock wave around the table. Everybody seemed to stiffen. The Archdeacon kept Christopher out of his line of vision but appeared to feel some sort of invisible stabbing coming from Christopher's direction. His whole body twitched.

"How do you mean exactly, Justin?"

Justin smiled at him meekly.

"Oh, well, you know. The altar being moved or the pews taken out. That sort of thing. I just wondered."

The Archdeacon shifted his position on his chair but still did not look at Christopher, who was eyeing him with an expression of extreme distaste.

"I can hardly say at this stage, Justin. Naturally, Mr Anthony and his colleagues will wish to form a more convenient worship space in the church and possibly form an area for, er, a music group. What I do know is that the Diocesan Advisory Committee is very sympathetic towards changes relating to fresh expressions of ministry and worship. A faculty would be granted very readily, I should think. Is that the last question? Come on, now. I'm here to discuss this with you. More questions."

There was silence. The Archdeacon fingered his papers restlessly, trying not to turn towards Christopher. But, finally, he could not resist satisfying his curiosity. With his head slightly lowered, he looked sideways at Christopher's face, only to avert his eyes almost instantly. Christopher was staring at him, not with hatred or irritation, but with a curling lip and a look of profound derision.

The Archdeacon stood up to leave, gathering his documents together clumsily. He had meant this to be a victory for authority and for himself personally, but his red cheeks and awkward demeanour seemed to suggest failure. He turned to leave and had reached the door before Hilda stumbled after him, bearing his coat. He took it hastily but, encumbered with his briefcase, struggled to get it on, first putting an arm in the wrong sleeve and then having to start all over again. Christopher cherished the moment.

But the moment did not persist. After the Archdeacon had stumped out of the church and slammed the church door, Christopher suddenly felt all in. His energy seemed to drain away and his head began to ache again. The other members started to murmur to each other in low tones, some with furtive glances at him. Caroline – to her credit, he thought – looked rather miserable. Justin kept trying to attract his attention but he pretended to be reading his agenda carefully, even though the words turned to mist in front of his eyes. He wanted only to escape. After a few agonising moments, he heard Caroline's anxious voice.

"Can I please call everyone to order? We ought to get on. I'm going to allow twenty minutes for general discussion. I wonder if Chris would like to kick off?"

He raised his head. Everybody looked at him.

"I'm sorry, Caroline. I've come over feeling a bit faint…"

"I knew you were looking ill!" exclaimed Justin. "You normally would have given the old Arch what-for! Hadn't you better go home, Chris?"

Caroline looked at him kindly.

"Yes, hadn't you better go and lie down, Chris? You do seem pale. I'm sure we can cope."

"Too right we can," added Simon audibly and sourly.

Christopher sighed and rose to his feet, stuffing his agenda in his jacket pocket.

"OK, I'm going," he replied wearily. "See you on Sunday."

As he worked his way down the church aisle, touching the end of every pew as he went past, he could hear the conversation in the vestry spring to life.

"He can be a pain in the backside." exclaimed Mark loudly, with an accompanying 'Shhh' from Justin. "Good thing he's left. I hope he stays away. I don't believe he's ill at all – only fed up. He's putting it on to get our sympathy. We can now have an intelligent conversation about these proposals. What does everyone think?"

"Caroline, you're too soft on him!" complained Simon, also very loudly. "He was being deliberately uncooperative in front of the Archdeacon. Anyone would think that he ran this parish properly! I don't think this is too bad an idea. Liven the place up a bit. It's as dead as a dodo at the moment. I vote for going with Christ Church. It's not perfect, but it's the best we'll get. People can always go somewhere else if they don't like it. It's better than what we've got now."

Caroline's voice could be heard, reasoning but indistinct, and then the two older women began twittering. Christopher, who had reached the back of the almost dark church, leaned against the end of the furthest pew and placed a hand on his forehead.

"God give me strength," he muttered.

Outside, the cold evening air revived him a little and he decided to go home on foot, hoping that the walk would make him feel better. After about twenty minutes' walking, during which time he had blocked all thought from his mind, he suddenly remembered his solemn pledge about Max and fumbled in his pocket for his mobile phone. Standing under a lamp post, he switched it on and peered at the screen to see if he had any messages. There was only a text from the phone company, informing him that calls in Europe were going to be cheaper, and nothing from Max. Although messages from Max had tended to embarrass him in recent days, he was nevertheless keenly disappointed at not finding any. He shivered. With a cold thumb, he picked out Max's home number and placed the phone to his ear. Jenny answered.

"Hello."

"Is that Jenny? It's Christopher. Is Max there, please?"

There was a brief pause. Then Jenny spoke more loudly.

"Chris! How are you? We haven't heard from you for ages! Are you all right? Max was getting worried about you."

"Yes, I'm OK. But I wanted to speak to Max. Is he there?"

Jenny sounded apologetic.

"Chris, I'm so sorry. Max is away on a course. It's to do with his promotion. But why not pop round for a drink or something? It would be so good to see you. There's only me and the kids here."

Christopher groaned inwardly.

"I can't, I'm afraid. I'm terribly busy. But when does Max get back?"

He could hear Jenny whispering, "it's Christopher" to somebody, probably one of the children. Then she spoke to him again.

"He's back at the weekend. I'll tell him you rang. But, Chris, love…"

Christopher ended the call. But, as he was replacing the phone in his pocket, it rang. He looked at the screen and, finding that the call was from Jenny, switched the phone off and stuffed it into the deepest corner of his coat pocket. Then, turning up his coat collar and warming his hands in his pockets, he trudged homewards to Islington.

Chapter twelve

It was a dismal Saturday evening in mid-December. The stinging sleet which had blurred the outlines of buildings and lashed the cheeks of passers-by earlier in the day had been cleared by a strengthening wind, leaving the twilight air bitingly cold.

Inside the church of St Benet-by-the-Wall, the air was not much warmer. The body of the church was in semi-darkness, but the chancel lights had been switched on, making the crucifix and silver candlesticks on the altar twinkle and gleam. There was also a flickering light on the few strands of gold and silver tinsel which had been draped around an artificial Christmas tree. There was more tinsel on the advent wreath, where two purple candles had burnt down a little and the remaining purple, pink and white candles were still in pristine condition. The brass plates on the walls of the chancel gave off their own comforting glow and everything seemed to shine with cleanliness.

The light was also on in the vestry, where Christopher was on his hands and knees in front of the store cupboard. Beside him on the floor were a heap of candles, several boxes of incense and three large boxes of matches. Reaching into the cupboard, he started to pull out boxes of charcoal and to stack them up next to the other things.

"Eight, nine, ten," he counted, as he stacked them. "Good. And there should be some old ones at the back."

He bent down to look into the depths of the cupboard and brought out two more boxes, slightly crushed and with a different design on the boxes from the new ones.

"They'll do," he muttered, scrambling to his feet. Still holding them, he remembered when they had been bought. It had been during Julian's time, when Christopher had frequently needed to buy charcoal and incense for the splendid services that Julian had conducted. It had not seemed a golden age at the time but, looking back, Christopher now thought differently. The large congregations, bright new vestments and Julian's melodious voice and polished sermons had given life and hope to St Benet's and complemented its beauty. The beauty remained. Sighing deeply, Christopher placed the boxes on top of the others.

After a moment's thought, he left the vestry and strode down the aisle of the church. Taking his keys out of his pocket, he unlocked the tower door, put the light on in the space just inside, and climbed quickly up the tower steps, trying to think only of getting to the top. When he got there, he opened the door and felt immediately on his face the cold, fresh wind. The clustering office blocks, some with windows brilliantly lit, ignored him on this occasion, as though they were gazing in a different direction. He selected a key – there was no doubt about its identity now – and opened the door which led into the roof space. The large polythene parcel was fairly near the entrance, although well out of the way of the damp area, and it took him only a second to pull it out carefully and re-lock the door. Gathering it into his arms as though it were a sleeping child, he returned to the tower steps and gingerly descended, frequently putting out a hand to the wall to steady himself.

When he was back in the church, he carried his burden to the vestry table and gently unfolded the polythene wrapping. The gold embroidery winked at him and he caught his breath, marvelling once again at the superb craftsmanship and undimmed colours. The crude polythene had now completed its task and was redundant. Christopher slid the rest of it from under the altar frontal and stuffed it in the litter bin, where it stuck up in grey peaks and folds. Taking his handkerchief out of his pocket, he wiped his hands before lifting up the precious frontal and carrying it into the chancel, where he placed it tenderly over the row of stalls. The altar was covered with a frontal of penitential purple, for advent, with a white cloth over it and six candlesticks on top of that, the large, silver-plated crucifix occupying the central position. Carefully, Christopher removed the candlesticks one by one and placed them on the floor of the chancel. The crucifix followed. Then he took the white cloth without folding or creasing it and draped it over the servers' bench. Next, it was the turn of the purple frontal, which Christopher folded up expertly and carried into the vestry, where he left it on the table. He returned to the chancel. The carved wooden altar stood bare, waiting to be robed. Deferentially, Christopher spread the embroidered frontal over the altar, smoothing it out until it was perfect. His previous attempts at doing this had been mere rehearsals. This was the real thing. The night of the play.

Slowly, almost as in a ritual, he placed the white cloth on top of the frontal. Then the crucifix and candlesticks. Finally, he stepped back a few paces and kneeled, prepared to allow the frontal to work its magic on him. With his eyes, he examined every part of it – the faded blue silk border and bands, the golden canopies, the swooping dove, unlike any real dove, the stylised roses and leaves, the angel and the graceful figure of holy St Benedict. White, gold, brown, blue, red and green. What did it matter that a few threads here and there hung loose? They had given service nobly. The canopies had ogee arches at the top, with curly patterns above and below, almost like sinuous dragons or crouching panthers, and the narrow columns that supported them were deeply patterned in gold.

He looked at the dove. Was this the Holy Spirit, linking heaven and earth, bringing power and strength and holiness to mankind? The roses were earthly roses and the stems had thorns. Christopher blinked. He had not seen many roses in his life. Only thorns. A picture inexplicably flashed across his mind of himself as a sixteen year old at a parents' evening at school. His father and mother, dowdily dressed as usual, were discussing his subject choices with his form teacher. Their fussy questions, ignorance of the subjects and repeated misunderstandings were making Christopher squirm with embarrassment and shame. His own attempts to explain the Latin syllabus or the French set texts only made the situation worse, because his parents told him to 'be quiet' or 'let them finish', as though he were a small child. Nearby, his main rival in the Latin exams, with his smartly-dressed parents and another teacher, was casting looks of pity and superiority in Christopher's direction.

Christopher shuddered slightly and tried to put the scene out of his mind. But, as he focused his eyes again on the embroidered picture, his empathy with it seemed enhanced. He felt more than ever that it was speaking to him, and to him alone. For a few moments longer, he considered it thoughtfully. Then he got to his feet and returned to the vestry, stiffening his back in a business-like fashion. There was more work to do. First, he put the purple frontal away tidily in a drawer in the chest. Then he stepped back and placed his hands together as though in prayer. This was the part that he did not want to hurry. From outside, he could hear the sound of police sirens some distance away, rushing to a suspected crime or an accident, shaking and jarring the London air. He waited. There was another siren, closer this time and rowdy, like a would-be rioter heading for a place of assembly. Gradually, it faded and the air fell back into relative quietness.

The minutes passed. Christopher approached the chest and, in one decisive movement, opened the lowest drawer. Swiftly, but with trembling fingers, he lifted out the Comper chasuble and carried it into the church. Without looking around him, he made straight for the priest's stall in the chancel and placed the chasuble over it, with the figure of St Benedict facing him. He stood back to survey its position and then stepped forward again to straighten it slightly, allowing the sides of the chasuble to hang gracefully on each side of the stall. The rest of the church, almost dark now, seemed to close in around the pool of light in the chancel. Once again, he took a step backwards and looked intently at the vestment, appraising its beauty as a connoisseur and its functionality as a student of liturgy.

Yet his eyes seemed blurred and he saw only merging colours – white, blue, green, brown, red and gold. Especially gold. He blinked, trying to clear his vision, and managed for a few moments to see St Benedict clearly, resplendent under his gorgeous halo.

"Benedict," he murmured. "Benedictus. Saying well. Do I say well? Does the Archdeacon say well?"

He knelt on one knee and continued to stare at the chasuble. But, again, his mind produced a quite different picture. Mentally, he had returned to a drinks party at his university, when he was a first year undergraduate. Later, he had given up enduring such events and avoided them scrupulously. But, when he was still relatively new, he had imagined it his duty to attend them. On this occasion, he was standing on his own against a wall, holding a glass of wine and wondering if he could pluck up the courage to talk to someone. In the middle distance, the bright colours of the students' clothing; red, blue, green, white and yellow, formed a kaleidoscope. Immediately in front of him was a group of students, seemingly oblivious of his presence, who were talking loudly about people whom they knew or had met. Some people were being praised enthusiastically, others were being criticised adversely and coarsely. Christopher listened to them without much interest until he heard his own name mentioned by a girl who had her back to him.

"What d'you think of Chris Jamieson?" she enquired, with a perceptible tone of derision in her voice. "He's in my seminar group."

Another girl, also with her back to him, laughed.

"Oh, he's all right," she replied. "A bit boring. Apparently interested in old churches. Not too bad looking. But hardly my type."

The first girl turned to look at her with surprise.

"Don't tell me you fancy him! He bores the pants off me. But you're welcome to him."

The second girl laughed again.

"Give over! I said he wasn't my type. It'll be a long time before I get interested in old churches."

One of the boys in the group spoke up, with a slight sneer.

"I expect he'll still be available when that time comes. I can just see you and Chris toddling around weedy old churchyards, hand in hand, looking at Perpendicular windows and Norman doorways!"

Another boy, who was standing next to him, suddenly noticed Christopher and looked embarrassed.

"Look here, you lot," he chimed in, trying to sound casual. "Can't you talk about something else for a change? You girls'll be starting on me and Kevin next. I dread to think what you'd say about me – or Kevin for that matter. Let's go and top our glasses up and see if there's any food."

Laughing, they ambled away towards the drinks table, leaving Christopher with burning cheeks and an ache of loneliness.

As the picture passed from his mind, Christopher buried his face in his hands.

"Oh God, what am I doing?" he muttered.

For several seconds, he knelt with head bowed. Then, dropping his hands and opening his eyes, he looked again at the chasuble, trying to draw its pure and soothing beauty into his sore brain. But, after a moment or two, something else entered his head. A noise. There was a tapping at the main door of the church, gentle at first but getting gradually louder and more insistent. Christopher listened, hearing it clearly but not, at first, believing that it was real. When it continued, he stood up, shook himself slightly and, with an uncomfortably beating chest, walked to the back of the church.

He pressed his cheek against the door. On the other side of it, a firm fist was thumping the woodwork. Thump, thump, pause, thump, thump, thump, pause.

"Here's a knocking indeed!" Christopher murmured. Then, clearing his throat, he raised his voice.

"Who's there?" he called out gruffly. "Who's knocking? What do you want?"

"Is that Chris?" came the muffled reply. "Chris, it's me. Max. Can you let me in? I'm freezing to death out here."

Christopher drew back in surprise. Max! What was he doing here? Should he open the door or tell him to go away? Half of him longed to see his old friend; the other half feared to meet him. As he stood, undecided over what to do, the banging began again. He endured it for two whole minutes before friendship won. His shoulders relaxed. Taking his keys from his pocket, he unlocked the big door and opened it just wide enough for Max to slide in.

"Chris! What do you mean, locking me out!" exclaimed Max, unwinding a long scarf from his neck and trying to look jovial at the same time as giving Christopher's face a covert look. The effect would have been slightly comical in different circumstances. Christopher locked the door again before answering.

"I didn't know you were coming," he replied simply. As he said it, he realised that it was rather a silly thing to say. Here they were, in a half-dark church on a bitter December evening, exchanging remarks that were better suited to an impromptu party in a warm and comfortable home.

"I'd keep your scarf on if I were you," he added, leading Max up the aisle of the church.

"Now, Chris," began Max again. "This won't do. I've been trying to get in touch with you for ages and, when I finally run you to earth, you practically don't want to let me in. I've been to your flat and thought that you'd be here if you weren't there, if you know what I mean. It's ages since we had a drink together and you don't even answer my texts. Don't you care about your old friend?"

Christopher motioned him to a seat on the front pew and sat beside him, but turned his body away. It was painful having Max there and yet, deep down, he longed to grasp his hand – or put his arms around him.

"Course I care," he muttered in a strained voice. "You've always been a great friend, Max. I haven't meant to snub you. I've just been busy, that's all. It was good of you to come here looking for me. Job all right?"

Max took off his leather gloves and stuffed them in his coat pocket.

"The job? Yes, it's fine. It's not changed much, by the way. I just got upgraded. Mind you, the powers-that-be might be dreaming up all sorts of horrors for me next year, to justify the pay. What about you?"

Christopher shifted his position on the pew so that he could almost face Max.

"Oh, just the same, you know. Boring as hell. I couldn't face the last conference. Wasn't it about conciliation in the workplace?"

Max smiled.

"Yup. Except that the first speaker had a bit of a row with the conference staff about the way they'd set up the room. He wanted us all in a semi-circle, luvvy-like, and they'd set it up with the chairs in rows facing front, usual style. You'd have loved it, especially when we all had to form a ring and hold hands."

Christopher grimaced.

"Yuck! Sounds awful. I hope that Bossy Brenda and her floppy friend weren't there."

Max's smile broadened.

"They were there, all right, Brenda leading the singing and the drippy friend joining in the chorus. It was all pretty chummy once the frayed tempers had died down. But I had to hold hands with Henry Stamford, who couldn't understand what it was all supposed to be about and kept saying that office workers didn't do things like that in his young days. I nearly creased up with laughing. I wish you'd been there. You'd have had a few things to say. Oh, and the food was especially disgusting."

Christopher smiled faintly.

"Pity I missed it. Did, er, Henry say anything else?"

Max directed a keen glance at him.

"Oh, well, you know old Henry. We talked about City dinners and things, and the Common Council, and all that. He asked after you."

"Oh? How come?"

"Well, he just said he hadn't seen you for a bit. I said that I hadn't either and we left it at that."

"I see. Sorry about that."

Max grunted sympathetically and there was silence for a few moments. Then Max spoke up brightly.

"I say, Chris, this is all looking super-duper. I've never seen things like that before – well, in museums, I suppose. Have you got a big service or something?"

Christopher nodded slowly.

"Hm, yes, sort of. I was just getting the place ready when you came. Do you like it?"

Max considered the chancel critically, with his head on one side.

"Well, it's very fine. That cloth on the altar and that robe thing are magnificent. I can see they're pretty old and precious. I suppose you only get them out for big occasions. But it's nothing like that place that Jenny and the kids go to – Christ Church. I'm not sure they have an altar or anything. And the parson wears a beautifully tailored suit. Best quality. He doesn't pay for that on a clergyman's stipend. I can't afford suits like that myself. And they have loads of people doing things. Henry goes there, by the way. I see him when I call for the kids. Oh, I say, Chris, do you remember that very smart couple who were sitting near you at that dinner when you were sick? The beautiful Asian woman."

Christopher coughed slightly, feeling his mouth going dry.

"Yes. What of them?"

"Well - Amy and Matthew, that's them – well, they take some of the services and they are going to be made ministers. Very nice couple. What do you have to do to be made a minister?"

Christopher passed his tongue over his dry lips.

"It depends. D'you think they're going to be ordained?"

Max gave him a quizzical look.

"Ordained? That means made a priest, doesn't it? I don't really know. The youngsters were asked to pray for them the other week. They bring a prayer leaflet home every week but I'm afraid I hardly ever look at it."

Christopher stood up abruptly.

"I'm going to make a cup of tea, Max. You must be frozen. I should have thought of it before. Just stay here. I won't be a minute."

Before Max could reply, he strode to the back of the church and let himself into the room under the tower. While he boiled the kettle and set out two mugs, two teabags and a spoon, he considered his position urgently. Should he tell Max? Should he ask Max to advise him? No, he could guess what Max would say. But wouldn't Max be right? Wasn't Max the most sensible person he knew? But Max didn't know much about the Church. Was that a good thing or a bad thing? How well did Max understand him? Perhaps he should tell Max to leave. How about confiding in him completely? But would he sympathise? Was it fair to lumber Max with this?

The kettle boiled too quickly. Christopher splashed the boiling water on to the teabags in the mugs and stirred the mixture hastily. There was an open carton of milk on the worktop and he grabbed it and was about to pour from it when he changed his mind and smelled it. The milk was sour. Grimacing, he poured the liquid down the sink and tossed the carton into the bin. Then he fished the teabags out of the mugs with the spoon and threw them in the bin as well.

Max was still sitting placidly on the front pew when Christopher arrived back, gingerly carrying the two mugs of hot black tea.

"Sorry, Max. The milk was off. But this should still warm you up. Mind – the mug's boiling."

Max gratefully leaned across to take the offered mug and tried to wrap his hands around it, but quickly changed his mind and placed it on the pew beside him.

"Thanks, Chris. It's a bit hot. Will it be all right there? It won't melt the varnish off or anything?'

Christopher placed his own mug beside his friend's.

"It doesn't matter. These are all going to be chucked out anyway. I don't care what happens to them anymore."

Max spread his hands over the top of his mug, trying to warm them with the steam.

"Why? They look all right to me. You're not going to have chairs instead, are you? I rather like the old pews."

Christopher shrugged his shoulders but did not trust himself to reply. The lump had reappeared in his throat. Max turned his hands over and gazed thoughtfully at the palms.

"I say, Chris," he remarked after a few moments. "This religion thing. I don't really get it. Jenny and the kids go off to that Christ Church place every Sunday and come back full of news about what they did and who said what, and it's all very jolly. But I don't seem to get the message. I've been once or twice and I must say the vicar preaches a powerful sermon. But this personal saviour thing. It sounds like make-believe to me. You somehow have to convince yourself that you are talking to someone who knows you and answers all your needs and you can't see him, but who isn't just a figment of your own imagination. And then there's the are-you-saved business."

Christopher glanced at Max's bent head.

"Are you saved?"

Max lifted his mug to his lips and took a nervous sip before deciding that the tea was still too hot.

"Yes," he replied apologetically. "I know that you know all about this sort of thing, but you must remember that I am an outsider. I know that the Bible says that Jesus died for our sins and all that, but I've never understood it. Mr Newton says that it was substitutionary atonement – I think I've got that right – whereby Jesus took all our sins on himself and was punished instead of us. But that all seems daft to me. If God is a God of mercy, why did he punish his son? Sorry to be so obtuse. I've never studied anything like theology and I even bunked out of Sunday school when I was a lad. You probably understand it all. You wouldn't go to church otherwise. Anyway, there's something about Mr Newton that I don't really like. He's very smooth and everyone at Christ Church adores him. But, well, I don't like him. I suppose I'm jealous of his suits."

Christopher began to feel close to tears.

"Max, you're not obtuse. Bloody Mr Newton can go to hell for all I care. There's a memorial in our chancel – look, that one on the left – that commemorates a former rector, James Seymour. He was worth twenty Mr Newtons."

Max looked at the chancel wall with interest.

"Why?" he asked. "Was he a saintly sort of chap?"

Christopher sighed.

"I suppose he was. He wouldn't have seen it like that. He actually loved all the poor people who lived roundabout. I can't seem to love any of them. He – he gave them everything he had and died going to visit a sick woman. He did all that because of his faith. He wouldn't have cared about smart suits or smooth manners or electronic things."

Max smiled and gulped down some tea.

"Well, he wouldn't have had anything very electronic. Let's see. Was the telephone invented then? But I think I would have liked Mr Seymour. He's my sort of chap – very decent. I don't suppose he had much to give, though, if he was a parson."

Christopher gazed down at his tea as though it were a crystal ball.

"He did, though," he replied quietly. "He came from a rich family but had nothing by the time he died. Practically only the clothes he wore."

"Definitely a saint, then. Except – I don't think you have saints in the C of E, do you? Or am I thinking of the Methodists?"

Christopher smiled weakly.

"We do have them but it's complicated. We haven't made any new ones since the Reformation, but we still recognise people who would be saints if we still had them. And we keep all the saints from before the Reformation. It's a typical Anglican compromise."

Max raised his eyebrows comically.

"Really? There doesn't seem to be anything very compromising at Christ Church. What's that tablet on the other side – facing my friend, Mr Seymour?"

Christopher was silent for a few moments while Max politely sipped his tea. Why was he finding it difficult to tell Max about Charles Aitchison? Max seemed to sense his reluctance and was just beginning a completely different question when Christopher chipped in.

"That's another rector," he said, diffidently. "Charles Aitchison. He was after Mr Seymour. He died in 1920. It's a very handsome plaque, isn't it?"

Max looked across at it, still clasping his mug.

"Yes, it looks fancier than Mr Seymour's. What was that chap like?"

"Do you really want to know?"

Max looked surprised and straightened his back.

"Why? Was there anything funny about him? He didn't abuse the choirboys, I suppose? You needn't tell me if you think it isn't suitable for my juvenile ears."

Christopher felt his cheeks go red.

"Of course not," he replied, hastily. "He was a sort of saint, as well. But in a different way."

"Well, tell me about him, then. I like hearing about saints, as I'm not one myself. What did Mr Aitchison do?"

Christopher drank the rest of his tea before replying and placed the mug on the pew beside him.

"Well," he began slowly. "He was very good to the poor, as well. He ran all sorts of classes and things for them and took kids to the seaside. He used to pack this church."

Max looked encouraging.

"Right. Well. Go on."

"And he was apparently an amazing preacher. Not the sort of apologetic stuff you get these days, but powerful Christianity."

"They get that at Christ Church," commented Max mildly. "But go on."

"Well, he did other stuff."

"What other stuff? Honestly, Chris, I'm starting to think that this Aitchison fellow must have been a very shady character. Why can't you tell me about him now you've got me all interested? You can tell me more about Mr Seymour, if you prefer."

Christopher turned his face away. Was Max deliberately keeping him talking for his own good? It was the sort of thing Max would do. He looked all innocent and genial on the outside but Christopher knew that there was more to Max than that. It struck him suddenly that Max was actually far deeper and more intelligent than he looked. Why had he never seen that before? Or had he? Why did the brain have these bewildering layers to it? And why had Max wanted to be his friend in the first place? There was nothing in it for him.

An involuntary movement of Christopher's arm sent his mug off the pew and on to the floor, where it rolled on its side and came to rest next to Max's right foot. In bending down to retrieve it, Christopher was able to avoid answering Max's question. Instead, he held up the unbroken mug as a trophy.

"They don't make them like this anymore."

Max grinned.

"What, the mug or Mr Aitchison? Mind you, I see what you mean about the mug. It looks like the one I had when I was in the scouts. I suppose I've never told you about my scouting career. My school chum, Alan, got me to join because he wanted someone to go with him on a camping trip. Gosh, it was awful! My mum bought a uniform and everything for me so that I could go, but I resigned the minute we got back and she had to sell it back, half price. We were forced to sleep in sweaty little tents and cook our own breakfast. Most of the food was either burnt to a cinder or raw. Never again! But I'm interrupting your story about the saint."

"I don't think you really want to hear."

The humour left Max's face and he looked at Christopher soberly.

"Yes, I do. This Christ Church business has made me bothered about religion. I just don't know what to think. I want to escape from it but don't know how to. Jenny takes it in her stride and so do the kids. What's it all about? It seems like a load of superstition to me and yet people seem so keen on it. Perhaps if you tell me more about this Aitchison fellow, I might just understand something. It must be easy for you."

Christopher covered his face with his hands.

"Max, it – it's not easy. I wish I were Charles Aitchison – or even Mr Seymour. But I'm not."

He took his hands away and focused his eyes on the altar frontal which seemed even brighter now that the body of the church was darker.

"Max, Charles Aitchison fought for this church. Almost literally. He had a mob attacking him because he dared to put six candles on the altar. For him, Christianity was not just ministering to the poor. Anybody can do that. It was something sublime, that deserved everything that was beautiful and well-made and excellent. God, this sounds silly."

Max put down his mug and stretched out a hand, as though to touch his friend's arm, but placed it on the pew between them instead.

"No, it's not. Was he the one who had that lovely cloth made? And that robe thing?"

Christopher swallowed hard and tried to speak without emotion. But his voice cracked.

"Yes," he replied stiltedly, and as though reading from a guide book. "He commissioned Ninian Comper, and a religious community, the – the Sisters of Bethany - made them."

"They're superb," replied Max, with a strange gentleness in his voice. "You must love them, Christopher. Just as you love this church."

Christopher passed the back of his left hand across his eyes and then stood up so abruptly that his mug took another dive and rolled under the pew.

"Max, I'm sorry. I must get on. You must go. I can't discuss this anymore. I can't."

Max also stood up and moved so that he faced his companion. Their eyes met. In agony, Christopher saw in Max's troubled gaze an infinity of compassion. He could not bear it. Wrenching himself round, he peered at the back of the church, where there was a pool of darkness.

"Max, you must go," he repeated. "I've got a lot to do. I'll – I'll be in touch. I'll let you out."

Walking unsteadily, he led Max back down the aisle towards the main door, closing his mind to the wave of generous sympathy which seemed to flow from the figure obediently marching behind him. He resolved not to turn around, not to give in to that sympathy like an injured child rushing into the arms of a loving parent. He walked on inexorably. But, when he heaved open the main door, he did turn and saw on Max's face the most desolate expression he had ever seen there. Nothing was said until Max was out on the pavement.

"Well, cheerio, Chris," said Max, offering a formal handshake. "Take care. We'll meet up soon. Don't do – don't do anything I wouldn't do, will you?"

Christopher touched his hand stiffly.

"Goodbye, Max. And – thank you for coming."

Max was gone. Christopher leaned his head against the closed door and listened until Max's firm tread had died away. What was there to do now but act? There was to be no thinking, no dreaming, no praying, no repenting. He went to the vestry and gathered up the boxes of charcoal, incense and matches, taking armfuls of them into the chancel, going to and fro mechanically until all the boxes had been moved. He had planned to make all this look like a boiler accident. But why should he ruin it all now by being cowardly? In an instant and despite his new resolve, he saw the tower blocks crowding around him accusingly, becoming taller and blacker as he crouched miserably before them. Cowardly. Cowardly. Pausing, with his arms full of the final load, and closing his eyes, he confronted them. 'I am no coward.' The little figure stood up and faced his accusers. For a second, there was deadlock. Then the tower blocks became only tower blocks once more, blind windows on blank walls.

It did not take him long to arrange the round cakes of charcoal in neat lines around the chancel floor and in front of the altar, making sure that all the cakes touched each other. He encircled the Christmas tree and advent wreath stand with them. He placed a special line of them on the floor close to the priest's stall and chasuble. When he had used up all the charcoal, he sprinkled the incense over it, shaking it out of the boxes with a practised hand, until every box was empty. Then he made two pyramids of all the empty boxes, one on the bench where Justin usually sat and the other on the wooden bench opposite. Beside each pyramid, he put a box of matches. The other box of matches was thrust into his jacket pocket.

But he had not yet completed his task. There were the candles to light. Returning to the vestry, he took a wax taper from the top of the cabinet and the box of matches from his jacket pocket. He carefully lit the taper, put the matches back in his pocket and paced slowly back to the chancel, where he held the burning taper to each candle until it lit. When all the candles on the altar were alight, he turned to the advent wreath and surveyed it for a few moments before lighting all five candles. The chancel now seemed alive with light, the candle flames bobbing and twinkling, the brass plates shining, the tinsel on the advent wreath and Christmas tree glittering and the silver candlesticks on the altar gleaming. There was an almost domestic cheerfulness in the scene, marred only by the strange rows of charcoal cakes and incense. Christopher nodded slightly as though in approval.

There was still another thing to do. Walking briskly, he went to the back of the church and took a prayer book from the back pew. The familiar little volume, with its well-worn cover and thin pages, almost broke his resolve not to think. He glanced down at it quickly and then turned his face away, feeling a prickling in his eyes. Now that the time had come, why was this all so painful? He had planned this event as his triumph, and yet, now that it was upon him, he longed to prostrate himself on the floor and weep and howl like a child throwing a tantrum.

In the chancel, he stood before the altar, opened the prayer book and read in a loud but quivering voice.

"O God, from whom all holy desires, all good counsels and all just works do proceed: Give unto thy servants that peace which the world cannot give; that both our hearts may be set to obey thy commandments, and also that by thee we being defended from the fear of our enemies may pass our time in rest and quietness; through the merits of Jesus Christ our Saviour. Amen.

Lighten our darkness, we beseech thee, O Lord; and by thy great mercy defend us from all perils and dangers of this night; for the love of thy only Son, our Saviour Jesus Christ. Amen."

It was finished. Christopher stood next to the pizza restaurant where he and Bob Bodkin had eaten lunch. Was that only a few weeks ago? It was now a fading memory.

He had left St Benet's when the wooden servers' benches had started to crackle and burn, the flames eating hungrily at the polished wood. The fire would be spreading around the chancel now, picking up anything that was flammable and being helped along by the charcoal. But what was that to him? He had vowed not to dream dreams or see visions. There was a dull ache in his head, an ache that made him feel weary, paralysing any thoughts or emotions. And wasn't that what he wanted?

He leaned his head against the cold brick wall and closed his eyes. Minutes passed. The December wind cut through his jacket and whipped his cheeks, as though he were some homeless nineteenth century urchin preparing to spend the night in a doorway. There was something almost comforting about this idea and, in an oddly detached way, he dwelt upon it, relishing the image of isolation and neglect, welcoming the freedom from hope. Mistily, he saw himself as a ragged child, thin, poor and chilled but stubborn and independent. Why should he worry about the cold darkness? Wasn't he used to it?

Suddenly, however, he opened his eyes wide. The wind, though still icy, carried with it a strangely familiar fragrance. He sniffed tentatively and straightened up. What was it? He sniffed more deeply. It seemed it was the smell of incense. Recollection flooded over him. And then, despite himself, despite the distant sound of a fire engine's siren, despite everything, he was back at that glorious farewell service almost a year ago, the church full, Justin earnestly swinging the thurible, Julian looking golden and graceful, and himself kneeling at the communion rail. There was a prickling in his eyes. For a moment, he struggled. What was the first hymn that they had sung that day? Yes, 'Love Divine.' Through nerveless lips, he whispered the well-known words until he reached the final verse.

'Changed from glory into glory.
Till in heaven we take our place.
Till we cast our crowns before thee,
Lost in – lost in – in – wonder-'

There were no more words.